W9-BUU-310

THE WAR YEARS

1

★ THE ★

FAR
STARS
WAR

FEATURING
DAVID DRAKE

EDITED BY
BILL FAWCETT

RoC

A ROC BOOK

ROC
Published by the Penguin Group
Penguin Books USA Inc., 375 Hudson Street,
New York, New York 10014, U.S.A.
Penguin Books Ltd, 27 Wrights Lane,
London W8 5TZ, England
Penguin Books Australia Ltd, Ringwood,
Victoria, Australia
Penguin Books Canada Ltd, 2801 John Street,
Markham, Ontario, Canada L3R 1B4
Penguin Books (N.Z.) Ltd, 182-190 Wairau Road,
Aukland 10, New Zealand

Penguin Books Ltd, Registered Offices:
Harmondsworth, Middlesex, England

First published by Roc, an imprint of Penguin Books USA Inc.

First Printing, July, 1990
10 9 8 7 6 5 4 3 2 1

Prologue and Interludes copyright © 1990 by Bill Fawcett &
Associates
''Band of Brothers'' copyright © 1990 by David Drake
''The Archimedes Effect'' copyright © 1990 by Todd Johnson
''Hero'' copyright © 1990 by Peter Morwood
''Trojan Hearse'' copyright © 1990 by Robert Sheckley
''Volunteers'' copyright © 1990 by Jody Lynn Nye
''Edge'' copyright © by Steve Perry
''Politics'' copyright © 1990 by Elizabeth Moon
''Museum Piece'' copyright © 1990 by William C. Dietz
''Grenadier'' copyright © 1990 by Rick Shelley
''Reunion'' copyright © 1990 by Diane Duane

FROM WAR TO PEACE

"Band of Brothers" by David Drake—Alien invaders have completed their first deadly attack on Earth and its colonies, and the only hope for human survival is the formation of a revolutionary alliance—the League of Man.

"Trojan Hearse" by Robert Sheckley—The war is in full swing, and fleet commander Darfur must join up with a group of mutant circus freaks to save the show—and the future of the League—from total annihilation by the enemy invaders of Gerin.

"Reunion" by Diane Duane—The Far Stars War has ended victoriously for The League of Man. But who will bring order to the alien and human chaos that remains?

Plus 7 more thrilling tales of interstellar warfare in the year 2237. . . .

THE FAR STARS WAR

CONTENTS

TIMELINE

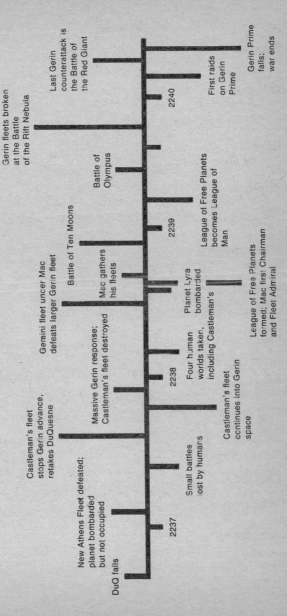

DuQ falls

New Athens Fleet defeated; planet bombarded but not occupied

2237

Small battles lost by humans

Castleman's fleet stops Gerin advance, retakes DuQuesne

Castleman's fleet continues into Gerin space

Massive Gerin response; Castleman's fleet destroyed

2238

Four human worlds taken, including Castleman's

League of Free Planets formed; Mac first Chairman and Fleet Admiral

Gemini fleet under Mac defeats larger Gerin fleet

Planet Lyra bombarded

Mac gathers his fleets

Battle of Ten Moons

2239

League of Free Planets becomes League of Man

Gerin fleets broken at the Battle of the Rift Nebula

Battle of Olympus

Last Gerin counterattack is the Battle of the Red Giant

2240

First raids on Gerin Prime

Gerin Prime falls; war ends

Prologue

The history of the Far Stars War, a war involving over a hundred systems and millions of participants, is the story of individuals. Its outcome was determined less by the decisions of Admiral MacDonald or the Gerin Supreme Triad than by uncounted minor decisions made on battlefields hundreds of light-years apart. It was a war that was marked by isolated battles, often fought by men who weeks earlier had been farmers or clerks.

By the time the war began, mankind had spread throughout much of its own arm of the galaxy. No government had been able to gain or keep control of the hundreds of human settled worlds. A lack of any means of faster-than-light communications encouraged the fragmentation of the race as it spread away from a depleted and backward Earth. The pattern of this expansion was hardly organized, and often simply haphazard. Though virtually every star has planets, perhaps one in ten thousand is not immediately inimical to human existence. Of these, less than 1 percent are habitable without extensive and prohibitively expensive artificial environments. All this still left an estimated fifty thousand human-habitable planets within our spiral arm alone. Carbon-based life being present on virtually all of these planets, it follows that in their two hundred years of expansion men have encountered several hundred other intelligent races, many having already perfected some form of space travel of their own.

Men also traveled outward, into the less densely filled regions farther away from the galactic core. The area, for obvious reasons, was designated the Far Stars by most stellar geographers. This was the nearest equivalent they had to "Here there be dragons" and other phrases signifying *stellae incognitae*. Among these stars, expansion tended to travel in lines, rather than bursts filling whole clusters. Each colony would often be weeks' travel from another human world, culturally and physically isolated from the rest of the race. The inhabitants, too, tended to be a hardy breed, more concerned for their independence and prosperity than for any larger concerns. Served only by tramp freighters, these worlds gave no allegiance to any higher authority and often lacked even a planetary government. It was because of all this that the first contacts with the Gerin, and their conquest of DuQuesne, went virtually unnoticed by even her neighbors.

The Far Stars War, it was decided long after the fact, actually began in the Terran year 2237. Actually, the monolithic Council of Triads that ruled all eleven Gerin worlds had decided to drive mankind and all other races from "their" portion of the galaxy years before. Other races had fought men, often to their detriment, and the Gerin moved cautiously. Their first action had been to conquer the frontier planet of DuQuesne nearly fifty years earlier, circa 2187. The octopoid Gerin had landed in overwhelming numbers, and aided by complete domination of the air and space above, they quickly crushed all opposition. Most of the planet's population died in the first few hours when the Gerin bombarded even the smallest villages. Those who survived were isolated, unable to contact each other, and any resistance was met by the complete slaughter of every human in the vicinity. Even so, for nearly two decades a few holdouts fought a hopeless guerrilla action.

By the time other men were once more concerned with the fate of the human population of DuQuesne, two generations had been born under the brutal domination of the Gerin. This interest was generated by a second Gerin assault, this time on the much larger and more prosperous planet of New Athens. Here they met surprising resistance and their landing forces took losses far greater than expected. The Gerin response was to withdraw and then bombard the planet until its surface was no longer habitable. Only a few survived, escaping in private ships.

These carried the warning to other human worlds, and also to the worlds of other races who feared the Gerin would turn on them next.

Though they didn't know it at the time, and perhaps have never realized it, the slaughter of New Athens and the enslavement of the remaining humans on DuQuesne, more than anything, inspired the unification of the nearby human planets. At first, though, only one planet, Castleman's World, chose to act. This planet had many advantages, including advanced factory complexes and space docks, which enabled it to construct a fleet of over a hundred warships in less than a decade. Many of these were purchased from the nearby League of Free Worlds; others were converted merchant ships. The loss of a recent minor war with another human world also provided Castleman's with a cadre of experienced officers and the need to reestablish her prestige.

At first the Castleman's fleet met with surprising success. It defeated three separate Gerin formations and retook not only a now lifeless New Athens, but also DuQuesne.

BAND OF BROTHERS
by David Drake

SANGER was the commando's point man this morning. Twenty meters beyond the abandoned farmhouse he walked into a Gerin killzone.

"Freeze!" ordered Rudisill, the artillery specialist, second in the six-man column and shocked out of the lethargy of a long march by the pulsing alert on his helmet display. "Sanger, your helmet's fucked. You're already in a killzone."

Coils in each helmet cooled the trooper's head and approximately half his blood supply, the next-best thing to total environmental control. The refrigerant didn't prevent DuQuesne's atmosphere from being a steam bath, though; nor did it do anything to lighten the commando's load of gear.

For concealment purposes, they'd been inserted by sea with ten kilometers to hike before they reached their objective. Sweat had been rolling off Rudisill's body with the effort of humping his helmet, weapons, rations—and the heavy spotting table—up and down forested ridges.

Now the sweat was cold.

"Everybody halt in place," said Captain Lermontov over the unit net. "I'm coming forward."

Lermontov's voice was more than calm; it was calming. "Sanger, you know the drill. You're safe unless you try to back up, so just stay where you are. Might be a good time to take a leak."

"I done that, sir," whispered the point man. Then, "Sir, you gonna be able to get me out?"

Commando 441 had carried out twenty-seven missions on this Christ-bitten hellhole without a fatality. The troopers of other units carried lucky charms. Four-four-one had Ivan Lermontov.

But it was going to take more than luck to pull Sanger from the trap into which his faulty equipment had dropped him.

"I don't see why not," said Captain Lermontov.

Rudisill heard the soft rustle of vegetation. The commando's leader was approaching with easy caution from his number-three slot in the column, a hundred meters behind the artillery specialist.

The heads-up display on Rudisill's visor showed pulsing blips as the computer-directed elements of the Gerin killzone maneuvered for optimal position. Pretty soon they'd encircle the whole commando, not just the point man. . . .

This killzone consisted of twenty separate elements, strung in a two-kilometer line almost parallel to the commando's axis of advance. If the commando had crossed to the left rather than the right side of the knob on the last ridge, they'd have been out of the zone's sensor range.

The troopers wouldn't have known—or cared—that the killzone was in place. Now—

Each element of the killzone was a twenty-centimeter sphere with sensors, magnetic lift engines, and a rudimentary control/communications computer. When a target entered the sensor range of any element, that computer alerted the other elements and the whole chain drifted closer to do maximum damage to possible following targets. Nothing would happen until the target started to move out of the zone's lethal area.

The magnetic motors had an electronic signature even in standby mode. Commando helmets could detect a killzone at twice the killzone's own fifty-meter sensor range.

Except that Sanger's helmet had malfunctioned.

The shell of each sphere was pre-fragmented ceramic, backed with high explosive. Sanger was within ten meters of one. At that range, the blast would shatter the trunk of thirty-centimeter hardwoods—it would atomize a man.

"Good work, Guns," Lermontov murmured, using straight voice instead of frequency-hopping radio as he came up behind Rudisill. "If you hadn't been looking sharp, we'd be in problems now."

That was oil, not reality. The helmet, not the artillery spotter personally, had done the work; but the words made Rudisill feel better nonetheless. "They're coming down on us, sir," he said tightly.

"Sure, that's what they do," agreed Lermontov as he paused beside Rudisill.

The captain was a man of middle height, with a gymnast's shoulders and slim hips. He'd slung his assault rifle and was punching keys on the miniature handset flexed to his helmet.

The face beneath Lermontov's raised visor looked unconcerned; a boyish lock of dark blond hair peeked out from beneath his helmet.

Lermontov smiled. "Got another job for you, Guns," he said. "Need you to tell me when I look like I'm a zone element myself."

Rudisill's rifle was aimed at the stretch of forest which concealed another of the mines drifting toward the target area. He brushed sweat from his chin with the back of his left hand and said, "Sir, you can't. These helmets won't—

Lermontov flashed a smile that brooked no more argument than a shark's did. "Don't you worry, troop," he said flatly. "These helmets'll sit up and beg for cookies if you know how to massage 'em. Your job's just to tell me—" Lermontov concentrated on the keyboard in his left palm—"when I've got it right."

Rudisill swallowed and nodded. His visor displayed the slow-moving elements of the killzone as blue dots on the ghostly relief map overlaying the reality of the forest. As Captain Lermontov touched his keyboard, another dot sprang to life beside the artillery spotter. The new arrival was fuzzy at first, but its outline quickly sharpened until it was nearly identical to the other twenty.

"You got it, sir," Rudisill said. "But I wish you wouldn't . . ."

"Okay, Sanger," Lermontov said over the unit push as he stepped forward. "We're golden. Help's on the way."

The undergrowth folded behind the captain, hiding him from Rudisill after a few long, gliding strides. On Rudisill's visor, the twenty-first dot moved smoothly toward the original one at a pace swifter than that of the other drifting deathtraps.

Lermontov's helmet was matching its own output to the commo and motor signatures of a killzone element. If the emanations were close enough, the Gerin sensors would ignore Lermontov until he switched the killzone off.

If the match *wasn't* close enough, the blast would be lethal within a fifty-meter circle.

Rudisill knelt carefully so that the ground took part of the weight of his pack. He pretended to ignore the drop of sweat that trembled on the end of his nose.

The dot that was Lermontov paused briefly as it reached the point man's position. Nothing came over the commo net, but Rudisill could imagine the captain patting Sanger on the shoulder, saying a few cheerful words, and moving on toward the waiting explosive.

Rudisill could imagine it because that had been more

or less what had happened to him when a laser toppled a tree across his thighs. The spotting table was smashed, so he couldn't call in artillery fire. He didn't have a prayer unless somebody crawled suicidally close to the Gerin bunker and dropped a grenade through its firing slit.

Which Captain Lermontov did.

The dot that was the commando's leader merged with the almost identical killzone element.

"Okay," said the captain's voice. "Now, everybody hug the ground for just a . . ."

Rudisill knew he should flatten from his crouch. He couldn't bring himself to move.

The line of oncoming beads faded to blurs or vanished as their motors cut back to standby power. The first element of a killzone to make contact became the master link; and Captain Lermontov had just shut it down.

"There, we're golden," Lermontov said. "Let's get moving, shall we? Heatherton, come forward and take point."

Rudisill finally let his breath out as he rose to his feet. "Negative," he said. "I'll take it, sir."

He moved forward, letting his eyes scan either side and the trees above him, as though he were already the column's point man.

"Guns," Lermontov replied cautiously, "we need you to spot when we reach the hostage pen."

"We need everybody," Rudisill said. "I'm here, and we know my hardware works."

He'd reached the clearing around the farmhouse. The inhabitants hadn't been gone for long. Chickens squabbled noisily beyond the palings of the kitchen garden, and the hog which snorted off among the trees was domestic rather than feral.

The pig's masters were probably hidden nearby. Rudisill didn't bother to try calling them out. The Dukes weren't going to come forward, weren't going to help even by dipping a gourdful of drinking water for the troops risking their lives to free DuQuesne from the Gerin.

The Dukes weren't shit.

Sanger was washing down a tablet of electrolyte replacement with tasteless water from the condenser in his helmet. He was nineteen years standard and could pass for twice that age at the moment.

Sanger stood, shouldering his pack. He didn't have the spotting table, but the MARS—multi-application rocket system—he and the other three troopers carried was equally heavy. "Thanks, buddy," he muttered to Rudisill.

"Hell, I didn't get you assigned to Lermontov's commando," Rudisill answered, speaking in a low voice because the captain was waiting only a few meters beyond.

Lermontov had clipped the keyboard back onto his helmet. His right hand gripped his rifle again. His left index finger was tracing designs on the mottled shell of the Gerin mine. The access plate in the top of the sphere was still open.

"Good job, Cap'n," Rudisill murmured.

Lermontov shrugged. "You watch yourself on point, Guns," he said.

"Always," Rudisill said without emotion. He stepped forward into the trees, following the azimuth projected onto his visor.

There were no more Gerin minefields, but the commando found repeated evidence of human occupation. Another farm; the prints of bare feet on trails the commando crossed but never followed; once the sound of a baby crying, tantalizingly near.

"I can feel 'em watching," said Minh, the last man in line.

"I'd better not see one," Heatherton responded. "I know damn well those shit-scared bastards're reporting to the Slime."

"None of that," Lermontov said sharply. "There's no evidence that the locals cooperate with the Gerin. They're just scared. Same as you'd be if your planet had been run by the Slime for three generations."

"Cap'n," said Sanger, "they don't have the balls t' live nor die neither. Any of *my* kin gets that scared, I'll cut their throats and put 'em outa their mis'ry."

Rudisill panted in time with the rhythm of his boots. His pack cut him over the collarbone and the jut of his hips. He'd glued sponge from fuse containers over the points of wear, but it didn't matter. In the long run, the weight and friction were the same, and the ulcers in his flesh reopened.

"I still say," Heatherton muttered, "that if *they* ain't interested in saving 'emselfs from the Slime, then I'm not interested neither."

"Look," said the captain. "When we release the hostages the Gerin are holding, then maybe we'll see some changes in the local attitude. That's what headquarters figures, anyway."

"Headquarters ain't sweatin' like pigs in the boonies," Sanger retorted.

They were climbing what Rudisill's projected map said was the last rise before they reached the target; but it was a kilometer of outcrops and heavy undergrowth, and the map was a best-estimate production anyway. Rudisill figured the Headquarters analysts must've been wrong, *again,* because if the commando were really that close to a Gerin base there'd be—

"Freeze," Rudisill ordered as his own body locked in place. But they were all right. . . .

"Sir," he whispered, "we've found it. I'm just about *in* the defensive ring, but they got half of it shut down so my sensors didn't pick it up till now."

"What're we talking about now, Guns?" Lermontov whispered back. His voice was a phantom in the artillery spotter's earphones.

Rudisill began unfolding his spotting table. "Sir," he said, "there's a plasma battery to right and left. I can't see them, but they're live. And—"

He swallowed. "And what I thought was a boulder right here in front of me, it's concrete. It's the cap of a missile site. They're loaded for bear, but I don't think they were expecting anybody to walk in the back way."

As Rudisill spoke, he clipped the leads from his helmet onto the spotting table. He could mark targets with a lightpen, but direct input was more accurate by an order of magnitude.

The meter-square table couldn't lie flat, but it had better be close enough.

"Okay," said Lermontov. "I'm coming forward—"

"Wait, sir," Rudisill said.

He focused on the "boulder," which was literally close enough to spit on, and pressed the enter key on his helmet's pad. Then he slid a meter to the side, focused on the same point, and clicked the key again. His helmet fed the triangulated data to the spotting table.

There was a muted *zeep* from the table. The relief map projected on Rudisill's visor echoed the processed date: three red beads, the Gerin sites identified either by sight or electronic signatures; and nine yellow beads spaced equidistantly around the remainder of the calculated circle.

"All *right* . . ." Lermontov murmured as he watched the same beads on his own display. "And you've got them . . . ?"

"Yessir," the artillery spotter said. "The data's sent to Support as soon as it's calculated. They're waiting offshore to launch as soon as they get the order."

Rudisill raised himself slightly to check the terrain of the estimated—and now confirmed—Gerin camp on the spotting table. The table's data came from the same satellite radar picture as the map on Rudisill's visor, but at least the display was better.

The ridge up which the commando was climbing fell away sharply at the crest. On the other side was a valley carved by the meanderings of a considerable watercourse. The plain's vegetation was kept to a height of ten meters or less by flooding, but giant trees from the crest spread their branches over the scallop a spring had carved from the cliff face.

Water pooled beneath the cliff before gurgling on toward the river half a kilometer away. The pool was the exact center of the Gerin's defensive ring.

"Bingo," said Rudisill.

"All the sites are vertical defense, right?" Lermontov said.

"Well, the plasma guns would be dual purpose," said the artillery spotter. "But yeah, there's likely antipersonnel stuff closer in that's shut down too."

Rudisill kept his voice steady, but he knew what the words meant. The normal way to eliminate a concealed defensive array was to take cover, spoof the system into life, and then blast the unmasked batteries with precisely aimed artillery. The other way of discovering the system was—

"Okay," said Captain Lermontov, "that means we gotta get real close. No point in our being here if we give the Slime enough warning they grease their hostages before we nail 'em, right?"

"No bloody point our bein' here," Heatherton muttered, a complaint but not an argument.

"Heatherton, Minh, Moschelitz," the captain continued. "You take positions on the clifftop. Guns, Sanger, and me'll circle to the low side and penetrate as close as we need to spot the Slime inner ring.

"Remember," Lermontov added, "take it easy."

His voice honed itself to just a hint of an edge, reminding them all that he knew they were hard men—but Ivan Lermontov was the hardest of them all, and he *would* be obeyed. "The first the Slime knows we're here is when Guns's salvo takes out all their defenses. If anybody shoots before then, he's responsible for the failure of the mission and the death of a hundred fifty civilian hostages."

Softly again: "Understood?"

"Roger," whispered five voices simultaneously across the commo net.

"Then let's move."

The other method of discovering a shut-down defensive array was damned dangerous. Maybe a little safer than jumping on a live grenade, but real bloody similar.

Not that Rudisill was going to argue with the captain.

Even shut down, the elements of an antipersonnel defense system could be detected if you got within a couple of meters. The danger was that if the Gerin had the inner defenses under observation, they could bring their weapons live while the human troops were right in front of them.

But then, if you figured to die in bed, you didn't volunteer for a commando.

It took Lermontov's three-man section over an hour to slink around to the opposite side of the Gerin base.

Their circuit confirmed the locations of four more batteries, but the outer ring defenses weren't really a threat. Even though the heavy plasma weapons could be put under manual control to fire on ground targets, there'd be a lock-out to prevent them from shooting toward the base itself. The whole commando was by now within the outer defended area.

The trees on the valley floor had soft, pulpy boles. They grew close together. Rudisill knew that every time he brushed one, the fan of leaves ten meters above him waved like a flag toward any of the Slime which happened to be watching.

Air didn't move among the dense trunks. Rudisill prayed there was enough breeze above the low canopy to conceal the foliage he moved in the broader patterns of nature.

His right hand was cramping. He deliberately took it off the grip of his rifle and flexed it, working fatigue poisons out of the muscles.

"Sir?" said Heatherton. "We're in position. I want to scope a look."

"Okay," said Lermontov. "Optics only."

Nonemissive viewing through the long fiber-optics lens each trooper carried was safe enough. Laser-ranging or using long-wave radar to pierce a curtain of vegetation might give useful information, but would be almost certain to arouse the Slime defenses.

Rudisill settled in place and spread his spotting table again. He switched his visor to play the take from Heatherton's periscope at full intensity. He could've crawled through the vegetation with Heatherton's data displayed as ghost images, the way the relief map had been; but the commando wasn't in a real hurry, and Rudisill wanted a good look at the lion before he stuck his head in its mouth.

The picture wasn't razor-sharp, but it was damned good for an image picked up by a one millimeter lens, piped down several meters of glass cable, digitized—and finally transmitted to Rudisill's helmet over a spread of frequencies.

It was good enough to kill by.

There were two Gerin in the spring-fed pool below the cliff. From Heatherton's near-vertical angle, they looked like short-limbed octopuses—or blots of slime that somebody'd stepped on.

That would happen real soon.

There was an armored transporter under camouflage netting, forty meters down the stream which gurgled over the lip of the pool. It was only a six-place vehicle, but its forward cupola held a plasma cannon.

A third Slime sat on the transporter's entrance ramp. Its tenacles waved idly in the water flowing to either side of the vehicle's plenum-chamber skirts.

Rudisill keyed in the vehicle as an artillery target. The spotting table whined happily.

"All *right*," whispered Sanger.

The analysts had been right for a change.

There was cave in the cliff directly beneath Heatherton. The gate at its mouth was invisible from this angle until another Gerin opened it. Shadows displayed the pattern of bars.

The guard was letting a pair of naked humans out of the cave. Commando 441 had the first sight of the hostages it was supposed to rescue.

Rudisill couldn't figure the byplay at the gate. The Slime had seemed to fondle the prisoners' necks before letting them run clumsily toward the plain, carrying tools and baskets.

Then Captain Lermontov said, "Okay, they're wearing collars. Explosives with radio detonators and antitamper locks, sure as hell. The Slime let 'em supplement their rations, but they make sure they come back."

"They give 'em knives, too," Sanger noted.

"Those may be trowels," the captain said.

"I'd open up a Slime with a trowel," Sanger retorted. "So'd they, if they had balls."

The hostages trotted into the forest; Heatherton's periscope gave only brief further flashes of them. They were operating at some distance from one another. They seemed to be digging and putting the results into their baskets.

The gate shut. The Slime guarding it remained in the alcove, barely visible in the strip of shade beneath the cliff face.

"Okay," said Lermontov. "We've got the right place. Let's move up and find the inner defenses."

"Sir, I don't think we'd better do that," Rudisill said. "We're already inside three hundred meters. The paradigms on my spotting table, they don't include one for antipersonnel arrays on less than a three-hundred-meter radius."

Nobody said anything for a moment. On Rudisill's visor, a Gerin rose from the pool with a splash. For a moment there were three of the ugly beasts within spitting distance of one another. Then one of the initial pair slipped deeper into the water and disappeared.

"Look, maybe they don't *have* an inner ring here," Sanger suggested.

"Unlikely," Lermontov said flatly, though he'd have liked to believe that as much as the others would. "The heavy weapons are too extensive for them not to have light stuff as well. They've just hidden it too well for us."

"Sir," said Rudisill, "we don't have a choice. Let's move back and I'll send in a drone. If we try anything without nailing the antipersonnel shit, we cut our throats and the hostages' too."

"Okay . . ." Lermontov said, but the word was a placeholder while he thought, not agreement. "This is what we'll do. The hostages themselves will have a notion where the defensive ring is hidden. We—"

"Maybe not," the artillery spotter interjected. "They maybe were brought here after the—"

"Chances are," Lermontov went on, "they'll know."

He didn't raise his voice, but his tone shut Rudisill up instantly. "All we need is one element to figure the whole array, right?"

"Ah," said Rudisill. "Two'd be better. But yeah, one'll give us a point and the radius. Chances are there'll be only one paradigm to match. If it's regular."

The Slime at the back of the transporter squirmed inside. A moment later, he or another Gerin reappeared with a food bar wrapped in one tentacle.

Slime worked in groups of three. That meant the vehicle's turret was probably manned.

"The outer defenses were regular?"

"Yessir," Rudisill admitted. "Like they'd asked a computer to lay it out."

Which they probably had. The Gerin had an accountant's taste for precision.

"Okay," Lermontov repeated. "We'll ask a hostage where the inner defenses are—or how they're camouflaged. Whatever it takes for us to locate an element. Then we're golden."

"Aw, shit, Cap'n," Sanger whispered. "Aw, shit. I don't like this shit."

"It's the only way we're going to get the hostages out alive," said Captain Lermontov. "So that's the way we'll do it. All right?"

"Yessir," said Sanger. Rudisill's mouth was too dry for him to comment, even if he'd wanted to do so.

"Guns," the captain continued, "one of the Dukes seems to be coming your way. Stay where you are while Sanger and me move in from behind her. Let me do the talking if possible."

"Roger," Sanger said. Rudisill either spoke the word or thought it while his mouth poised to scream.

He had too much imagination. It was all right when shit started to happen and there was nothing to do but react to the terror that stalked in with blast and fury. But for times when he had to wait and *know* how much could go wrong with a plan . . . for times like this, Rudisill had too much imagination.

The soft dirt wasn't perfectly regular. He edged sideways into a low patch and flattened, wishing he were back in the base camp, or up on top of the cliff, or any damn place else in the world.

The hostage's tool echoed against a root with a hollow *chock! chock! chock!* Bare feet shuffled closer to Rudisill's hiding place.

He caught a glimpse of leg among the narrow trunks. The skin was the pasty white of a cave creature's.

The hostage stepped into plain sight, five meters away. She didn't see Rudisill. His helmet and uniform took on the mottling of his surroundings with the perfection of a chameleon's hide; and anyway, the hostage was looking for fruiting bodies like the dozen or so she already carried in her basket.

She was about fifteen years old and stark naked except for the metal collar. He body was as filthy and scrawny as that of an alley cat.

Sanger and Captain Lermontov slipped out of the trees just behind her and moved in from either side.

The girl was humming something beneath her breath. She knelt by a tree two meters from Rudisill. Her eyes caught the regular outline of the spotting table.

Before the artillery spotter had time to react, the girl spun erect, kicking gritty loam back toward him.

"It's all right," said Captain Lermontov with his arms spread. "We're here to free—"

The hostage screamed. She flung her blunt-bladed machete into Lermontov's visored face, then sprinted between him and Sanger.

For a moment, Rudisill had a flash of what the girl was seeing: a trio of grim figures like monsters sprung from rotting vegetation. Camouflage made the men faceless blurs; only the arsenal of weapons they wore had firm outlines.

"*Geddown! Geddown!*" Rudisill shouted as he uncaged the red firing key on his table. The girl would warn—

"I got 'er!" Sanger cried as his hand rose. Not with a gun, because the shot would be worse than the screams. . . .

Sanger's hand was vertical. A long-bladed knife rose from it like a torch, hilt-down for a short throw. At this range, Sanger's arm would send the point pricking out above the girl's breastbone while the crossguard rapped her shoulder.

"No!" said Captain Lermontov, but words didn't matter now, not even *his* words, so he tackled the trooper.

Rudisill pressed the red key. He forced himself into the dirt, exhaling so that he'd be that much flatter when—

The first sound was the snarling roar of a backpack rocket, fired from the clifftop on Rudisill's warning. The next sound was a whine, *through* the damp soil and then above it, as the Gerin antipersonnel array deployed.

Gerin lasers were firing even before the MARS warhead's blast and the rippling secondary explosions of fuel and ammunition aboard the Slime transporter.

The commando hadn't been able to locate the inner ring defenses because the elements had been buried deep in the ground. Three meters *behind* where Rudisill cowered, a thick post thrust from the soil like a cylindrical toadstool. Its high-energy laser scythed through tree trunks in bursts of fire and live steam.

Rudisill's helmet went black, saving his vision from the blue-white dazzle a centimeter above his head. He poked his rifle backward like a huge pistol and fired blindly while hell roared and ravened above him. The bare skin of his hands and throat crinkled.

Far around the circuit, a plasma weapon started to pulse skyward. Then the artillery support Rudisill had summoned burst overhead.

Rudisill's rifle had antipersonnel ammunition up, but a lucky round snapped through the laser aperture. His visor cleared when the glare paused, and he had a chance to throw the switch on his magazine to armor-piercing.

Rudisill's aimed shots punched the laser unit into a colander before it could rotate a replacement lens into place.

The air bursts spewed a rain of self-forging fragments. Each one struck within satellite-computed centimeters of the targets the spotting table had sent them. The circle of Gerin plasma and missile batteries, gutted by molten penetrators, blew skyward in alternate bubbles of ionized light and flattened mushrooms of flame-streaked smoke.

The spotting table was *zeep*ing again as it transmitted the coordinates of the inner defensive ring.

Rudisill twisted, loading another magazine to replace the one he'd emptied on the automatic defense unit. He had a good view of the Slime positions now, because the laser had sawed the trees in a jumble of steam and thrashing feathery branches.

Sanger was okay. He'd been saved—like Rudisill—by irregularities in the ground they'd scarcely have noticed while marching. Sanger was shooting toward the guard at the cave mouth. Purple blood spurted from the back of the Slime as it tried to unlock the gate and squirm for shelter.

The laser's beam of coherent light had sliced off the feet of the running hostage, then cycled back as she fell and touched her again. Her hair smoldered, and the top of her skull lay a little distance from the rest of her body.

Captain Lermontov had been on top of Sanger when the laser began to cut. Now he lay very still.

His torso was separated from his hips.

The remains of the Gerin transporter were still burning fiercely. Rudisill had targeted it for the artillery, but the fragment's impact only fanned flames which the commando's own rocket had ignited.

The men of Heatherton's section must have destroyed the automatic defenses nearest to them, because they were able to shoot instead of cowering beneath the ravening lasers. Bullets blew forth from the pool and combed Sanger's shots in a sparkling crossfire.

Rudisill heard a familiar howl in the sky. "Watch yourselves!" he warned over the unit net. "Incoming!"

He spread himself flat again. These were shells he'd summoned, but no fire was friendly if you happened to be at the point of impact.

Instead of ducking, one of Heatherton's men fired his MARS down into the pool. A geyser of water lifted, carrying with it the bodies of two Gerin. Steam puffed out around the bars of the cave and the Slime corpse which lay there shivering as bullets continued to rake it.

The world paused for the triple low-altitude blasts of incoming shells and the hypervelocity shock waves of the glowing spearpoints they spewed. The ground rippled like a trampoline, flinging Rudisill into the air as mud gouted thirty meters high at the point where the laser unit had been.

The inner ring of the defensive array vanished. Bits of metal and plastic dribbled down with the columns of gritty mud the penetrators had lifted.

"Have we got 'em?" Rudisill called. "Have we got 'em all?"

Sanger was reloading his rifle. He paused in mid-motion as he noticed Lermontov for the first time. Sanger was a veteran. When the shooting started, he must have rolled into position and fired by reflex, ignoring every part of the equation except what was in his sight picture. . . .

The head of a Gerin wearing an armored battlesuit rose just above the surface of the pool. It fired up at the cliff. The Slime was using what by human standards was a light cannon. Rock crumbled around the bright orange shellbursts.

Minh yelped over the radio and a rifle went flying, but there was no body in the mini-avalanche which bounced down the cliff in response to the blasts.

"They killed the captain! They killed the captain!"

Rudisill fired at the Gerin. The angle was hopelessly bad, but his bullets sparked and splattered on the rocks across the pool. The Slime ducked back beneath the surface and Heatherton, on the cliffs above, churned the water again with a vertical burst.

Minh still had his MARS. He launched the heavy rocket into the pool while Heatherton and Moschelitz kept the Slime down with rifle fire.

Rocks and steam spewed even higher than before, because the water level had been dropped by the first warhead. The cliff was black where water darkened the dun stone.

More steam belched from the cave. Shadowed figures moved beyond the bars. Rudisill thought he heard shouts and crying.

"They killed the captain!"

Even in an armored suit, the Gerin couldn't survive a direct MARS hit. Rudisill's left hand stung. He looked down and noticed for the first time that his left little finger was missing. The automatic laser had—

"That must've got the—" Heatherton started to say.

The Slime rose from the bubbling water of the pool and raked the clifftop again with explosive shells.

Heatherton screamed with frustration. He triggered a

wild burst as he lurched back from the spray of grit and shell fragments. Rudisill fired also, nowhere near the target that ducked away, back under the water.

"I know where it's going!" Rudisill cried. "The pool connects with the cave, so the Slime gets out of the water and clear of the shock wave!"

Moschelitz fired his rifle into the pool.

There was a *thump!* as Sanger launched his MARS, the only rocket left in the commando. Its backblast slapped Rudisill like a hot, soft pillow.

The warhead detonated with a yellow glare that filled the interior of the cave. The half-open gates blew out in a tumbling arc. They splashed to the ground between Sanger and the sectioned hostage who'd tried to escape him.

The pool burped a gout of steam. No question now about it and the cave connecting. . . .

The Gerin staggered from the mouth of the cave. It was amazing that the Slime survived even wearing armor, but it had lost its weapon in the blast.

Rudisill, Heatherton, and Moschelitz emptied their rifles into the creature. A few of the bullets spanged and ricocheted from its battlesuit, but only a few. The corpse wasn't even twitching by the time Sanger snatched up his rifle again and reloaded.

Sanger fired off his whole magazine anyway.

The silence that followed was broken only by the ringing in Rudisill's ears.

Rudisill stood up, loading a fresh magazine by reflex. The spotting table was still attached to his helmet. He jerked the leads out, careless of whether he damaged them. He walked over to Sanger and Lermontov, a few steps and a lifetime away.

Nothing moved within the cave except whorls of smoke.

Sanger cradled the captain's head in his lap. Lermontov's helmet had fallen off. His pale blue eyes were open and sightless.

Rudisill knelt and put his arm around the shoulders of the living trooper.

"The bastards," Sanger whispered. He was weeping. "The bastards. I swear I'll kill 'em all!"

Rudisill figured he meant the Slime, but when he looked toward the smoldering cave he wasn't sure.

Rudisill wasn't sure that he *cared* which Sanger meant, either.

Defeat in Detail

After their initial victories the Castleman's fleet settled onto the defensive. Had they been dealing with a human opponent, their supposition would have been that they had inflicted a defeat sufficient to discourage further attacks. Instead, they had only managed to upgrade man from a local menace to a major threat. Where the original Gerin invasion force had been composed of fewer than two hundred ships, the Gerin retaliated with over fifteen hundred ships, including dreadnoughts and carriers. There was never any question of the result.

The Castleman's fleet was crushed in the first encounter. Its remnants was rallied around a heavy cruiser commanded by Captain Chu Lee MacDonald. This officer led the survivors on a fighting retreat. At one point Mac-Donald's fifty survivors turned and destroyed over a dozen Gerin cruisers. The unfortunate effect of their success was to reinforce the paranoia of their attackers, convincing them that all humans represented an immediate threat to the survival of their race.

A second ambush by the Castleman's ships destroyed at some cost to them a Gerin headquarters ship. The effect of this astonished everyone as the Gerin force suddenly lost cohesion, fighting individually and in threes. This bought Castleman's World exactly three extra days. The running battle continued until they were fighting within the actual atmosphere of Castleman's World itself. Of over two hundred original human ships less than a dozen fought their way free after their planet suffered the same fate as New Athens.

Having destroyed Castleman's World, the victorious fleet split into several groups to enable them to strike at a number of human worlds simultaneously. For many of these planets the first knowledge of the loss of the Castleman's fleet was a Gerin bombardment. Others, warned of the danger, still refused to give up their sovereignty and make a joint response. Seeing the human forces in disarray, many of the nonhuman races chose to limit their support to carefully observing the continuing Gerin success. Unified as a race, the Gerin see division as a weakness and are quick to exploit it. For the next months a dozen human worlds fought hopeless battles against overwhelming odds.

THE ARCHIMEDES EFFECT
by Todd Johnson

Awwwk! Frag the lieutenant! Frag the lieutenant! Arawwk!'' The bird's noise pierced the steamy midday air.

In the tense silence that followed, Charlie Poindexter knew he was in trouble. "Quiet, Archy! Quiet!'' he whispered.

It was too late. Dressed in battle armor, helmet off to let some of the steam that had so recently been sweated seep into the equally steamy day, the marine lieutenant turned to focus a harsh, killing glare on the parakeet standing on Charlie Poindexter's left shoulder. Ahead and behind him were the hardened troops of his platoon, trudging warily on either side of the dirt road. The tropical sun beat down on the silent clearing with murderous intensity.

The gunny sergeant and the others of the combat platoon were suddenly gathered around on either side of their lieutenant.

"Frag the lieutenant! Awr-eek!" the bird screeched as Charlie batted him in mid-squawk.

Three days of wakefulness and lots of casualties stared out of the lieutenant's eyes as he asked in a voice made gruff from screaming too hard too long: "That bird bio'd?"

The bird was suddenly quiet and Charlie could feel his sweat chilling in his one-piece shipsuit as he lied.

"Him! No sir, natural as can be!" Damn this humidity, he swore to himself, it's playing hell with all the electronics! "Just a dumb bird."

"Dumb dead bird soon," one of the grunts behind him grumbled.

"Araak! Sir to an officer!" the bird screeched. Charlie batted it desperately. "Frag the lieutenant!" Charlie batted it harder but the bird dodged aside. "Incoming! Incoming!"

Shit! Charlie swore to himself. He matched stares with the lieutenant. "The bird's just a joke, a gift from some old buddies. It's a real Earth parakeet."

His left arm started up to his pocket but spasmed halfway, vibrating so quickly it hummed, and then froze as far down as the wrist, while the hand began clawing and shuddering like a lost spider. Hastily, Charlie reached over with his right hand, opened the pocket, and thumbed open his wallet.

"They thought it was a good joke."

The lieutenant swallowed hard, took his eyes off the clawing hand attached to the spasming arm, and looked at the ID on the wallet.

The man in the picture looked younger and tougher than the man in front of him, but he could see the resemblance. His eyes went up to the man and back to the wallet again.

The gunny took that moment to approach and peer at the wallet ID himself. It included Poindexter's service record. The noncom straightened suddenly and turned around to his platoon.

"All right, you bunch of slugs! No more goofing off.

Let's get set up around here!'' He herded the rest of the platoon off with one respectful backward glance at Charlie, his arm half raised in a salute, hastily dropped in shame.

Charlie took the time to move his left arm to his side, pressing some special spot in the underarm which caused it to jerk suddenly and remain still. ''This damned moisture!'' Charlie swore.

''Yeah, it gets into all the electronics,'' the lieutenant agreed hastily. He looked up again carefully and asked, ''Why the parakeet?''

For a moment Charlie Poindexter remembered the charge and the explosions and the laser fire, his cheerful men being set alight like so many fireworks, how he'd held together the remnants, struggled through the night to regroup them, dragged bodies into cover, and how they'd cheerfully cursed him throughout it all.

''Frag the lieutenant!'' It had been a big joke up to that point, a game he and his men had played. When the flarefire—that strange burning weapon that looked so much like a laser and acted so much like powdered white phosphorus, burning and sticking to everything it touched—had got him as he signaled the last remnants to safety, they in turn had pulled him back. Pain-racked but sure his men were in no danger of fleeing, he had joked back: ''Lieutenant fragged!'' On the battlefield, where body parts and burned flesh were the order of the day and the only thing to hold out for was the buddy who was holding out for you, it had been high humor. It had been so funny that the whole platoon, all seven of them left out of the fifty men of the day before, had burst out laughing; laughed their sides out.

''Battlefield humor,'' he replied, remembering how his old men had come to the hospital, subdued, respectful, until one of them remembered the joke and they all laughed. He sketched the details to the lieutenant quickly, adding: ''Then the next day, the parakeet.''

''Sick,'' the lieutenant agreed. He looked over at the parakeet again.

''You sure he's not bio'd?''

Charlie stared back and lied again: ''You think I made

that bird say those things? Mister, I've still got some living to do!''

The lieutenant shrugged. ''I've never seen a bio'd bird, that's all.''

''Me neither,'' Charlie agreed, lying cheerfully. ''I can understand bio'd dogs, it'd be kinda useful to have a dog you could link with, but a dumb bird?'' The parakeet turned its beak and took a nip at Charlie's ear.

The lieutenant was getting fidgety. He'd spent enough time with Poindexter and—that arm. ''My men're setting up,'' he said. ''You want a hand with that arm? My tech's pretty good with the small stuff.''

''No, no thanks,'' Charlie replied quickly. ''I just have to reset it every so often in this damned muck!'' He swirled his good arm in the heavy moisture that lay around them.

The lieutenant looked doubtful. ''Well, if you say so.'' Suddenly he asked: ''What're you doing out this far from town, anyway?''

The tone had Charlie instantly alert and he struggled not to show it. Instead, in nostalgic tones: ''Heard there might be some action here, and—well, you know.''

The lieutenant did not know what Charlie was talking about, but nodded anyway. ''Better head back to town soon,'' he replied. ''What do you do there?''

''Trader,'' Charlie replied. ''Got a one-manner over at the yard.''

''Risky business,'' the lieutenant said disapprovingly. ''You must make a fair profit.''

Charlie bridled realistically, raised his left arm, and intoned haughtily: ''I rather think I have a right to make up for this.'' The lieutenant looked away. ''Besides, I don't have much else to do and I still can help out.''

''Whatever,'' the lieutenant allowed. He turned toward his platoon. ''You'd better get back to town soon, sir.'' There was more tone in his ''sir'' than there would have been had Poindexter been a civilian. With that the lieutenant trudged off, battle armor whirring as hot motors fought for traction.

''You damned bird!'' Charlie swore as soon as he was

sure the lieutenant was out of sight. "I ought to break your neck right now!"

"What, and feel it, Charlie my boy?" the bird quipped back in a poor brogue. "Bio'd!" Archy sniffed.

Poindexter had no time for the simulac's pride. "What'd you get?"

"You got it all," the bird told him. "KG-30 silicon gear oil with a hydroscopiscity of thirty percent, delamination of the main breastplates of ninety percent of all combat effectives, forty percent failure of all communications gear, inaccuracies of up to one hundred percent in all heads-up displays—"

"That stuff is shot. If these are typical, they're gonna be slaughtered!" Charlie Poindexter exclaimed. "C'mon, we've got to get back to the ship!"

"What about informing the authorities?" The simulacrum inquired.

"Oh no! Not after the last time!" Poindexter replied, picking up his pace.

The guard at the spaceport freight yard was the first human Charlie had seen since his conversation with the marine. Tandin, the capital of powerful Isslan, was ghost-town empty. At least it was some indication that the authorities had finally come to take the alien threat seriously.

"Too late," Archimedes declared, responding to Poindexter's unspoken thoughts. Poindexter sighed. The evidence was overwhelming: the humans were going to lose the planet.

"If the local governments had banded together immediately into one military coalition there was only a forty percent chance of successfully countering the enemy's military forces."

Charlie pursed his lips. The problem was that the enemy insisted on killing every human found. The evidence was only just coming to light and still hotly contested by most of the nations of the world. They contended that it was just the Alliance's way of getting more military aid. The politicians conveniently forgot the destruction and conquest of the states of the Coastal Coalition and made no mention at all of the Royal Islands of Anseen. The New Adriatic Alliance was composed of those island states which surrounded what had once been called the Coastal Coalition, which itself had surrounded the Royal Islands.

The planet Skylark had been inhabited centuries ago by humans, who established thousands of monarchies and anarchies among the many islands of the water world. The military forces that existed had evolved only to protect the various nations against any possible "misunderstandings" and so were purposely token in nature. If ever a nation got expansionist tendencies the surrounding nations would band together in a loose coalition and contain the perpetrator. Things being as they were, the military forces were always underequipped and overcharged by the civilian sector. Equipment was nonexistent or faulty, as Archimedes had noted of the Alliance marines assigned that sector of Tandin's defensive perimeter.

"There has to be something," Poindexter declared. To the parakeet simulacrum he said: "List me their known weaknesses."

The simulacrum ruffled its feathers, muttering: "It's a sign of inferior design to always vocalize your thoughts." Poindexter grabbed for the simulacrum but it dodged away and began: "Known weaknesses of the Gerin—"

"Start with what we know about them instead," Charlie interjected.

"The Gerin were first encountered on the lesser island of Marjea in the Royal Islands. Only fragmented radio reports from the islanders made it to the mainland," Archy intoned. "When coast guard ships attempted to contact the islanders they were obliterated before they could report back. Aerial observation of the island was interdicted by some unknown form of antiaircraft weaponry later termed 'inkjet incinerators.' The Royal Space Station was attacked and destroyed without warning."

The bio'd parakeet had settled back on the merchant's shoulder.

"At this point a company of Royal Marines were loaded aboard a seawater destroyer under orders to reoccupy Marjea. Simultaneously, overtures were made to the three largest republics nearest the Royal Islands to form a military coalition while the Royal Intelligence Gatherers attempted to determine which of the neighboring nations had coveted Marjea.''

The robot bird's presentation was clipped and toneless. It had been a week since Charlie had been given the bird and ship. Ever since he had been unable to decide just how smart the enhanced bird was. Charlie wondered if the bird remembered he had been a Royal Marine. There certainly was no hesitation as it continued its recitation.

''The devastation of the company of Royal Marines was not complete, although three of the eight survivors were thought to have been eaten by some sea animal previously not known but later identified as the Gerin themselves. Neighboring space stations were destroyed on the night of the first landing of the Gerin on the main island. Within three days the Gerin had reached the outskirts of the capital and the neighboring nations had agreed to form a military coalition with troops arriving within the week.''

Charlie shuddered. They didn't get the week. He remembered how his company had been annihilated in twelve minutes, how his shattered platoon had ''held the door open'' for the remnants of the Royal Battalion. He remembered the long torturous night and the agony of his seared arm. The fleeing Royal Islands forces were evacuated to the nearest unoccupied islands, but those were overrun in the following days.

The Gerin attacked in threes, one in the lead and two on either side. The leader invariably was better equipped and tore through defenders with a ferocity that left limbs and entrails strewn over meters. On the ground, the Gerin were unstoppable. In the air, the Gerin had developed sophisticated aircraft capable of outflying all the manually controlled aircraft the Coalition and now the Alliance could pit against them. The space forces of the Alliance were engaged in the strictly defensive role of trying to maintain exterior lines against interior forces. The Gerin fought a reverse siege—the humans on the defensive outside of the conquered territory, the Gerin savagely expanding their conquests from the inside.

From above they were aided by their space force, which maintained not only a low earth orbit, but both geosynchronous and geosynchronous transfer orbits. High above the planet Skylark a battle fleet hovering constantly over one spot conducted the war. Transports looped in from it to supply topcover to the assault fleet, which itself provided a stream of airspace transports downloading supplies and fighter aircraft. Surprisingly, the Gerin seemed to ignore unarmed ships which avoided the war zones. Poindexter closed his eyes and called up the graphics which showed the orbits as two circles—the geosynchronous and low-earth orbits joined by an elliptical geosynchronous transfer orbit. It was this newly arrived assault fleet, a relatively new development, which finally awoke the politicians of more distant island states to the danger the Gerin posed. Far away, however, the threat looked unreal or at least transient, and certainly not global.

"The destruction of all space stations, completed just this week, will ultimately cause larger coalitions to form," Archimedes continued. "Unfortunately the destruction of the stations and the few free-flying communications satellites has rendered coordination of defense nearly impossible and has already reduced commerce of all forms by thirty percent." The simulacrum paused, the result of a trillion new calculations. "The restriction of commerce is projected to increase arithmetically until the planet is conquered by the enemy."

"The assault force is in retrograde orbit. Why?" Charlie asked of the fake parakeet.

"Unknown," it answered. "Most probably due to original orbital inclinations."

"What about the composition of the GTO force?" Charlie asked, searching the possibilities open to them.

"GTO—ambiguous—expand," Archimedes responded in computer confusion.

"GTO: geosynchronous transfer orbit," Charlie explained with a sigh. Every so often the simulacrum would remind him that it was nothing more than a very sophisticated set of molecular electronic devices linked to form an excellent imitation of intelligence. Only an imitation.

It couldn't think; it could just repeat what had been programmed into it.

"Information regarding the enemy's space forces is classified as an Alliance top secret," the simulacrum responded primly.

"I thought you were going to break into those systems," Charlie insisted.

"Certainly," Archimedes replied. "However, you have been occupying too much of my computative facilities to permit me to gain access."

"Okay, okay! I'll shut up," Charlie responded. Electronically he called ahead to his spaceplane, *Risky Lady*, to lower the boarding ramp as they approached. Once inside, the merchant pressed the retract button and strode determinedly into the cockpit. There he deposited the strangely still form of the parakeet on the armrest of one of the pilot seats and sat himself in the other.

Risky Lady was a standard aerospace plane which still had conventional displays and controls as well as the ever-present biolink the avian aliens had given him which enabled properly "wired" pilots to connect directly to the onboard intelligence. It was incapable of getting farther off Skylark than a high orbit, but could put him anywhere on the planet within minutes.

Charlie connected with *Risky Lady*. Softly he subvocalized, *Hey, baby! How's it going?*

All systems are functioning normally, the ship replied in dry controlled tones. *However, I have noted on the military wavelengths that there is an increasing number of military craft in the air and suborbital space which indicates that—*

Yeah, I know. Rough times ahead, Charlie interrupted. Having your ship controlled by a second enhanced computer programmed to be primarily concerned with its own survival could be a problem. *What about the cargo?*

All cargo has been successfully off-loaded, the ship responded, adding with a note of discomfiture: *However, the simulacrum Archimedes conducted all business transactions on our behalf.*

So? Archy do something wrong?

A profit was made but not as great as could have been realized.

Charlie smiled. *Risky Lady* was also programmed to maximize profits.

Overhauls cost money! the ship protested.

Archy was acting under my orders, Charlie informed her. *Don't worry about the profits. I thought we were gathering vital information.* He sensed silent shock from *Risky Lady.* Whoever had programmed her really liked his profits. *What about back-freight?*

The prospects of profit are dismal, the ship responded, feeding him raw data. Charlie stiffened involuntarily as the data were downloaded into his implant. Instantly, he had a list of over a thousand items which could be purchased from the port's automated warehouses all over the beleaguered capital. His implant and *Risky Lady* both had already decided which items from the list would maximize certain slightly different requirements: profit and usefulness. One item stored near the port itself caught his attention: *Umbrellas?*

Tanning umbrellas, silvered, two meters in diameter with bimetallic sun sensors. They open automatically in sunlight. "Ideal for the beach!" the ship intoned in response, even to the point of switching "voices" to reproduce the advertising blurb at the end.

Here? That's insane! You don't need a tanning umbrella on Skylark! Charlie laughed. The clouds rarely parted anywhere on Skylark—it was just too humid. Apparently they were intended for off-planet export.

"The same tanning umbrellas that the natives of beautiful Skylark use!" Another line from the commercial.

"I have succeeded in gaining the data on the enemy space forces," Archimedes announced suddenly, startling Poindexter. His entire conversation with the ship had taken 11.2 seconds.

"And?" Charlie prompted the enhanced parakeet.

"The data are very interesting. It appears that the largest craft of the Gerin's geosynchronous space force always alters to transfer orbit—GTO—before a major assault is launched."

"How often is GTO in sync with the LEO?" Charlie snapped.

"Ambiguous phrases: sync, LEO, please clarify."

Charlie responded in computer, wondering who had programmed such marvelous memories and hadn't entered so many commonly used terms. "Sync: short for synchronous. LEO: low earth orbit." Charlie finished in exasperated tones. "Bloody parrot!"

"Understood," Archimedes replied evenly. "This simulacrum is a parakeet, *not* a parrot," it continued in hurt tones.

Charlie rolled his eyes heavenward. Whoever had programmed the personality was a sanctimonious SOB, too. "Just give me the answer!"

"Geosynchronous transfer orbit and low earth orbit synchronize once every seven low earth orbits, nearly in exact time with the orbital period of geosynchronous transfer orbit," the simulacrum answered.

Charlie paused to turn that answer into something more human-readable: transfer orbit matched with low earth orbit about once every ten hours, roughly. That big ship . . . "What sort of communications data do you have?" Charlie asked.

"Ambigu—"

"The big enemy ship—how much communications traffic does it have?" Charlie expanded.

"Information indicates that the largest enemy ship has the greatest amount of communications traffic," Archimedes answered. Then, reaching Charlie's conclusions: "However, that does *not* make that ship the command ship—it could just as easily be a hospital or repair ship."

"Something important whichever way." Charlie decided.

"You must remember that the rules of war do not allow hospitals to be attacked," Archimedes informed him.

Charlie swore. "Bird, those mothers' sons don't give one flying—" He caught himself as he realized he would have to spend several hours explaining the meaning of his swearing to the simulacrum. "Disregard. The enemy do not seem to be playing by the rules of war." He thought to himself for a moment. "Do you have any idea when that ship will be in LEO again?"

"That ship does not take a low earth orbit," Archimedes responded primly, accepting the acronym and ignoring the meaning of the question.

Charlie sighed in exasperation again. "When is that ship going to be at perigee of the GTO again?" he asked, rephrasing the original question in a manner understandable to the computer intelligence of the fake bird.

"The ship will probably participate in an assault on the three remaining capitals of the Alliance in eighteen thousand four hundred and fifty-three point three-four seconds." Archimedes sensed the question from Charlie before he asked. "Or five hours, seven minutes, thirty-three point three-four seconds."

"If only we could get that ship . . ." Seeing the tattered remnants of the island's defenders had affected Charlie more than he expected. He *had* to do something.

"The effect of destroying that enemy vessel is not known, as its exact purpose is still unknown," Archimedes responded. "However, if that ship is the command ship for the alien assault they would be discommoded only for the length of time required to receive another command ship; doubtless their assault would continue in the interim, diminished by an unknown factor."

"Bird, you talk too much!"

"Our purpose in being here is to gather information so that—"

"Don't say it!" Charlie cried, pointing a silencing finger at the bird. "I know why we're gathering information on the enemy, but it won't do a bit of good if they're going to wipe out the whole planet!"

"As long as the information is stored in a manner that allows it to be retrieved at a later date it does not matter whether the planet is devoid of human life," the simulacrum replied dispassionately.

"It does to the humans who die here!" Charlie replied hotly, forgetting for a moment to what he was talking. He cooled off. "Besides, how are we supposed to preserve this information?"

"That," the simulacrum responded, "is why I was united with a human being—to allow him to make that determination. That is your function, your sole function, so far as I am programmed to respond."

"Five hours, huh?" Charlie mused. *How is our fuel?* he asked *Risky Lady.*

Fuel types for all stages of ascent and descent were ordered and are at maximum, the ship responded.

Charlie could have sworn it sounded a bit smug. He leaned back in the pilot's seat.

Decisions must be made soon. The situation grows risky as the enemy gets closer, the ship prodded him in a twittering voice. Charlie wondered if the voice belonged to the genius that had programmed her, then pulled in on himself, thinking. After a few seconds he threw two switches on the control panel and all external contacts cut out, ship, simulacrum, even his artificial left arm. Bitterly, he mulled over the information he had. The planet was lost. It was only a matter of time. He thought of the children he'd watched playing just outside the walls of the marine compound on the Royal Islands, and felt helpless. Surrender was pointless, overflights had found no sign of a living human being in any enemy-held lands. Fighting was pointless; the enemy would overwhelm their meager defenses, and only a totally committed planet-wide defensive stood any chance of checking the enemy until help from other human worlds came—if it could be persuaded to come. There was no hope.

"Dammit, I won't give in!" Charlie swore, jerking forward as images of his men dying around him mixed with the death-tired eyes of the marine lieutenant and his platoon—all too soon to be annihilated. "There's got to be a way to hit back, or at least to give them a hotfoot!"

Charlie stopped. A look of amazement crossed his face and he fell back in the seat, thoughtful. A smile crossed his face, and then he laughed, loud and long. He reconnected to the rest of the electronic world, forcing his left arm to take a thrower's stance and jerking it as though throwing an unseen javelin. He speeded the arm up, faster, and then stopped.

"Archy?" he called. The simulacrum looked at him.

"What's the fastest cycle time on this arm? How fast can it move?"

"I cannot tell. The specifications are altered for each human recipient," Archy replied.

"Well, here, take it and see what you can find out," Charlie responded, releasing control over the artificial arm. He watched, slightly perturbed, as the arm flexed and loosened repeatedly and then suddenly performed a series of jerks so fast that he thought the circuits must have blown again.

"It has a cycle time of about forty-nine milliseconds, but I would not perform that operation repeatedly without getting modifications made to the limb's mechanics."

"How about eight thousand cycles?" Charlie asked.

The simulacrum was silent as it thought. "I can reasonably assert that the artificial limb can repeat that number of cycles for a limited time without sustaining immediate failure."

Charlie was instantly active. "Call the tower and get a clearance for Phoenicis," Charlie told the parakeet. Internally he ordered the ship, *Buy the umbrellas!* They were already in a container and should take only a few minutes to load.

The umbrellas are not *profitable*, the ship objected in haughty tones. When Charlie overrode the objection, *Risky Lady* allowed: *They may be useful as samples. How many did you want?*

All of them! Charlie replied, getting a bit impatient. *How soon can you get them aboard?*

There are eight thousand umbrellas for sale, the ship responded. If it was possible for mere circuits to sound confused, she did.

I know! How long to get them aboard? Charlie asked, wondering if it was possible to outrage a computer.

Two hours and twenty-three minutes to receive the container and reload all eight thousand umbrellas, the ship responded after consulting her computer counterpart in the automated warehouse.

I want them loaded so that we can access them from the airlock, Charlie said. *Risky Lady* acknowledged the order, revising her estimate to exactly three hours.

"Take off in three hours and five minutes," Charlie informed the simulacrum as he settled back into his seat again.

"Tower wants us to leave as soon as possible," Archy responded, adding, "Enemy action outside the capital is beginning to threaten air access."

Poindexter ignored the parakeet's warning, demanding instead that Archimedes calculate a series of orbits and orbital maneuvers that either so engaged or so confused the simulacrum as to render it speechless. Of *Risky Lady* he demanded detailed emissivity and absorptivity data of all paints commercially available. He finally found what he needed in Phoenicis, which was one of the few other ports still operating. Then, after overriding the ship's troubled objections that the paints he was most interested in getting were already imported and not a profitable cargo, he ordered Archimedes to buy all they had.

By the time *Risky Lady* was taking off, the Gerin were on the outskirts of the city and the simulacrum had struck a deal with a Phoenician trader for the paint. The flight to Phoenicis should have been completely atmospheric, but Charlie Poindexter chose to go suborbital. He rapped the simulacrum on its beak with his finger to get its attention.

"I have not completed your calcuations! One is needed for each launch," the parakeet objected.

"Fine, later," Charlie said. "Link in with the *Lady* and see what sort of sensor information you can get on that big Gerin ship. Confirm that it's coming down to LEO."

"I cannot possibly see what the position of the Gerin's largest ship has to do with the safety of the information I possess," the simulacrum complained.

"That's why you have a human being with you, bird beak."

Archimedes started to reply and stopped. After some time it spoke again, this time in a new voice. "There is no possible way for you to attack it with the equipment on this vessel!" it objected. "There are no ship's weapons and it would have allowed none to be added."

"Just get the readings!" Charlie ordered. He linked with *Risky Lady* and added: *Continue approach.*

Descent in ten minutes. On the descent Charlie remembered all of the lies he had told the marine lieutenant. Likely the young officer was dead now, he and the men he had led. What Charlie regretted most was the lie about the simulacrum: his men had not given it to him.

"Just take it with you wherever you go. It'll feed you all the information it has or gleans," the birdlike ITC trader had said to him. "All we ask is that you let us take a data dump when we pass this way again."

"What if I don't make it until then?" Charlie had asked.

"Then just leave it someplace safe. We'll find it," the trader had replied.

In return, Charlie Poindexter found himself leasing an amazingly low-priced spaceplane capable of making geosynchronous orbit and so of trading directly with the Interstellar Traders Collective. If they ever returned to the system. The bird and ship represented some of the strangest technology he had ever encountered. He was amazed at the abilities of the ship and surprised at the simulacrum, which was not really a parakeet at all but some artificial creation styled to look like a small household pet of the avian race that had crafted it. Something about that whole deal still nagged at the back of Charlie's consciousness. Sure, the aliens were traders, but why did they need information on the attacking Gerin? Sure, any new military tactics were instantly salable—military intelligence was always salable. But there was hardly anything new about the Gerin's attacks. They always had overwhelming numbers. Besides, traders avoided wars, they didn't sneak into war zones just to get standard intelligence. But the birdlike trader had been so persistent, so dedicated to getting Charlie to accept the offer.

Phoenicis Tower calling, the ship informed him.

"Tell them that we are just landing long enough to pick up our cargo," Charlie replied. "And tell that trader to have the goods ready as soon as we stop."

To Archimedes: "Get ready to download our first orbit into *Risky Lady* as we land."

The fake parakeet squawked. "She's gonna refuse! And the tower will read her program and refuse you permission to launch."

"Override her," Charlie replied calmly. Twenty minutes later, as *Risky Lady* launched at full throttle, Archimedes, on a command from Poindexter, overrode the ship's intelligence and replotted its course. *Risky Lady* altered angle immediately after retracting her gear and went supersonic, to the loud protests of Phoenicis Tower.

"Blame it on the war effort!" Poindexter told them. High up in the atmosphere, as the air grew too thin for the ramjets to operate, *Risky Lady* was switched to scramjets, which rapidly boosted her speed up to Mach 25. Instead of trimming for a low-energy Hohmann orbit, on Poindexter's orders the simulacrum kept the thrust on to form a direct-ascent orbit.

"This is gonna play hell on the fuel-cost balances!" the parakeet remarked.

"We've got fuel to spare," Charlie responded. "It's the time I worry about. How are we?"

"We're right where you want us to be," Archimedes responded. "It cost more fuel because of that hold at the gate, but we're right on time."

Minutes later, *Risky Lady* was shifted from her scramjets to pure rockets, burning a combination of her standard hydrogen fuel with onboard oxygen. In seconds she was in a well-formed circular orbit three hundred kilometers above the planet's surface. The former marine officer activated his magnetic soles and undid his seat harness.

"We are within risk of detection by the enemy," the parakeet noted. "It would have been wiser to shape a retrogade orbit with the planet between us."

"And have the GTO force and the GEO ships spot us?" Charlie shot back. "Get the airlock ready," he ordered as he hurried toward the hold. Once inside the airlock, Charlie sealed a helmet over his one-piece shipsuit, then opened the lock connecting the cargo hold to the airlock bays. Using his pilot's implant, he overrode several safety connections and caused the air in both the combined hold and the airlock bays to be evacuated. He found the paint in the cargo bay and hauled it toward the airlock, carefully stacking the magnetized containers. Then he looked at the stacks of boxes that housed the umbrellas.

"Time!" he called to Archimedes, not bothering with his implant. When he got no answer he shouted, repeating on his implant: "The second program, is it running?"

"Affirmative. Time is seven eight zero, seven-nine, seven-eight . . ." Charlie shut out the droning of the simulacrum as he started a large clump of boxed umbrellas through the cargo hold and into the airlock bays. Through his ship connection he engaged the ship's conveyor system. Not waiting to see the result, he manhandled another set and started them on the way. Somehow the parakeet got separated from him.

"Just what is it you are trying to do, human?" the simulacrum asked in pompous tones.

Charlie did not respond, setting the final group of boxed umbrellas in motion. Archimedes continued: "Even granting that the combined velocities of this ship and the enemy craft will be in excess of twenty kilometers per second, there is insufficient mass or rigidity in these umbrellas to pose a hazard to the enemy."

"That's okay," Charlie replied. He clambered around the massed umbrellas and climbed up to the airlock's exit, an umbrella in each hand. He stopped, staring down at all the other ends that waited to be opened. With a shrug, he picked up an unopened umbrella in his artificial arm, ensured that it was properly aligned, and with a quick thrust forward popped the umbrella out into the darkness of Skylark's shadow. He watched approvingly as the closed umbrella, looking like a thin javelin, streaked backward away from the ship.

"The trajectory was not correct," Archimedes chided. "In order to correctly align—"

The ship silently started to rotate as control jets and then maneuvering jets cut in.

"Time?" Charlie called.

"Seven fifty-three," Archimedes responded automatically. Then, "Human, this can't work!"

"Sure it can," Charlie replied. "One umbrella every seventy-nine milliseconds"—another umbrella out and another as Poindexter spoke—"while we traverse inclination from plus twenty-eight point five to minus twenty-eight point five." Another umbrella.

After a few hundred umbrellas Charlie's shoulder began to feel stretched. With his "arm" moving almost too fast to watch, the mechanism was remaining sound, but the flesh and blood attached was beginning to show the strain. Breaking only long enough to open another box of five hundred, he continued the process.

By the time two thousand umbrellas had been jettisoned, his shoulder throbbed painfully. Two hundred later, the agony had spread until it was hard to breathe. After five hundred umbrellas, a tiny trickle of blood ran down the straining merchant's chest. Still he couldn't and didn't halt. At one point, he distracted himself by reciting the roll call of his lost command. The ordeal seemed to last forever.

"That was six hundred umbrellas," the bird noted, "and each is taking longer."

"That's all I need, and more," Poindexter replied. Another umbrella.

"That was eighty-eight milliseconds," Archimedes chided. "And the one before was—"

"If you've got a better idea?" Charlie asked, straining to grab for another umbrella while chucking the first one.

"Computers don't have ideas, they analyze data," Archimedes corrected him. "Data analysis: attach unit to fixed surface."

Charlie Poindexter stared at the simulacrum.

"That'll work!" he exclaimed, quickly unstrapping the physical connections to his artificial arm. The opening was raw and his shoulder bled where he had to pull the leads out of muscle and skin. At other times the action would have made him feel crippled, but not now. There simply wasn't time. Twenty seconds later, Charlie Poindexter, one-armed, was feeding umbrellas up to his artificial arm, at the end of which Archimedes sat to control minutely its speed and accuracy. With the parakeet's help he had precisely positioned the arm with magnetic clamps on the outside of the lock, securing both arm and simulacrum to the outer hull of the ship. Two minutes later, after one hundred and twenty seconds, the simulacrum had counted off one thousand five hundred and nineteen umbrellas.

Charlie soon found that he had to climb back down into the hold in order to push the masses of umbrellas forward to get them onto the ship's conveyor belt. Above him, through the link, Archimedes continually harangued him for not getting umbrellas to the arm fast enough. "That one was twenty microseconds behind, and its orbit is one thousandth of a degree off true!" the fake bird snapped.

Charlie grimaced, pushing more umbrellas up with his remaining arm.

"More!" the bird called.

"Last one," Charlie called back. He was sweating in his suit as he climbed up the ladder to the outside. Turning, he could see nothing of the last umbrella. All eight thousand were already lost in the darkness.

"Are they on course?" he asked the artificial bird as he returned the arm to its socket. Without the imbedded connections, it felt awkward.

"Nominally," the parakeet responded, returning control of the arm to Charlie, adding after a long pause: "I fail to calculate—"

It was abruptly cut off as the artificial arm grabbed and threw the simulacrum in a totally opposite direction from the distant umbrellas.

"The information is safe!" Charlie called after the disappearing bird. Archimedes' circuits had been too heavily involved in analyzing Poindexter's reasons for the madness of throwing needlelike umbrellas in the enemy's path to note the surging link between the human and the artificial arm. Now, floating helplessly in space, the simulacrum found time to be fleetingly intrigued that a slow human brain, even augmented with implants, could, outpace a well-programmed simulacrum.

On board *Risky Lady,* Charlie Poindexter stared in the direction of the simulacrum for long moments. He shook himself.

"Nothing but time on my hands," he said. Then he laughed. "Boy! That damn bird must be pissed!" He undid the magnetic clamp on his artificial arm and carefully reattached it to his shoulder. With a mental sigh he flexed it once or twice and smiled, in control once more. He sobered suddenly, chiding himself: "What about the *Lady?* She'll be sore!" He hurried to the bridge and freed the restraints Archimedes had put on the intelligence module that normally controlled the *Risky Lady.*

THERE IS NO PROFIT IN THIS! Risky Lady shouted immediately, using all uppercase to print out the same message on every screen on the bridge. *You must restore this ship to full functionality!*

Sorry, babe, Charlie responded. *No dice.*

He turned around, facing in the direction of travel. *Sun's going to come up soon, and we'll be in a polar orbit,* he remarked conversationally to the *Lady.*

How could you waste so much fuel? the ship demanded.

It doesn't matter, Lady.

Charlie sighed contentedly, turning back to stare out the forward port at the darkest side of the planet as they headed toward the terminator. His arm still ached, but he would soon see if it had been worth it. They had also been up here a long time; they were lucky no Gerin patrol had spotted them. Soon they would move into direct observation of the Gerin fleet. After more than a minute he spoke.

Listen, in about ten minutes it's going to get pretty hectic. I want you to do me one last favor.

I cannot see how ownership can be changed, the ship's computer responded. *You will tell the Gerin ships that this is a trading ship, intended only for peaceful profit! Maybe then they'll not blow us apart. I am not programmed to attack. Only military ships are capable of such.*

Charlie filed that bit of surprising information and then responded, *You've just been commissioned.*

The merchant expected to find himself either ignored or restrained for piracy. After all, the ship was just a loan. Surprisingly, *Risky Lady* responded in yet another new voice. *By whose authority?*

Poindexter was taken aback. He had not for a moment expected that the ship's programming would include a change of prime purpose. Finally he managed, *By the authority of my appointment as an officer by the king of the Royal Islands.* Bitterly he tried not to remember the Royal Islands had been overrun six weeks earlier.

That will do, the ship acquiesced. *What do you want of me? We can charge into the enemy and probably . . .*

Charlie found the difference between the merchant and military programming of his ship startling. *Nope. I want you to stay on this course until I tell you and then thrust us directly above the enemy's formation. All of the time send that we are a merchant interested in selling information. They must have seen traitors before.*

The enemy will destroy us when we approach too closely or remain too long, the ship informed him. *This is not a good battle plan. I could suggest a number of approaches more likely to achieve success. One has an almost eleven percent probability of successfully damaging a Gerin warship.*

Charlie raised an eyebrow. Could they have programmed this baby for military operations? he asked himself. Sure, he decided. If they can stick all the books ever written onto a molecular chip one centimeter square, why not throw some basic tactics onto a trader? Especially one which, he was sure, was especially made by those bird-brain ITC traders. It was a shame to waste it.

My plan will have to do, Charlie responded as they arrived at the terminator. Below him the day faded to night.

Enemy ships are seven thousand kilometers away, and closing, the ship informed him.

Contact in nine minutes, Charlie responded.

And eighteen point five seconds, the ship corrected. *Based upon prior behavior, I predict that they will detect us in two hundred and twenty-four point seven eight seconds.*

Let me know when you get a definite contact, Charlie responded. *As soon as I tell you, start that maneuver.*

How far above the formation should I arrive? the ship wanted to know.

Near enough to scare 'em, I don't care, Charlie responded. He climbed down the ladder. *Maneuver now so that this airlock is pointing on an intersecting path.*

Jets coughed, stars whirled, jets coughed again, and stars stabilized.

Done.

Charlie looked out, but saw nothing in particular. With great care he centered himself on the airlock docking marks. With his artificial arm he began heaving out the two hundred one-gallon cans of paint. His shoulder began to ache again, but the pain was tolerable and he didn't dare risk the dullness a pain-killing drug would have as a side effect.

Are you throwing out some form of secret weapon loaded while I was inactive? the ship inquired.

Sort of, Charlie replied as he heaved another.

Radar lock! They have spotted us, the ship's computer warned.

Great. Hold steady. Charlie kept heaving. *Ninety. Ninety-one, ninety-two,* Charlie counted to himself.

I detect small arms being fired at your projectiles, the ship told him. *They have vaporized the first four.*

Beautiful! Charlie allowed himself a smile. *One-forty-two, one-forty-three . . .* he counted as he threw the paint out of the hold. He was panting. His artificial arm might be doing the throwing, but the rest of his body was doing the lifting and countering the recoil. Once more he found himself working in a fog of pain.

Energy beams! We are just beyond range, the ship warned.

If they shoot at us, execute that maneuver! Charlie responded. *One-eighty-nine.* Suddenly his view changed and he felt himself being pushed against the floor. The new bruises didn't make his shoulder feel any better.

They fired at us, the ship explained. *Their beams are following us! Missile launch! One hundred seconds to intercept!*

* * *

The airlock glowed brightly, then red-hot. Charlie Poindexter shielded his eyes as he dived for the ladder to the bridge. He never reached it.

Far back in space, the simulacrum Archimedes detected the thermal signature of plasma weapons as they tore through the hull of *Risky Lady*. In seconds, nothing was left of the spaceplane but a molten mass. Dispassionately, the simulacrum noted that its calculations had been correct. The paint flung out of the ship and fired upon by the Gerin had spread into a large vaporized cloud which wrapped the enemy fleet like black ink from a squid. As the fleet emerged from the cloud, the simulacrum noted that some of the ships, including the largest, had been well coated with the black paint. The simulacrum devoted some microseconds to calculating the average temperature rise if the aliens did nothing to remove it. Dispassionately, it noted that the rise would be well within standard limits. It would have no effect. Further, Archimedes calculated that the paint would not provide sufficient interference to reduce the enemy's ability to detect and avoid ramming the thousands of umbrellas which would shortly clear the planet's shadow and . . .

With a sudden burst of understanding the very sophisticated computer known as Archimedes almost *wished* it could turn around to see the umbrellas opening.

Each electronically neutral and unthreatening umbrella orbited slowly toward the Gerin fleet. As the Gerin fleet and its trailing swarm of umbrellas cleared the planet's shadow, each umbrella heated slowly until the bimetallic springs reached a critical temperature. One by one, but in increasing numbers, the umbrellas fanned open to catch the sun's rays and shine—in a nearly perfect parabola with constantly changing focus, directly on the largest ship of the Gerin fleet!

With the speed of its kind, the amazingly complicated microcomputer that almost resembled an Earth parakeet completed its calculations. Each umbrella was coated with a near-perfect reflective surface. It had often noted how humans always used their best materials for their luxuries. Perhaps five thousand of the umbrellas, each spread about a meter apart, retained their alignment. Each umbrella was two meters in diameter, and the light intensity of this star at this distance was 1,400 watts per square meter. That was a total reflected energy of 4,398 watts per umbrella. As they entered the sun, the otherwise inoffensive umbrellas opened and concentrated the sunlight on the still unshielded Gerin ship. The Gerin flagship, not being threatened by anything electronic or massive enough to attract attention, was not even at alert.

The simulacrum watched the bright white spot form on that large ship, glow as the hull grew hotter and hotter, as twenty-two megawatts focused on that one spot for slightly over three hundred seconds. The large ship distended and finally, with alarming speed, exploded in a large cloud of debris as its hull was fatally and unexpectedly ruptured.

With an almost human glee in the silent void of space, Archimedes crowed at the cooling mass of debris that had been the *Risky Lady,* "Frag the flagship! Frag the flagship! Craaaaw!"

The Gerin

Aliens are, by definition, different. They have different physical structure and developed in often radically varied environments. The Gerin's differences made the Gerin a challenging opponent. Their similarities made a collision with man inevitable.

The Gerin are true amphibians. A Gerin is octopoidal—that is, it is radially symmetrical and has eight arms. These arms are much stronger than those of any earth octopus, as they are adapted to carrying weight as well as to locomotion. Each arm ends in two "fingers." The average Gerin weighs over two hundred pounds and is stronger than a human. A large centralized eye is capable of discriminating fine details and is supplemented by two much smaller light-sensitive organs that are barely visible higher on the Gerin's face.

This race developed in oceans that resemble Pliocene Earth's. These waters were filled with creatures more vicious than any Terran shark. There were probably very few moments when the primitive Gerin felt secure. A healthy degree of paranoia was required for survival and has become ingrained in all Gerin attitudes. Also, as amphibians, the early Gerin were limited to a habitable zone comprising only the shallow waters at the continent's edge. This created intense competition between Gerin for the hunting grounds available.

The Gerin individually are driven more by their instincts than are humans. Strong among these instincts is the need to protect the race by destroying any intruders into "their" territory. It is these same instincts that make it nearly impossible for a Gerin warrior to surrender. But more than anything else, the Gerin are driven by racial and personal need to dominate or destroy any potential opposition.

In combat as well, instincts drive the Gerin to fight in patterns laid down in the shallows eons earlier. As reflexes developed in the waters of an ocean are three-dimensional, these often serve the Gerin warrior well in space. They also can be used to an opponent's advantage, in that they often make Gerin tactics predictable.

In nearly every combat situation, the Gerin fight in multiples of three. Their smallest unit is the triad. This is led by an experienced warrior, who is supported by two younger Gerin whose position is similar to that of a twelfth-century squire. On a higher level the theme of threes seems preferred, but is often sacrificed to necessity. All command is centralized and failure is often rewarded with punishment; some Gerin commit suicide. The entire race is ruled over by a Supreme Triad whose decisions are implemented by three further triads, served themselves by nine triads in an ever-expanding pattern of threes.

A combination of extended lines and stiffening resistance slowed this second Gerin onslaught. Many of the remaining human planets had at this time small or weak navies. Most of the planetary forces were composed of nothing larger than a few destroyers supported by unshielded fighters, these being more experienced at rescues than at combat. Everywhere among the Far Stars, worlds strained to produce ships capable of self-defense. During this crucial time the entire burden of defense fell upon the those few ships and men that were ready.

HERO

by Peter Morwood

HE was a little man, with thinning hair, and sad eyes, and a dead son, and he came to the fleet field at Skandurby on a gray winter's day when the rain was slanting down from a sky the color of ancient lead.

The armed military shuttle settled into its preassigned bay for only a few moments, just long enough to leave off the only civilian passenger who had any business here, then powered up its ion drivers and lifted silently away into the lowering clouds. The passenger stood for a moment and watched it go, then looked around him in helpless confusion until he saw the guard post by the gate.

He looked at the sentry, and the sentry looked at him, but only the sentry saw no threat. Behind the rain-spotted clearsteel visor of his helmet, the soldier's face looked as harsh as the slugthrower he carried. The little man held out an ID card in a hand that was trembling with age and something more, then took off his hat and wrung it in his hands while he waited for a verdict. The rain ran down his face like tears.

For a moment the soldier studied the ID, looking up twice to compare its holo image with the small figure standing in the rain. Then he handed it back, and slammed a formal salute-and-present so that the raindrops sprayed from his armor in a glitter of mock dia-

monds. Behind the visor his hard features shifted into a
configuration that now represented stern sympathy. He
tabbed open a channel on his helmet comm, spoke briefly
into it, and then opened the door of the guard post. "Mr.
Prescott, sir, you're expected. If you'd like to come in
out of the weather, there'll be someone out from the officers' mess to collect you right away."

"Thank you, er . . . Corporal."

"That's Sergeant, sir."

"Oh. I . . . Thank you." His mistake must have made
the little man feel even more uncomfortable, because
when he came inside he sat in a corner and from the look
of him seemed to be trying to fade through it. The sergeant offered him tea—which was refused—and then,
greatly daring since even having it in the sentry post
would put him on a charge, held out a mess-kit beaker
and a flask of armagnacois brandy.

"Just for medicinal purposes, sir," he said, and if the
muscles of his face hadn't long before forgotten how to
shape the softer expressions he would have looked shy.
"It, uh, it keeps the cold out as well as electric under-
wear, and tastes a damn sight better."

"Thank you, Sergeant," said the little man, and took
the beaker. He stared for a few seconds at the familiar
unit crest on its side, then held it out for the proffered
nip of brandy. "Real Armagnac, from Earth?"

"I wish," said the sergeant, smacking the stopper back
onto the flask. "No, we just used the name because the
synth was already making something that was going by
the name of cognac brandy, so when Johnny got this out
of it, we . . . I'm sorry, Mr. Prescott. That was out of
order."

"Not at all. I'm glad he had a good time. He was a
fine boy."

"Yes, sir." The sergeant turned away, put his brandy
flask back into whatever cubbyhole it had appeared from,
and stared out across the gray expanse of the landing
field. There were only a few ships still bayed here and
there; the rest were in the belly of a cruiser somewhere,
or in action, chopping the Gerin into sushi. Or being
chopped. That happened too. He was glad when the field

tender arrived for Johnny Prescott's father before the silence could stretch long enough to be uncomfortable.

An officer with captain's tabs at his collar came through the door, and managed to acknowledge the sergeant's salute with great precision without once breaking the rhythm of slapping raindrops from the shoulders of his uniform. His smile as he took the little man's hand was equally precise, a nice balance of welcoming good-fellowship, official regret, and some personal feeling. "Captain Piper, Mr. Prescott," he said briskly. "I'm the squadron adjutant. Sorry I wasn't here waiting, but even though we were advised you were coming to Skandurby, nobody bothered with an ETA. Well, you're here now, and safe enough, and the boss wants to see you. Any luggage?"

The little man blinked, slightly overwhelmed by the young officer's approach. Then he gathered himself together. "None, Captain. I'm just passing through, but since I was on-planet, and this was . . . was Johnny's last posting, I asked the squadron commander if I could visit."

"Quite so. And perfectly understandable. Now if you'd like to make your way out to the wagon . . . ?" Captain Piper stood to one side as the little man went out, watching him with that same odd mixture of emotions in his eyes before turning to face the sergeant. "Well?"

"No luck, sir. He doesn't know."

"Damn."

"Sir." There were many occasions when the sergeant wished he was an officer, but many more when he was happy to remain a noncom, and never more so than right now.

"All right. Thanks for keeping an eye on him. Oh, and one last thing."

"Sir?"

"I've got an absolutely rotten sense of smell, but you might just want to open a window for a while. People like Provost de Kuypers can imagine the strangest things."

"Sir!"

"Carry on, Sergeant."

* * *

The few flight crews in the officers' mess had been hastily warned in advance of Mr. Prescott's arrival. Consequently there was no uneasy falling-off in conversation when the visitor entered, since what little talking remained had already been muted from its usual real or forced bonhomie down to a discreet murmur. That was why the silence that spread from the open door like ripples in a still pond seemed not so much wary suspicion as respect. One of the snubship pilots set down his drink and stood up; then another, a third, until one by one every man of the squadron who remained dirtside today was on his feet, gazing quietly at the small, rumpled figure who had stopped, embarrassed, in the doorway of their private world.

"Two-one-seven Squadron," said somebody, they didn't know whose voice, or care, "*atten-shun!*"

Weary backs straightened and the heels of combat boots came together in a ripple of sound like a smallbore volley. There were no hats worn in the mess and therefore no salutes, but the young crewmen remained at parade attention while Johnny Prescott's father went by, until the connecting door had closed behind him. Then they relaxed again, and wondered why they'd bothered.

It's the usual stuff, thought Major Yevgeny Alexandrovich Nakashima as he pushed a small box across his desk and watched while Mr. Prescott opened it. *I've packed those bloody boxes far too many times, and always it's the same stuff, more or less.*

There was a wristchrono, the squadron crest engraved on its band as if for dress wear, but dirty and scratched and with part of its metal slumped into shiny droplets. There was a bundle of letters, both chip and printed hardcopy, tied with strapping plastic; some money; a tobacco pipe and a pouch of what passed for tobacco on Hekla; a scarf of red silk with white polka dots; a bar of medal ribbons and the cased decorations that they represented; and a dog's collar.

There had been a couple of vidisks as well, but they had been destroyed. There were some intimate parts of a man's private life that had no need to outlast him. Nakashima had acted as censor before. He was good at it, as good as anyone might be with his amount of practice at sorting personal effects. He would have to do it again when the present raid came back, and he would do it as always to the best of his judgment, without a qualm, and be ready to answer for his decisions to the highest level.

Mr. Prescott looked at the pipe for a long time, turning it over and over in his hands as he polished the bowl with the spotted scarf. "Like something out of history," he said.

"History, sir?"

"Yes. From the early flying wars. When pilots were supposed to swagger, and dress in a certain way that showed they were . . . different."

"They still do, Mr. Prescott." *Although the way they dress usually ends with a zippered rubber bag—if they're lucky.* Nakashima felt suddenly uncomfortable in this old man's presence, and knew that he would continue to feel that way until he had the answers to a great many questions. "Sir," he said, not so eagerly that it was obvious, "would you like a tour of the station?"

"Is that permitted?"

"If I permit it, yes. There's nothing sensitive or classified on view. Most of that stuff"—Nakashima smiled crookedly—"is probably in action right now."

"Will you be showing me around, Major?"

Nakashima managed to keep shock at the very idea from showing on his face. "I'd like to, but"—he gestured at his desk, neat enough but with ominous racks of data chips awaiting attention—"keeping the place this clear needs work, and I'm behind on that already." He thought for a moment, sorting through names and faces before deciding on the safest candidate and switching on his annunciator. "Lieutenant Glass, Captain Piper, to my office."

The two officers arrived so fast that Nakashima suspected they might have been waiting for the summons— Piper because he was the squadron adjutant and likely to be called upon at any second by the boss, and Glass for no other reason than that he was observant and intelligent.

Young Phil Glass was already well aware that he had been posted to the 217th as a replacement for Johnny Prescott. Commander Nakashima credited him with enough sense to realize that his presence was likely to be required in this situation for just that reason—as well as various others, all interconnected with a lack of seniority, a lack of experience, and a consequent ability to say quite honestly, "I don't know about that, sir."

"Lieutenant Glass," said Nakashima when the brief ceremonies of introduction were out of the way, "I'd be grateful if you could give Mr. Prescott our official two-cred guided tour of the station. Reserved," he continued with a thin smile at the elderly civilian that included him in a private service joke, "for top brass, politicos, and all the other sorts of people we hope will vote us funds when the next defense budget comes up for review."

There were no laughs, because it wasn't really a very funny joke whatever side you were on. Then Glass took Johnny Prescott's father out of the office to show him around the stark base where his son had lived and more recently died. The feeling of relief that followed his departure was almost as shaming to Yevgeny Nakashima as the embarrassed discomfort preceding it had been.

"I thought we had buried this one with Prescott," he said, poking at the little box of personal effects while staring carefully at nothing in particular. "Evidently not. I'm sorry to rake it all up again, Jochen, but official notice might just have to be taken after all."

"Notice of what, boss?" said Jochen Piper, and shrugged, dismissing the problem that he saw as no problem. "He lived, he fought the enemy, he's dead. Nothing unusual about that in wartime."

Nakashima set the security interfaces and stood up, setting his uniform cap on his head and becoming with that one small gesture no longer just "the boss," but the squadron commander with all of the rights and responsibilities that went with the rank. "It depends on the life and the death. There's too much unusual about this one.

I need to talk to the people who knew Prescott better than I did. Come with me.''

Piper followed in silence, and listened in silence as Nakashima began a questioning session in the mess that came pretty damn close to an interrogation. The late Captain John E. Prescott was not a subject which the normally garrulous young men of the squadron wanted to talk about. Major Nakashima soon found out why.

"He got here on the same shuttle as Wollacott and Vass, sir,'' said Nick Hudson. "Last fall. Same time as most of B Flight, when you think about it. . . .''

"Bugger brought a personal flitter with him,'' chipped in one of the other pilots. Nakashima raised an eyebrow, inviting elaboration. He knew about the flitter, but had never wondered before what the other members of the squadron thought about it. "It was an ancient grid, of course,'' the pilot continued, in a tone that suggested none of them had expected anything else. No fighter jock who played the part that Johnny Prescott had chosen for himself would ever drive a *new* sports wagon. "A '28 Boulton Turbo-Ten. He used to drive it like a mad bloody bastard.''

"And,'' said someone else, "he had a dog.''

This time Major Nakashima blinked as astonishment slipped through the impassive mask of his official face. Promoted and posted to Skandurby only a few months back, he hadn't known about the dog—and had only barely known about Prescott. "A dog?'' he echoed.

"Yes, sir. Some sort of terrier. He called it Toby.''

"It pissed on my boots,'' said a voice from the back of the group. "Twice.''

"So let me get this straight,'' said Nakashima. A long time ago he'd been interested in military history, enough at least that he'd eventually ended up in a uniform himself, and lots of images from wars centuries past were tangling with what he had just heard, cluttering up his mind so that he was properly confused by now. "The man had a dog, smoked a pipe, wore silk scarves, and drove a . . .''—he rummaged in his mind for the archaism—''. . . sports car.''

"He drew a line at a mustache, though," said Jochen Piper helpfully.

"Oh, good." Major Nakashima felt and sounded venomous, as if the dead pilot had somehow managed to pull some sort of long-term practical joke on everyone remaining in the squadron. "I'm so pleased to hear that he wasn't a total cliché. So tell me about him. Everything"—he sent a slow stare around the pilots and crewmen of League Attack Squadron 217—"that was somehow left out of the official reports."

Johnny Prescott had been transferred to 217 Squadron during a slack time in the war, just after the victory at Ten Moons had changed Admiral MacDonald from a reasonably capable fleet commander into a genuine chrome-plated hero. Eight new flight crew got off the shuttle—eight, and Prescott. He wasn't new, except to the squadron; he was already famous, with a chestful of the sort of decorations that showed how brave he was and how lucky he was and how long he'd managed to stay alive. They said that he, too, was some sort of hero, and he took care to behave that way.

There had been the Boulton sportster, for one thing, which he drove right to the edge of its envelope; and the way he was able to drink anyone in the squadron under the table and still be on the flight line at dawn, looking fresher than any human being had a right to when an alien system's primary was still barely able to peek over the horizon. There was the way he flew, too, like a fallen angel. Everybody wanted to be there the first time Johnny Prescott went up against the Gerin with the 217th, and nobody, but nobody, wanted to be wearing the sushi's tentacles on that day.

It came soon enough.

Sensor-linked, Skandurby's scramble klaxon went off with a screech in the same instant that 217 Squadron's designated carrier cruiser downwarped into the Hekla system. By the time LCC-1702 *Lanoe Hawker VC* slid into a high geosynch, all of the ships detailed for that particular tour of duty were already prepped, cross-checked, and lifting through the atmosphere for rendezvous and departure.

"Fast enough for you, kid?" said Prescott to his co-pilot. Miklos Istvan, one of the young replacements who had come in with Johnny, nodded in dumb amazement. Seven minutes was all that it had taken, from uncomfortable suited-up dozing in the ready room to lining up a final docking approach with a cruise in high orbit. That was enough to impress most people, never mind someone who had already spent an entire transfer run just being impressed with the company he was keeping.

"All right then." Johnny Prescott moved his command chair back and opened a channel to the cruiser's flight deck. "*Hawker* Mayfly Control, this is Ranger Zero Three, at the perch and on course. Intercepting glide slope threshold in seventeen seconds from my mark, bay Bravo-Two docking clearance confirm, over?" Long before the reply came back, Johnny slid his hands out of the primary control gauntlets and grinned sidelong at his co. "You have control."

"But sir, I—!" squeaked Istvan, then made a grab for the secondary command grips and jabbed his fingers into them. "I have control, sir!"

"*Zero Three, this is Mayfly. You have a go for dock, Bravo-Two confirms clear, acknowledge, over.*"

"Zero Three, acknowledged, over. Well, you heard the lady," said Prescott, and leaned back to look as ostentatiously relaxed as his pressure suit allowed. "Take us in." In his headset he could hear someone else in the heavy fighter's four-man crew laughing softly, and he smiled.

He was smiling again later, but this time there was no humor in it, just a cold skinning of lips back from teeth as his helmet gunsight laid itself squarely on the crew compartment of a Gerin escort.

The two ships had chased each other for fifteen seconds through a shrieking outer-atmosphere furball in which it seemed that every Gerin escort vessel in the quadrant and every other League fighter but themselves had appeared on screen or had gone flickering over, un-

der, or on either side. The sushi's more maneuverable
ship had hammered into a tight right-hand left-hand scissors, both to throw the Leaguer's gunnery off-track and
in an attempt to force an overshoot beyond the three-nine
line into a target position.

It might have worked with most people, but not with
Johnny Prescott. He had laughed at the hasty scissors and
rolled inverted through the Gerin's six, then instead of
pulling through into what should have been a standard
split-S disengagement, rolled again and swept back up
into his present perfect knife-range firing slot, where he
sat, and sat, and did nothing, for two whole age-long
seconds.

"Why don't I shoot?" Prescott snapped suddenly.

"FOD, sir," Miklos returned just as smartly. Foreign-
object damage caused by the bits of an enemy chopped
up at close range could splash a fighter just as efficiently
as being on the wrong side of that same enemy's gun-
sights. In the instant of his reply the junior co flared Zero
Three's drag brakes into whatever atmosphere was available for them to hang on to, and punched in just enough
retro from the reaction thrusters to open the distance.

The Gatling laser pod scabbed onto Zero Three's belly
went active. Despite its apparent multiple barrels, the
deuterium fluorine laser did not actually rotate like the
old projectile weapon from which it took its name; but
its variable-wavelength energy did, emitted from each
lasing rod in turn at a rate of six hundred shifts per second and an average power output of ten gigawatts.

There were no ravening beams, and in deep space there
would have been nothing to see at all except for the damage at point of impact. Here, skimming the atmospheric
envelope, Prescott's ship was linked to its Gerin target
by a narrow string of sparks as what little air was present
ionized in the blast of power.

The Gerin pilot ionized too, and became nothing more
than Leaguer slang. Sushi—except that usually sushi was
raw, and this had been most emphatically overcooked.
Its ship tumbled out of control, hit denser atmosphere at
far too steep an angle, and became just one more bright

score across the sky above the unnamed planet's night-side.

"Splash one, splash all, that's the lot." The allcall was from Matt Devlin on the ECM and monitor station. "There's not a sushi ship left on the screen, people. *Hawker* just nailed the command globe. Let's go ho—"

That was when they hit the loose torpedo.

It might have been League, or it might have been Gerin. None of it mattered to the torpedo except that even though its propulsion charges had run out, its warhead was proximity-fused and there was something entering that proximity. Although none of that mattered to the target ship at all. . . .

. . . johnny . . .
Johnny . . .
"Johnny? . . ."

He came back from the darkness through a sheet of fire to air that was cool and fresh against his blistered skin. The suit, and the armored chair back, had taken most of the blast, and then the automatic ejectors had cut in and blown him clear. Zero Three had been tumbling by then, swapping ends and top for bottom once every second after losing most of her main drive to the plasma torpedo.

The bang-seats were designed to fire sequentially, so that the rocket igniters of one wouldn't roast the occupant of the next in line. That sequence was once every quarter second. Johnny had gone first, then Matt, then Miklos, and finally Jules back in navigation. He had been fired upward at twelve o'clock high, away from the planet, out toward where the rescue tenders were already vectoring on his ship's last known position. And as he left, Zero Three pitched inverted, so that Matt and Miklos and Jules had gone the other way.

His co had been lucky: Miklos was shot ballistically at six o'clock low, a fifteen-gee acceleration straight down into atmosphere, and lasted maybe seven seconds. The other two were fired out at three and nine level, skimming along the edge of the atmosphere envelope so that it took more than a minute for the gravity well to drag them down to where the air friction waited to do what the ejector exhausts had not. They were wearing nothing more heat-shielded than vacuum suits, and there was hardly even a streak of fire to mark their passing.

But Johnny saw. And right up to the point when the noises on the comm channel flashed to static, he heard. All the way.

After the medics had checked him over and declared him still intact, the brass gave him a medal. And then they put him right back in the line.

"Buckshot Red Leader to Buckshot Red Flight, I have twenty-plus bandits at green two-zero-five, range one-four-niner-seven, closing fast, tallyho, tallyho."

"Red Leader, Red Two, roger your tallyho on twenty-plus," said Johnny Prescott. "That's only three apiece." Then he half turned to the new co in this new three-man ship. "Ever flown an attack mission before, kid?"

Nguyen Van Bay shook his head. "First time, sir," he said, unable to take his eyes from the hypnotic dance of sensor blips on the main targeting screen.

"It's simple enough: we're here, they're there. Put a salvo of torpedoes down our approach vector, then follow up with beamers. Got it?"

"Uh, yes . . ."

"Then you have control."

"What . . . !"

"Take it, kid." Prescott pushed clear of the control consoles, then unbuckled his acceleration straps and grabbed the overhead, pulling himself back to the empty seat beside the navigator's station. Dave Westley looked at him with worried eyes, but Johnny only grinned. "What's the matter, Dave?"

Westley looked pointedly at the flight deck, then switched on his commpack's privacy channel. "Johnny, it's Van Bay's first time out. Are you sure about this?"

"Don't you trust my judgment, Lieutenant?" said Prescott softly, and though he was still smiling, now it was the smile usually reserved for a gunsight and the locked target beyond it.

Westley lifted his eyebrows at what sounded like an unnecessary threat to pull rank, and squashed down irritation that Prescott should think that it was necessary. "You know I do. But you're the big hero and he's—"

"—never going to get the chance to be one himself without something like this. So why not now, when there's a . . ." The grin thawed again. ". . . a big hero on board to keep an eye on him."

"Hah."

"And I'm not sitting up there beside him to breathe down the kid's neck. If he needs help he knows where I am." Johnny Prescott settled himself into the vacant seat and secured its straps, glanced forward at where Van Bay was flying the fighter all by himself, and then did something very odd. He polarized the faceplate of his helmet, taking it right down to opacity, and disabled his comm-pack's output channel. Westley was tempted to say something, however rash that might have been, given Johnny's apparent mood—except that right then the first Gerin single-seater lined up on the incoming raid, and conversation of any sort went right out of the window. . . .

"I have control."

Lieutenant Van Bay glanced jerkily at where Johnny Prescott had returned to the left-hand seat, and nodded, but it took him several seconds to unlock his rigid fingers from the control gauntlets, and rather longer for him to acknowledge. "Y-you have c-c-control, s-sir," he managed at last. His voice was shaking, and there was so much sweat inside his suit that the environmental scrubbers hadn't cleared all of it yet and a silvery cloud of water droplets hung in zero-gee just inside his faceplate.

"How many did we get?" said Johnny. Then he laughed, and if it sounded just a bit forced that was only to be expected. "I mean, how many did *you* get?"

"Three, sir, one with the torp and two with guns." Van Bay's voice was right back under control, and despite his very own private fog screen he was starting to look pleased with himself.

Johnny grinned at his co and once again took his hands from the gauntlets. "Okay, whiz kid, then I think you should be capable enough of taking us back to the *Hawker* in one piece. Do it." He swung half around in the command chair and stared at Dave Westley, silently prompting him to get rid of whatever might have been on his mind. The navigator stared right back in silence and raised his right fist; then flipped its thumb up and began to laugh.

Buckshot Red Two slewed down and sideways in a manner its designers had never intended, its hull the bright, fast-moving source of a long trail of chaff and IR flares. Gerin fire from three points intersected at where it should have been, but wasn't, and then one of the Gerin ships blew apart as Red Two broke hard left and its laser cut a ragged gash across the Gerin's main drive compartment fuel cells. The second and third came through the expanding globe of fire and fragments that had been their companion in a staggered turn that was meant to catch Red Two in one or the other's boresight. It should have worked, and given three seconds longer in the turn, it would have worked—except for the Leaguer ship's wingman.

Larry Stewart in Buckshot Red Four had hosed his own Gerin by the time the sushi lined up on Two; now he pulled up into the climb and inverted roll of a high-speed yoyo that cut the curve on the Gerin's more maneuverable ships and dropped him astern of the nearest. Luck or skill or judgment had the pipper of his gunsight already blinking a lock on the Gerin fighter's main drive. Larry smiled thinly and squeezed his trigger twice.

As its remaining warrior apprentice disintegrated, the last Gerin pulled clear of the fight in a high half-loop that might have been an attempt to escape—or equally the beginnings of a move to get around and down into the lethal cone behind the two Leaguer's tails. It didn't work: as the Gerin made its play Larry and Red Four were already slamming into a vertical rolling scissors that tracked the enemy vessel's climb and blocked both any getaway and any potential attack. At first the two ships ran level, but when Larry's barrel-roll reversals began to swing wider, the Gerin fell into the trap of a slow-speed overshoot and on line for Red Four's off-boresight targeting predictor. It didn't live long enough to realize its mistake.

"Red Two, this is Red Four: God *damn* it, Johnny, are you asleep or somethin'?" Stewart was furiously angry, the anger born of fear for a friend that can only really find expression in a shout. His rage cut off short, stumbling over surprise, when another voice than the one he had expected spoke to him over the comm.

"Red Four, this is Red Two . . . er, Captain Prescott isn't available right now. . . ."

"What the bloody blue blazes . . . ?" Stewart rasped, shocked for just a moment into forgetting proper comm procedures. Then he got a grip again, even though he had to restrain himself from taking a precautionary sideslip down into firing position on Two's tail. "Red Two pilot, identify yourself. Where is Captain Prescott . . . ?"

Lieutenant Price listened miserably to the exchange between Dave Westley and what sounded like the entire crew of Red Four, wincing inwardly every time his own name was mentioned and cringing in sympathy as Captain Stewart savagely disposed of every excuse that Westley offered for Johnny Prescott's conduct. Both ships had been set up for an autodock approach to the *Hawker*, which meant that he couldn't even take refuge in pretending to be busy. Price could have shut off his commpack until Red Four broke its connection, but there was a horrid fascination in hearing what Stewart had to say about his piloting skills, and his combat abilities, and his prospects of surviving this tour, and a dozen other things.

It was the same fascination as he found in staring at Johnny Prescott, self-strapped painfully tightly into the navigator-B seat and staring . . . at nothing at all. As Price watched him, a long dribble of saliva trailed out of the captain's slack mouth and hung inside his helmet, unnoticed, just as everything on Two had gone unnoticed by him since the Gerin's first attack had looked likely to kill them. One of the near misses had shorted out some of the cockpit circuitry, including the polarizer overrides to ports and helmets, and for the first time since the death of Ranger Zero Three, Johnny Prescott's face was visible during combat.

Price shivered. During this tour there had always been something of a competition among the new pilots to get the co on Johnny Prescott's ship. It had never been admitted, but it was common gossip knowledge that if you did get the right-hand seat, and were very, very lucky, Johnny P might just let you fly the combat mission itself—and then credit you with any kills, as well. He wondered, but didn't want to know, what it took to make the face of a popular, much-decorated hero look like what he saw. Then Lieutenant Westley gripped him by one shoulder. Price realized suddenly that the comm channel was dead, and had probably been dead for several minutes now. He swallowed, and tore his gaze away from the drooling apparition that had been Johnny Prescott.

"You," said Westley, speaking slowly and carefully as if to a child, "did not see this. You will not talk about this. You will leave the clearing-up of Red Two's messes to its regular crew. Do you understand me, Lieutenant Price?"

Price nodded dumbly. It was the truth; he did understand, quite clearly. Even though it was the only thing about today that had been clear at all.

They grounded Johnny Prescott when the *Hawker* brought 217 Squadron back to Skandurby; but the grounding was for medical reasons, pending further multilevel checks concerning the long-term consequences of his involvement in the destruction of Ranger Zero Three and the death of its crew. When someone was an established hero, the phrase "lack of moral fiber" was not bandied about so lightly as it might be in the case of a recruit. Reputations had to be preserved: the reputation not merely of the hero, but of those who had made him so, for fear their judgment in this, and therefore other things, should be called into question.

To the more senior crewmen, those aware by one means or another of High Command's little secret, the whole situation seemed unhealthy. Their opinion was straightforward—either restore Johnny Prescott to his former status and stature, or kick him out, ignominiously and with publicity so that the legend could be laid to rest; but whichever course was chosen, let it be chosen quickly, rather than trundle along in this half-light of doubt and double-talk. It seemed to make no difference to Johnny, either in the way he behaved or in the way that successive intakes of younger squadron members treated him, with a respect that seemed often to border on adoration. Red silk scarves were blossoming like poppies in Flanders, some of the young men were making their first splutter-ing experiments in pipe-smoking, and at least two of them were actively canvassing the civilian population of Skan-durby Town for a dog, any dog, just so long as it could walk to heel and fetch a stick the way Johnny Prescott's Toby could.

Until the day when Toby was fetching sticks for the off-duty maintenance crews, and chased one right into the repeller field beneath the station tender. There wasn't a great deal left to bury, but they scraped it up and buried it just the same, in a little grave out by the station bound-ary. And then they took the collar and their regrets to the officers' mess, and to Johnny.

Who went right off the deep end. "You stinking gutless bastards!" he screamed at them, and would have lunged at the electronics corporal who had actually thrown the fatal stick if Dave Westley and two of the other officers hadn't grappled him to a standstill. "You hadn't the balls to chop me, so you did it to the bloody dog, didn't you!" There was saliva glistening on his chin, and foam at the corners of his mouth. "That's where you want to see me, isn't it? Shoveled up and shoveled in! Just like Toby. . . ." And then he began to cry.

"The dog was his luck, sir," Westley said later during an uncomfortable session with Squadron Commander Kincaid. "Apparently it's been with him since he joined up in '35, and neither he nor it has ever come to any lasting harm. Not until Ranger Zero One, and now . . ."

"Now he thinks that someone's trying to kill him by proxy?" Kincaid sat back in his chair and snorted deri-sively. "Ridiculous!"

"Sir, there's little enough in the way of honors or decorations left for the man to win." Jochen Piper hesitated as his commander's full attention settled balefully on him, then swallowed down his nervousness and continued. "There might be a suspicion at the back of his troubled mind"—*Christ, but that sounds stagy,* thought Piper, hoping that Kincaid would let it pass,—"that the only thing he hasn't yet gained is a worthwhile death in battle. It's possible that he believes he should have died with the crew of Zero One, and that he sees his continued active participation in the war as somehow . . . improper."

Major Kincaid stared at his two subordinates for several seconds, then drew in a slow, deep breath. "Captain Piper, when I think about the drivel you have just spewed up I find myself wondering whether it's really Prescott and not you, sir, who should be waiting for the medical board's findings. Both of you are dismissed."

The two officers saluted, about-faced smartly, and got out of the office before one or both blew up just as thoroughly as Prescott had done. "The Old Man," said Piper disgustedly, "he doesn't want to be," he cleared his throat to give the mock headline its full value, " 'the Squadron Commander who Destroyed the League's Favorite Hero.' "

"If he doesn't do something with Johnny, that's what he'll be anyway." Dave Westley shrugged. "It's the uselessness that festers. I know Johnny Prescott well enough to see that much. Bring him back or let him go, but don't keep him standing on the trap with the noose around his neck."

"If he was sent up against the Gerin tomorrow, would you go with him?"

"Bloody right I would!"

"They you're as mad as he is. Because I wouldn't. Prescott's a corpse looking for a funeral, and I'd as soon send flowers long-distance."

"Very funny, Jochen. Abso-bloody-lutely hilarious."

"Quite so. I thought you'd get the joke." Except that neither Piper nor Westley was smiling. . . .

* * *

Kincaid finished his mission briefing and managed to look uncomfortable rather than just unpleasant. "Deep-interdiction strike tasking is invariably hazardous, gentlemen," he said. "Each squadron taking part will be supported during its attack by full ECM backup centered on their individual carrier cruiser, but be advised that this Gerin globeship is command-level. In order to create sufficiently divergent approach vectors to confuse the Gerin defenses, all five squadrons involved in the mission will need to field every available pilot. This therefore includes Captain Prescott."

The subdued but definite cheer that murmured through the briefing hall was evidently something he had neither expected nor approved of, but there was little enough that Kincaid could do about it that would not make him look and sound foolish. "Sir," said an anonymous voice from the back of the room, "does that mean Johnny's been reinstated?"

The commander didn't try to find out the source of the question. Instead he simply shrugged. "Recall what I said. It means only that he qualifies as an available pilot, since no evidence has so far been received to indicate the contrary. I would remind you all that the destruction of this command globe deep within what the enemy consider inviolable space is of paramount importance, both strategically and in connection with morale. To this end I am prepared to set aside rumor and innuendo, and I trust that the members of this squadron will do the same."

He reached down to shut off the holoprojector that had been displaying nav and target coordinates, then swept his gaze across the eager, nervous, wary faces. "217's carrier cruiser for this mission will be LCC-1864 *Frank Luke Jr.* If it's of interest to you, considering the object of the mission, I understand that Frank Luke Jr. was a famous balloon buster in the First Flying War. Preflight in eight hours, scramble in ten. Dismissed."

They were already deep into Gerin-held space when they finally left the *Luke* and dispersed into attack formation alongside the fighters of the other four squadrons; space so deep and quiet that not a single threat receptor in the whole task force registered so much as a molecule of stellar hydrogen out of its supposed place. That was what Dave Westley claimed, at any rate. On a slightly less exaggerated level, there was no sign of the expected Gerin perimeter-patrol vessels, and no emission trail to even suggest that they had been through the sector before the League interdictors warped down onto station.

"Military intelligence," said Westley, as if announcing the punch line of an old joke. "No matter when, no matter where, a contradiction in terms." At which, on perfect cue, the proximity alert went off.

They had taken the Gerin globeship by surprise. That didn't mean the sushi in it were presliced and needing only some wasabi; far from it. The huge command vessel launched a swarm of single-seaters that outnumbered the League fighters by at least four to one. "Hey-ho, the usual odds," said someone on comm channel D in a voice that feigned boredom, or used it to cover a less easily admitted emotion. "Why can't they vary it once in a while, just to be different?"

Only a matter of seconds later, the first League ship and the first Gerin fighter erupted in fire and fragments as each vessel's plasma torpedo slammed into its opposite number in an orgy of mutual destruction. There were no stylish tactics about the first part of the combat, just a long-range slugging match with torpedoes as each side tried to obliterate the other while sides could still be seen as being different.

There were few enough tactics about the second part, at that: a frenzied whirl of ships, trying to break through or trying to prevent a breakthrough, while on the far sides of the sprawling dogfight the ominous bulk of the command globe and the carrier cruisers maneuvered for the single massive killing shot that such leviathans directed at one another.

Dave Westley had intended that he would spare at least some of his attention for Johnny, but it was a vain hope. All of his concentration and all of his time were reserved for Red Two's defensive countermeasures: electronic, chaff, flares, and antilaser particulation. He just had to hope that Prescott was justifying the trust placed in him and in his reputation by an entire squadron. No: by an entire task force.

It seemed that he was. At least, he rather than Sanjit Singh, the co, was piloting the ship, and Red Two was still intact, against all the odds that said both the fighter and its crew should have been a drift of dust and ashes long ago. More than that, if Johnny kept flying the way he had done up to now, they looked likely to be the first, or the only, League fighter to break free of the dogfight and out into clear space. Somewhere ahead of them, beyond the Gerin defensive screen, was the command globeship, and once they got through they would have a clear shot with the battery of plasma torps that crammed the weapons bay in Red Two's belly.

Make that *if* they got through. . . .

Dave's head jerked up from his control board, and he slapped the side of his helmet, hoping that it would clear away whatever sound interference had begun to clutter his headset. Instead it increased in volume, and an apprehensive chill crawled down his spine as the background mutter became recognizable as the human voice it had been all along.

Something made Dave glance at the local-area nav monitor, and what he saw there made his face turn putty-pale. Except for the erratic curves of evasive maneuvers, Buckshot Red Two was steering an almost straight course through the tangle of opposing fighters. And once beyond the dogfight, the vector projection was unmistakable. Not an attack course on the globeship, but a collision. . . .

"Johnny," said Dave carefully, "what goes on?" The low mumbling stopped, interrupted by a deep, sad sigh. "You're doing bloody well, Johnny—but are you all right?"

"Fine." There was another sigh, and a sound like a choked-off sob. "I'm all right. Everything'll be all right soon. . . ."

Oh shit! thought Dave after another glance at the projection visor. His fists closed, and if he hadn't been suited up, his nails would have dug into his palms deeply enough to draw blood. "And what about us, Johnny? What about Sanjit an' me?"

"You're getting all the choice I got," said Prescott, infinitely sad. "I'm sorry, Dave, Sanjit, but it's the only way for me."

"Johnny, I'm scared. . . ."

"I've been scared for years, but they wouldn't let me talk about it like you just did. They wouldn't let me say my own bloody words, Dave. I had to hide behind the medals, and I've been there so long I can't come out again."

"Then let us eject, Johnny. At least let *us* get out."

"I can't. People would wonder. They'd talk. All I've got's my rep, Dave. That's the only thing I can leave behi—"

The sentence broke in a grunt, because all the time he had been talking Dave had been working his way forward from the nav station, and now he wrapped one forearm around Prescott's throat and wrenched him backward with all his strength. It should have worked, and it almost *did* work—except that they were in deep space and zero gee; except that they were both suited so that the attack looked like teddy bears wrestling; and except that Prescott was combat-strapped into his seat. All that leverage went only into flipping Dave off his feet in the opposite direction to the one in which Johnny Prescott should have gone, and when Dave regained something like equilibrium he found himself looking at Johnny, up now and out of his seat, and at the broad razor-edged blade of an issue combat knife. Issued for the express purpose of opening up a suit, and then its occupant if hard vacuum or hostile atmosphere hadn't done the job already.

"Captain Prescott," said Sanjit Singh quietly, "put down the knife and fly the ship." Prescott waved the knife at him as well.

"Look, this is your chance to be heroes as well," he said, quite reasonably for all that his voice was trembling. "And you won't have to be scared for anything like as long as I was. . . ."

Sanjit didn't grab for the knife hand; instead the Sikh copilot chopped the edge of his own hand down hard on Prescott's wrist, and suited or not, there was enough force riding on the blow to send the weapon spinning some-where to the rear of Red Two's crew compartment.

Then the attack alarm screeched, and without letting him think about any of the other things that had seemed so important an instant ago, Johnny's combat-ingrained reflexes swung him back to the control console to throw Red Two into an evasive corkscrew break. And an instant later the degraded remnants of an off-target Gerin beamer punched through the side of the ship, and through the side of the flight deck, and through Johnny Prescott's side as well, just as he began to grin that old grin at a fine piece of flying.

Johnny didn't stop grinning, not for an instant. He just stopped breathing. And being scared.

Sanjit Singh rammed his open hands into the auxiliary gauntlets and took Red Two into a combat-evasive sequence that skimmed the fine line between inspiration and insanity. The damage-control boards became a single scarlet constellation of stress-violation lights before he eased up on the pressure for an instant and snapped, "Stand by on torpedoes!"

Dave suspected that the Sikh's spatial awareness was the result of some special arrangement between crazy fighter pilots and the more violently inclined of the old North Indian gods, because without recourse to lock-ons or targeting predictors, Singh had put Red Two into a near-textbook firing position—although Johnny Prescott's attempt at immolation had done a lot to bring them in this close. Fingers spread wide, Westley's gloved hand came down on the fire controllers, and the fighter shud-dered as she lost ten tonnes of weight in a ripple of fire that lasted half that many seconds.

The globeship didn't shudder at all. It became a small, localized sun that flared and faded in the time it took Red Two to curve back toward the safety of the *Frank Luke Jr.*'s hull. None of the remaining Gerin tried to attack them as they went; instead, shorn of their deep-space support vessel, the sushi conserved what energy and air they had and broke off the engagement, heading for some safe haven, somewhere, anywhere, so long as it was far away from the Leaguer ship that wasn't scared of anything. . . .

Major Nakashima sat for a long time, very still and very silent, lost in his own thoughts. Somebody broke into the silence, a soft voice, unsure that what it was saying was right, or wrong, or even if the valuations made sense any more. "Sir, Prescott was a coward. He killed himself, near enough, and tried to take his ship and his whole crew with him. The old man doesn't know. Maybe he should be told."

"Why? What good would it do now?"

"Because it's the truth, sir."

"Have you any idea of how far the truth can go in wartime?" Nakashima held up both his hands, index fingers out and separated by the thickness of a mapping stylus. Then he pressed them tightly together and said, "Not that much. Maybe his father *should* be told. Maybe everybody should be told. So somebody should tell them. But that somebody will not be me. What about you?"

The pilots and crewmen of 217 Squadron looked abashed, and neither spoke nor met their commander's eyes.

"Good," said Yevgeny Nakashima after a few uneasy seconds. "Even after so short a time, I know my squadron—and I'm glad my guess is right." The major looked up, then stood up. "Gentlemen, our guest is back. Entertain him. And—" his hand sketched the briefest of salutes, then removed his cap as he came back off duty,— "thank you. All of you. I have been . . . honored."

He left the fleet field at Skandurby on a gray winter's day when the rain was slanting down from a sky the color of ancient lead, but he walked toward the waiting shuttle with his head held high, as if the chill of the falling rain were a benediction. He was just a little man, with thinning hair, and proud eyes, and a dead son.

But a son who had died a hero.

Total War

The next months were a period of outright terror on most of the worlds in the Far Stars region. Slowly, the planets began to band together for mutual defense. There was little thought of revenge, much less of liberating those planets enslaved by the Gerin. Even then, jealousies and man's stubborn independence interfered constantly with those more altruistic motives. Chu Lee MacDonald found himself a revered hero, the only man to have "defeated" the Gerin. The "admiral" quickly found that politics took precedence over even military decisions as he warned of the Gerin threat. The films taken by the survivors tended to guarantee a near-total effort.

With all the zeal of a prophet, Mac preached his gospel of unity and revenge. On other levels he fought to gather the diverse defense forces of every world into an effective human fleet. Since this meant the defenders of each planet had to leave their homeworlds virtually defenseless, few would consent to his plan. Still each world bowed to his fervor and contributed a few ships, until Mac commanded a force of over a hundred ships and twice that number of fighters based on converted freighters.

The first resurgence of the Gerin offensive came at Gemini. Here the home fleet was able to stop the first attack, even allowing time for the evacuation of the planet's main satellite. This also bought time for Mac to lead his ships to the system. When he arrived, Mac observed that the attack on the planet had been renewed. Over three hundred Gerin ships had pressed the eighty remaining Gemini ships back to the fringes of their planet's atmosphere. In an effort to trap the remaining defenders, the attacking fleet was formed into half of a globe. The open end faced the planet, and this allowed every ship in the Gerin fleet to concentrate its fire on the shields of the defenders.

Without hesitation the Castleman's commander threw his forces at high acceleration against the rear of the Gerin formation. Passing along the outside of the globe, the human ships themselves formed a much thinner half globe. Suddenly the Gerin found themselves trapped between the planet and Mac's fleet. Minutes later, Gemini launched every planet-based missile, and her fleet counterattacked. The Gerin broke, their formation splintering with all command control lost. Nearly half were blasted before they could find escape in FTL space.

Following this victory the entire Gemini fleet placed itself under Mac's command. With his newfound prestige and credibility, Admiral MacDonald began uniting the human worlds. Everywhere, men began to find new ways to slow or even defeat the numerous Gerin fleets menacing their systems.

TROJAN HEARSE
by Robert Sheckley

THE yeoman entered Commander Darfur's office, stood to attention, saluted. He had a yellow flimsy in his hand.

"Is that what I think it is?" Commander Malang Darfur asked.

The yeoman hesitated.

"Go ahead and tell me. I know you've read it."

"Evacuation order, sir," the yeoman said. "Back to Point Brave." The relief was evident on the yeoman's face as he handed Darfur the paper.

Commander Darfur read the evacuation order with mixed feelings. On the one hand, he was relieved that his small group of people and their solitary cruiser *Co-*

chise were being withdrawn from their lonely duty on Alicia. They were dangerously exposed on this worthless little world of mixed human and alien peoples. Despite the fact that they were technically allies of earth, the Alicians had not been especially friendly to Darfur and his men. Earth was growing unsure of the value of its alliances with the worlds on the periphery of the great struggle.

Darfur was the youngest man in the Point Bravo sector to command a cruiser. He had been merely one more fighter pilot when the war began. The little ships had needed a lot of officers to man them. They were often Earth's first line of defense. Darfur had gotten his break when he had been on picket duty out past Lohengrin's Star. After a long and unexciting tour of duty, he had been ready to turn for home when he got a signal on his warning system. He looked down at the controls. Yep, enemy action taking place nearby. He could run home and get reinforcements. Or he could try to do something about it now.

Then a globeship appeared, popping down from FTL space. Almost instinctively, Darfur had put his ship in a position that left the sun of the local system behind him. From here he had a moment to look over the enemy. The mother ship, a huge globe, had released two little fighters, short stubby affairs equipped with plasma torpedoes.

He knew that the thing for him to do was to cut and run as fast as he could. The enemy fighters, side by side, were coming in fast, the big sphere of the mother ship moving along behind them. From the faint dimming of the stars behind it, Darfur could tell that they were getting up their shields.

Darfur had been a first-class knife fighter on his home in Zylene. Boys there began their lives on the great plain that so resembled the Serengeti Plain of their distant homeland. The two Mtabeles came suddenly out of a thorn thicket. Darfur was alone, with only his knife. He knew that either man was a match for him with their heavier pangas. But some instinct told him that his only safety lay in driving straight ahead.

He pretended to turn and run as they came at him, their

dark skins gleaming with red and ocher stripes of war paint. Then, as they came up behind him, he suddenly whirled, and, in movements as choreographed as any ballet sequence, ran between them, ducking low. Their pangas, swung in furious reaction, sliced each other. Before they got over the shock, Darfur was behind them, stabbing with the knife, then taking to his heels as the main Mtabele war band came up.

The feat won him a scholarship at Zylene's Space Academy. And now, years later, he was ready to try it again.

At full acceleration he swung his little ship, kicking it into a 180-degree turn. The two Gerin were startled to see him coming directly at them. As he started to pass between them, Darfur put the ship into a fishtail maneuver, the bow swinging first right, then left. He let go his plasma torpedoes and kept on going.

The Gerin aboard must have been too full of fighting lust to care that they were in danger of disabling their partners. That was one thing you could count on about the Gerin—they were individualists all the way, even when that way could put their winning chances into peril.

One of the fighters took a hit and blossomed into a brilliant fireball. The second one managed to intercept the oncoming torpedo and to bring its torpedo tubes to bear on Darfur's ship. Darfur frantically swung his ship again, expecting at any moment to take a torpedo up the spout. But the Gerin ship was hit by wreckage from its partner before it could fire. Darfur's automatic cameras had caught the whole thing.

The cameras also caught his hasty retreat into FTL space when the globeship released five more fighters. But that was not held against him. He had succeeded against daunting odds. The affair was written up in the squadron newspaper. The CO of his squadron sent in Darfur's name for a medal. This was turned down—there were a lot of medals given out that month. But he did receive his promotion to commander, and was put in charge of the cruiser *Cochise*.

Duty had not been dangerous on Alicia, but it had been dull. The planet's main city of Morgels was a one-horse town with little in the way of entertainment for off-duty personnel. Commander Darfur had counted himself lucky that a circus had come to Alicia recently. Watching the various acts and strolling through the sideshows had given his crew something to do.

Darfur had his doubts about spacekeeping circuses. It was said that circus people weren't like others. They had special talents. Dealing with them could be tricky.

In such disrepute were they held that some of the countries of Earth barred circus people from landing or performing.

They had caused Darfur no trouble here, however. He had enjoyed their performance himself. Now, however, it was his duty to tell Jon Blake, the circus director, that he and his cruiser were pulling out, and he was prepared to take Blake and his people with him.

Darfur was also prepared to cram aboard as many of the Alicians as he could. But so far, from the evasive answers the Alician dignitaries had given him, it looked like they would be content to stay on their home planet and deal with the Gerin as best they could. Probably by joining them, Darfur thought angrily. It was always the same on these little isolated worlds. The inhabitants forgot their ties to the League of Free Planets when any inconvenience was involved. You couldn't blame those who were outright aliens—the G'tai, for example, and the Neuristii. Even though the League of Free Planets had many alien allies, not all aliens were interested in joining their fortunes with those of the League. Especially now, when it was looking a little dicey for the Terrans. But people of human stock ought to stick to their race. That's what Darfur thought, and it's what he expected all right-minded humanoids to think.

Straightening his uniform and setting his cap at a rakish angle, Commander Darfur left his office, waving off the guards who were supposed to accompany him. He walked down the dusty main street to the edge of town. Long before he got there he could see the big aluminum-colored bulge of the Circus Ship. A few Alicians nodded to him as they passed. Darfur was going to regret giving up this, his first independent command. Soon he would return to the Earth base, and then he would be just one more young commander among many.

The Circus Ship, several hundred yards long, lay in a field just on the outskirts of town. It had been costly in terms of fuel to bring the ship down to planetside rather than leave it in geosynchronous orbit. But once down, the ship served as quarters for the circus acts, and as commissary, and it even had its own built-in theater set up in the big storage areas where cargo had gone, back when the ship was a trader for the OddJohn Corporation.

Darfur went to the Circus Ship, well dressed in his pressed whites and very aware of his dignity. Darfur was almost seven feet tall, skinny, dark-skinned, and dark-eyed, with clean-cut features inherited from his Somali-Arabian ancestors.

There was confusion around the Circus Ship, as always seems to happen at circuses. Darfur pressed his way through the crowd of scruffy, pale-eyed Alician urchins who were trying to sneak in free, like youngsters everywhere. The ticket-taker recognized Darfur and let him through, directing him to the backstage door to find the impresario, Blake.

There seemed to be even more confusion backstage. Men rushed back and forth carrying cardboard scenery and painted wooden sets. Jugglers practiced their acts one last time; the dancers were warming up. Darfur noted that these circus folk looked thoroughly disreputable and probably deserved the evil reputation that clung to all interstellar circuses. And where in all this was he to find Blake?

"He's in the animal sector," a roustabout told him. "One of the elephants has gone spooky."

Commander Darfur thanked him and walked quickly to the animal sector. But he forgot to duck his head as he passed through the entrance. His cap was knocked off his head by a guywire. He picked it up hurriedly, brushed it off, set it back on his head, and marched stiffly off. He was aware that several of the performers seemed to find that funny.

Some of the people he passed were obviously of human stock, especially the jugglers and acrobats. Some of them derived from a bewildering mixture of alien and human races. Some of them had been mildly gene-teched. Others appeared to be the result of unfortunate mutations. There were startling man-animal combinations. Some of the circus people were feathered and some were furred, some walked on two feet and others on four. And then there were the winged men, the first Darfur had ever seen, though he had heard of them. How had they gotten that way? Implants on earth-type people? Or was there a race of winged humans somewhere out there among the thousand or so worlds that had been contacted since space exploration had begun?

There was sawdust on the floor. It made the footing uncertain for a man in polished military boots.

A sweating groom working with the team of horses used for the big chariot event pointed him in the right direction. He went past a group of Neanderthal-looking jugglers tossing several small balls back and forth, then introducing other objects into their act, objects thrown to them by people outside their circle, until the air around them seemed filled with flying objects—balls, small chairs, combs, pocketbooks, glasses, anything light enough to lift and throw.

Darfur ducked past them and saw, far down one side of the hold, a good-sized gray elephant being backed with difficulty into a cage. The elephant looked ready to turn on the man at any moment. That was Blake. Darfur recognized him from their earlier meeting. Blake was not as tall as Darfur but he was burly-chested and muscular. His floating blond hair was held in place by a woven gold circlet, and he was overawing the elephant by sheer force of character. Although the elephant looked as if it wanted to stomp the man, Blake kept steadily advancing on him, a cigar clamped into the side of his mouth, talking steadily and without much inflection:

"Back away there, Daisy, and no sense you keep on

glaring at me with those little red eyes of yours, you know I'm the boss and you are going into that pen where we can strap you down and do something about that toothache of yours, and don't try anything with me 'cause I'll hit you right between the eyes."

Brandishing a light whip, Blake finished backing the elephant into her cage, then turned away as a groom ran forward to secure the door of the cage. Blake noticed Commander Darfur and strolled over to him.

"Is this a social call, Commander?"

"Not in the slightest," Darfur said. "I've come to tell you that I have been ordered to close down the League station on this planet and get my men back to Point Bravo."

"Well, that's life in the service," Blake said. "Here today, gone tomorrow."

Darfur was annoyed but struggled not to show it.

"My departure," Darfur said evenly, "has been hastened by information that a Gerin fleet is believed to be heading this way. I will be happy to escort your ship back to Point Bravo, where the forces of the League of Free Planets can protect you."

"Mighty kind of you, sonny," Blake said. "But we've got other plans."

"Might I ask what they are?"

"It's none of your business," Blake said, "but you might as well know I'm taking this ship on to Rhea."

"Rhea? Next planet out in this system? They've just got a few hundred thousand people there."

"That's a good audience for a circus, Commander," Blake said.

"I would advise against it. There's a possibility the Gerin will move this way."

"Sure. And there's a possibility they'll show up in a hundred other places, or even vanish right up their own tail pipes. It's no concern of mine. This planet's played out. We're moving on to Rhea."

"And if the Gerin come?"

Blake shrugged. "We're from Pelops, and we're non-combatants. None of us are original Earth stock."

"Do you think the Gerin give a damn where you were born? You look like humans and they'll treat you as such."

"What I've heard," Blake said, "is that some humanoid worlds have gone over to them and they haven't suffered for it."

"You wouldn't do that!" Darfur said. "You still owe something to the human race."

"Because they gave birth to me? Extend that back. I also owe the entire line of primates, who were the forebears of all of us. And the rodents and reptiles before that. And so on, to lichen and algae and finally to constituent chemicals."

"You can make anything sound absurd," Darfur said. "The fact is, no matter which planet you were born on, you're still humanoid and you owe something to the rest of the race."

"You think so?" Blake said. "Let me tell you, the human race as represented on our homeworld hasn't been so nice to us. Do you know about the Pelopian doctrine of True Breeding?"

Darfur nodded.

"We're the culls."

Darfur knew about Pelops. It was a case study in repression frequently lectured on in Military College. Many of the humanoid-occupied worlds had small populations, kept under distressingly rigid dictatorial control by the self-elected authorities. This was especially true on the planet Pelops, where the clique known as the Lords of Force ruled and had ruled since the founding of the civilization. It wasn't only political control the Lords were after. They were obsessed with racial purity. Their doctrine was called True Breeding. With the help of their scientists they had drawn up a Code of Protocol. It dealt with both physical appearance and mental attitude. The first test, the most important test for a young Pelopian, came on the day he would be checked by the Psychometrics Board. They would test his deviation from the idealized Pelopian norm. The Lords had stringent ideas about what humanity should be like. Any unusual skills or talents were forbidden. Anything resembling psychic talent was absolutely proscribed.

The Lords, taking a lesson from Earth history, didn't want to breed geniuses. We're a down-to-earth people, they said. Everybody is doing well here. We are not going to rock the boat. Those who did not pass were subject to outshipment. They were given a short period of time in which to settle up their affairs and make their goodbyes, and then they were shipped off-planet. Any who exceeded the period of grace were subject to immediate seizure and incarceration. After a trial whose outcome was a foregone conclusion, the Outcaste would either be summarily executed as a criminal against the social order or marooned on one of the little planetoids at the edge of the Pelopian system. Here he would have to live on a planetoid never designed to support human life. These were prison worlds. It was an open prison: you could leave and go elsewhere, if you could find some place that would have you, and would be willing to pay your way there. There were few planets which gave them that opportunity. Life was tough for everyone; each world was still trying to make things work for its own population, and none had time left over to take in strays. And, too, each of these worlds had its suspicions about people who didn't fit into its own social matrix. Life on the Outcaste worlds tended to be short, brutish, and painful.

Many governments of human-occupied planets did not approve of the Pelopian methods. In a multiracial universe, these doctrines of racial purity were sinister, unethical, and certain to lead in time to fatal inbreeding. The Lords didn't care what people of the other worlds thought. And because of the great struggle against the Gerin, the Pelopian fleet was badly needed. So dire was the plight of the League of Free Planets that the usually liberal League government refused to get involved and refused to take in Outcastes for fear of offending the Pelopians.

"All of us here in this circus," Blake said, "human and alien alike, are mutants as well as Outcastes. That compounds our untouchability. Humanoids dislike people with mutant abilities. Even minor mind-reading skills freak them out. They think all our people are reading their minds, learning their shoddy little secrets. It's untrue, but it's one of the lies they spread about us. We've been kicked off quite a few earth-settled worlds. We're not allowed on Airies, or on Earth itself. Did you know that?''

"No, I didn't," Darfur said.

"It's true. So I say, let the humanoids go their way. Good luck and all that, but I think we'll just sit this one out.''

"If the Gerin let you," Darfur said.

"Hey, we've dealt with a lot of aliens in our time. No trouble. Once they see we're truly neutral, they'll leave us alone.''

Commander Darfur had to be content with that. He left the ship and returned to his headquarters building. Everything was in readiness. Everybody had been expecting orders to come through at any moment to take them off this dreary little world of Alicia. They were ready to go.

The formalities were brief. Within twelve hours, the cruiser *Cochise* upwarped.

Not long after that, the converted cruiser *P. T. Barnum,* having run out of suckers and spectators, rang down the final curtain. The circus people were well schooled in quick exits. Sometimes they were necessary when things didn't go right on the world they were entertaining. No problem this time, but they got off quickly anyhow.

When Commander Darfur came out of FTL space to Point Bravo, he found a scene of confusion at fleet headquarters. Ships had been recalled from many points along the vast volume of space guarded by Point Bravo. So many had come at the same time that it posed a traffic-control problem for the local fleet headquarters of Admiral Clark Van Dyne, commanding MacDonald's 4th Flotilla.

Darfur had to remain in space for three standard days. From his ship's observation post he could see the waiting ships keeping station in long rows, their winking lights like stars across the panoply of space. At last, orders came through. Darfur had the navigator set the parking orbit and ordered the crew to stand easy. There would be nothing for them to do until Darfur had made his call upon the admiral and given further orders.

It took three Earth-standard twenty-four-hour days before Van Dyne's calendar was clear. Then Darfur was summoned. Dressed in his best whites, hat under his arm, he took his launch to the admiral's dreadnought and was piped aboard.

Van Dyne was a busy man. Short, narrow in the shoulders, potbellied, he didn't look as if he could be the famous Van Dyne of Temple Pass fame, the man who had taken his ships through the narrow straits between the crowded planets of Temple Pass, to break through the Gerin gauntlet and live to fight another day. He was known as one of MacDonald's best fighting admirals, and most men considered it an honor and privilege to serve under him.

So had Darfur. Until his interview with the admiral.

"What do you mean, you let the Circus Ship go on to Rhea?" Van Dyne demanded. His eyebrows knotted. His eyes were glittering gray slits. Darfur felt his stomach knot.

"Why, sir, I didn't like to let them proceed. But I have no authority to order around civilians."

"Is that a fact?" Van Dyne said, sarcasm dripping from his heavy-edged voice. "Do the articles of the Universal Emergency Declaration mean so little to you, then?"

Darfur had to admit that he didn't know the articles. He tried to add that he had been in space, keeping station, when the Declaration was made. But Van Dyne refused to let him off the hook.

"You should have had a copy of them with you anyhow. Any man with a gram of sense knew they were sure to be adopted sooner or later."

"I . . . I heard it was a close vote in the council, sir," Darfur said. "People said it could have gone either way."

Van Dyne glared at him until Darfur could feel his cheeks going crimson. The commander was embarrassed and furious, and he knew that he'd better watch what he said or he'd be in even worse trouble than this.

"What should I have done, sir?" he asked, biting out the words. "When they refused to accompany me, I mean."

Van Dyne shook his head at the naïveté of this young commander. "Darfur, you should have brought them back at gunpoint if necessary. For three reasons. First, we are not allowing people of Earth stock to get away from us so easily. Second, losing a civilian Circus Ship, of all things, to the enemy is the worst possible propaganda on the home front. And third, why put a perfectly sound ship into the hands of the enemy?"

"I understand, sir," Darfur said. "I did not know my orders allowed me such latitude. It will not happen again."

"That's the spirit," Van Dyne said. "Get back there, Commander, and bring that damned ship in. I don't care how. Bring it back or don't come back yourself."

"Yes, sir!" Darfur stood to full attention and saluted. Despite the admiral's harsh tone, he knew he was being given a second chance. He could still wipe this error off his record.

When the admiral returned his salute, Darfur turned to leave.

"I haven't dismissed you, yet," Van Dyne snapped.

"Sorry, sir. I just thought that it would be best for me to get at this as quickly as possible. Given the situation with the Gerin, sir. So I wanted to put my crew on standby for immediate takeoff."

"You're right about the need for speed," Van Dyne said. "But you won't need your cruiser for that. Temporarily I'm putting command of *Cochise* into the hands of your second officer. You can go by fighter. That way, if you flub it this time, we won't lose a major ship of the line."

"Yes, sir!"

"Dismiss." The admiral turned back to his papers. When Darfur reached the door, Van Dyne looked up.

"Oh, and by the way."

"Sir?" Darfur stopped.

"Good luck, sailor."

"Thank you, sir!" And Darfur was running as soon as he was outside the admiral's door. There was a lot to be done and he wanted to be underway in an hour.

The planet Rhea was a farming world populated by a lizard-evolved species who called themselves the Ingoteen. The tall, mild-mannered lizard farmers and fishermen had little in the way of hard cash. Nor did the Ingoteen have any background for understanding the Earth-based skits, the plays and dancing, the singing and miming, that were a part of the performance.

As Blake had learned before, it didn't matter. Entertainment on these isolated worlds was difficult to come by. Anyone, human or lizard, would drop what he was doing in order to watch a show and hear some music, even if the show was incomprehensible and the music jarring.

So it was here. There had been no trouble getting landing privileges. The Ingoteen Director of Landings had been effusive where he welcomed the troupe.

"Delighted to have you," he radioed back to Blake. "Do you want a parking orbit?"

"I'd like to bring the ship down," Blake said. "That way we have all our stuff with us. There's no mess and no fuss for anyone else. We're so self-contained we even have our own stages and auditorium."

He didn't mention that it was nice to have your own ship when dealing with a world whose psychology was unknown to you. It gave Blake and his people a controlled place from which to operate. He didn't have to tell the Director of Landings any of that. The fellow probably understood it anyway.

The ship came down slowly, majestically. A huge group of Ingoteen gathered to watch and cheer. It was the biggest event on the planet since a comet had almost clipped them ten years ago.

Blake set up in the designated place, negotiated the amount of the profits the local government would siphon off, and set up his ticket booth.

Inside the ship, the circus people went about their well-remembered tasks of preparing for the performance.

Blake was relaxing in his office with a bottle of genuine Sargassian vodka when there was a tap on the door.

"Come in."

Commander Darfur, in his dress whites, came through.

"This is a not very pleasant surprise," Blake said. "I told you to get lost. The circus folk will go where they please."

"I'm afraid not," Darfur said. "I am under orders to bring you and your ship back to the fleet at Point Bravo."

"You can't back up that order," Blake said. "Not even with your cruiser."

"I didn't bring the cruiser," Darfur said. He took a small handgun out of his pocket. "Just me. And this."

Blake stared at the weapon, incredulous, then burst into loud laughter. "You're threatening me, you pup? I'm going to take that thing out of your hand and make you eat it."

He advanced on Darfur, moving quickly for so large a man. Abruptly he recoiled and was slammed back hard against the wall.

"I have it set for pressor beam," Darfur said. "There are lethal settings, but I don't think they'll be necessary. If you won't do as I request, I'll leave the gun on press-lock, keep you against the wall, and con this ship back to Point Bravo myself."

Blake struggled but couldn't free himself from the grip of the beam.

"I'm sorry I have to do this," Darfur said. "But it's for your own good. Believe me, you wouldn't want to be around here when the Gerin get here."

"Release me at once," Blake said, "or I'll kill you when you turn this beam off."

Darfur ignored him and turned to the control panel. He was just sitting down to type in his first instructions when he felt something sharp press against his back. He turned. Silvestre Smoothfoot, the Clownmaster, had slipped into the room and was holding something against him. It felt very much like a needle beamer.

"You can't go pushing your weight around here like that," Silvestre said. "Turn off your beam."

"I'm only trying to save your lives."

"I know you mean well," Smoothfoot said. "But you can't do it this way."

"I'm going to take this ship out of here," Darfur said.

"If you do, I'll have to shoot," Smoothfoot said.

"I don't think you'll kill me," Darfur said. "Too bad there isn't a better way to do this." Ignoring the needle beam, he examined the flight control panel. Some of it was a little unfamiliar to him, but Darfur had taken extra instruction in different panel setups, as well as armament arrays both humanoid and Gerin. He thought he could figure it out without much difficulty.

He started to set controls. Smoothfoot bit his lip and his hand tensed on the needle beam.

"Give it to him," Blake said.

It is hard to say what Smoothfoot would have done then if he had not been interrupted by a man in a red-and-white clown suit bursting into the room. He had the transparent features and watery eyes of one type of human mutation.

"They're here!" he said. "The Gerin! They're here!"

Darfur turned off his pressor beam. Blake stepped away from the wall and quickly flicked on the ship's screens. They showed Gerin soldiery racing through the ship's open hatches, moving quickly despite their bulky armor, weapons at the ready, moving in their familiar three-point formation, a warrior ahead, two squire slaves behind. The circus people had been taken completely by surprise.

"They'll be here any moment," Blake said. He opened a closet, rummaged in it, and found some gaily colored clothing. He threw an armload to Darfur.

"Here, get into these."

"What are you talking about?"

"From what I've heard," Blake said, "the Gerin kill human warriors on sight. You're not a bad guy. Got guts, anyhow. Join the circus and save your life."

Darfur didn't have to be asked twice.

* * *

Usq-Usq-Tweed, senior officer in charge of Gerin forces, settled back in the portable tub his aides had brought for him. When he had the final word that the inhabitants of Rhea were offering no resistance and that the circus people were secure, he knew that his coup had succeeded and he could take a well-deserved soak. His comrades faced outward as Usq-Usq-Tweed, minus his armor, lowered his eight-limbed body into the tub. His body glowed with a heavenly blue color of satisfaction. This Rhea could be a valuable little world. But what was even more interesting was the Earth-manufactured ship which contained the circus.

The Gerin had no circuses, but they were familiar with the notion of entertainment. This often took the form of combats with them, but there were also musical contests featuring the resk, an instrument like an enormous pan pipe, with a bellows that could be manipulated by one tentacle. Usq-Usq-Tweed had read of circuses in the concise histories of Earth that were required reading for Gerin of the commanding class, and especially for those with a political leaning. You couldn't hope to get ahead in the chain of command unless you knew something about the enemy whose planets you expected to take over.

Usq-Usq-Tweed was familiar with Interlingua, the tongue in which the Circus Ship's log was kept. He used that knowledge now as he read over the log of the *Barnum*.

The last entry was of great interest.

"We have been requested by the League of Free Planets authorities to return to Point Bravo and the protection of the fleet. We have refused. We are neutrals, so we have no reason to run."

"And so," Usq-Usq-Tweed said aloud, "they refused to return. They thought they could deal with us. As neutrals."

Juu'quath, one of his squires, indicated by the lilac flushing of his foremost tentacles that he understood that his captain was proposing a fine irony.

"We Gerin are not entirely merciless," Usq-Usq-Tweed said. "We will send these poor fellows back where they came from. And we won't harm a hair of their heads.''

Juu'quath flushed purple, waiting for the punch line.

"No, we won't harm them," Usq-Usq-Tweed said. "But we'll do a little work on their ship before sending it back, eh?"

Heliotrope and scarlet make a strong combination. Not all Gerin approve of it. But in their military, a tentacle showing those colors is saying, ''That's just beautiful.'' That is what Juu'quath displayed now.

"First, however, let's find where the pilot of the League fighter has hidden himself.''

"Do you think he could be among the circus people, sir?''

"He's probably gone out of town and is hiding in the hills. But if he's among the circus people, we'll soon find out. Send their head man to me.''

The call went out: Blake waited in the commandant's office.

"No, you've got it all wrong," Silvestre Smoothfoot told Darfur. The old Clownmaster had been instructing Darfur for the past hour, and the fellow didn't show the slightest aptitude. Not even for Form 4 clowning, one of the most direct and easy to learn.

"Try for a sadder expression of the features," Smoothfoot said. "You look merely angry, not forlorn.''

"I *am* angry," Darfur said, standing there in a white satin suit with red polka dots, with big flappy shoes three times as long as his real feet, with an orange fright wig, and suspenders that were supposed to let down so that he could drop his trousers with comic effect, but that refused to budge off the commander's square shoulders.

"Turn the corners of the mouth down!" Smoothfoot said. "But look comically miserable, not as if you wanted to kill me!''

They were in the little dressing room off Stage One. They and all the rest had been told that they had one hour in which to mount a performance. Blake came in to check Darfur's progress.

"I don't think the Gerin figure you're hiding out among

us," Blake said. "I told them that I'd known every man here for the better part of ten years and that you're all skilled performers. So I'm for the high jump if they catch onto you. They'll do for you, too, not that that will be too great a satisfaction to me."

"But I don't know how to be a clown!" Darfur said. "Haven't you something else I can do?"

"Like what? Trapeze artist? Elephant dancer? Juggler? Musician? Tumbler? Acrobat? What are you suited for?"

"Fighting the enemy with a ship," Darfur said.

"Circuses don't use fighters. Either be a clown or die."

"I'll be a clown," Darfur said. But it was proving difficult.

"Now, try that fall again!" Smoothfoot shouted. Darfur fell.

"Too graceful!" Smoothfoot shouted. "Do it clumsily. Haven't you any sense at all?"

Darfur was trying, but he was finding it almost supernaturally difficult. He was a man in conflict. Of course he was frightened for his life. But that wasn't his only concern. He was oppressed now by a sense of failure. It was bad enough being overtaken unawares by the Gerin and having to disguise himself as a clown. If he lived through this, the story would come out and he'd be the laughingstock of the officer's mess. That was bad enough. But having to pretend to be a clown, at this moment of supreme disaster in his life—that was asking too much. The thought occurred to him that it might be better to die with dignity than to live on the basis of silly antics.

One of the circus dancers stuck her head in the doorway. "Come, time for practice is over. They have commanded the performance to begin."

"But he's not ready yet!" Smoothfoot said in despair. "You're not going to make anything of him in another ten minutes, no, nor ten days, either!"

"This fool is going to be the death of us all," Blake said. "What an idiot I was to put myself into jeopardy for an officer of the League of Free Planets! I'll never make that mistake again!"

No one pointed out that he would be unable to.

They all looked at Darfur, standing tall and proud.

Then Smoothfoot came forward. Perhaps he understood something of what the officer was feeling.

The old Clownmaster said to him, "Darfur, please, for me, act the fool."

Darfur stared at him. His features contorted. Smoothfoot giggled. Then Blake took it up, then the others.

Darfur said, "I can't do it!"

Smoothfoot said, "You're doing it!"

"They want us now!" the dancer said.

Even though for them it was an entirely alien performance, the Gerin enjoyed themselves very much. A circus is a universal thing. The Gerin were smart enough to see that the circus people were poking fun at themselves. They were making fun of humanoids. That was enough to put the Gerin in good spirits. They slapped their tentacles on the seats in front of them and made loud honking sounds with their beaked mouths.

They were especially fond of one tall young humanoid clown in red and white polka dots. The fellow never could seem to get his balance. Wherever he moved, some other clown was there to knock him down. He was really laughable, that skinny, silly-looking Earthman. The Gerins weren't connoisseurs of this sort of thing, but it was apparent to them, and especially to their commander, that the tall fellow was the chief performer of the troupe.

The Gerin put work parties onto the *Barnum* the next day. The seats that had been set up in the bays were torn out. Heavy equipment was brought in. Torpedo tubes for the plasma torpedoes were mounted fore and aft. Gatling laser guns were sweated into position, set up on their special platforms. FTL coils were brought in to supplement those that were already aboard. Day and night there was a hammering and a hiss of escaping gases as welding went on, replacing the shielding, fortifying the most vulnerable points on the hull.

There were a few regrettable incidents when circus people got too close to the Gerin working at the installations and were pushed back. Several circus people were killed, toppled off catwalks or smashed against steel doors, because the Gerin weren't shy about using their strength. The rest of the circus people soon learned to stay out of the way.

In the quarters he had selected for himself, Usq-Usq-Tweed set in motion the final portion of his plan. By fast fighter courier he had established contact with the Gerin fleet in his sector. His scheme was weighed in high councils while the final work was being done aboard the *Barnum*. Finally it was agreed to try it. This was a signal honor for Usq-Usq-Tweed, because he was only from an auxiliary branch of a noble family. By the complicated status rules of the Gerin, this would give him a chance to take his place among the high councillors of the race.

Usq-Usq-Tweed was aware of this, but it was not his primary motive. What interested him most of all was this opportunity to smash one of the great fighting fleets of the League of Free Planets. If he could get Admiral Van Dyne's force out of the way, a path lay open to the humanoid-colonized Inner Worlds. Success in this could mark the beginning of a decline in the League of Free Planets' power, mark the moment when the League's defeat was irreversible, and signal the beginning of Gerin hegemony throughout known space.

It was a daring chance, and risky. But it could not be overlooked. The military expected this ship to come in to the safety of Point Bravo. But they did not expect it to be armed and filled with fighting Gerins.

Usq-Usq-Tweed thought, *We'll be within their lines when we cut loose. They won't be really able to fire on us because of the chance of hitting their own ships. We should be able to hold out for quite a while, meanwhile occupying all their attention and all their forces. If, at that time, an entire Gerin battle group were to downwarp into the zone and take up the battle—we could roll up the Point Bravo position! And that would secure this entire sector of space for us.*

His mind flashed on the possibilities. If he could tie up the Point Bravo fleet long enough for the Gerin battle group to come through, this battle could be won, and its victory would mark the beginning of mankind's end.

By God! This attack has to be made! The entire war can be won right here!

Darfur, having thought of the same scheme, was thinking the same thoughts, in the small cabin he had taken for himself. For him it was torture of the most exquisite sort to clown through his performances, all of the time aware that the octopoidal creatures in the audience were about to nail the lid down on humanity's coffin.

He sat alone in his cabin and thought. And finally a plan came to him. He went over it in his mind. . . . Yes, he thought it might work. But first there was something he had to find out.

The circus impresario, Jon Blake, was in deep sleep, yet so hyperalert were his senses that he caught the faint sound of a footstep on the deep pile of the carpeting. He came awake in an instant and grabbed for the pistol he kept under his pillow. Before he could come up with it, a long form had launched itself from the darkness, pinning the hand that seized the gun. Blake struggled, and he was a man of very great strength, but it was in vain against the whipcord-and-steel power of the being who held him fast.

"Take it easy," Blake grunted as the gun was wrenched from his hand, almost breaking a finger caught in the trigger guard.

The man released him and turned on the light. Blake had known, by the absence of the characteristic smell, that it was not a Gerin who had attacked him. He was not surprised to find Darfur, in dark clothing now rather than his clown suit, standing over him with the gun.

"You pick a hell of a time for an assassination," Blake said.

"I don't care if I kill you or not," Darfur said. "What I must know is the location of the grand cable junction box. You have the ship's plans in here somewhere."

"May I sit up?" Blake said. When Darfur released him he sat up, touching his bruised throat with delicacy. "You want the main junction box? The power splice? Planning to blow us up?"

"That's it," Darfur said. "I don't know what deviltry

the Gerin are up to, but they're not going to get a chance to do it.''

"I know what the Gerin are planning," Blake said.

"How do you know that?" Darfur asked. "You're pretty friendly with the commander, aren't you?"

"I wouldn't say he was close to anyone," Blake said. "But he did have to tell me the destination, since I will be running this ship. Under his orders, of course."

"And what is the destination?"

"Point Bravo."

"Are they crazy?" Darfur asked. "They're going to fly into the midst of the Earth forces? Even with armament aboard this ship, they wouldn't last half an hour once the deception was discovered."

"Half an hour might be long enough," Blake said.

"Long enough for what?"

"To tie up the League forces and spread confusion until the rest of the Gerin advance fleet shows up."

Darfur sucked in his breath, then let it out slowly. "You think they'll commit an entire battle group to this?"

"Usq-Usq-Tweed didn't tell me so in so many words, but the implication was clear."

"It could work, too," Darfur said. "Damn! If only we could tell Point Bravo. My scout ship—"

"No longer on-planet," Blake said. "They took it to join the rest of their fleet."

"No way to send a message," Darfur said. "Even if we had control of the radio, which we don't. Well then, there's no alternative. I have to blow up this ship."

Blake shook his head. "The thought occurred to me, too. But I've had my people check. The area of the main junction box is under continuous guard, as are the other key points."

"We'll have to try to suicide attack," Darfur said. Then he looked at Blake. The man was grinning.

"But I forgot. You're on the other side."

Blake shook his head, "I said I was neutral. But that was before they started killing my performers. Now I find myself definitely biased against them."

"That's nice," Darfur said bitterly. "A little late to do any good, however. I suppose the only thing we can do is try to take over the ship before they can get it aloft. They'll probably kill us all, but at least we can delay them and take some of them with us."

Blake shook his head. "I'm annoyed at the Gerin, that's for sure. But that doesn't mean I'm ready for suicide. It would serve no purpose, anyhow. I have a better idea."

Darfur had an angry retort on his lips, then he smothered if. It would do no good being petulant. He had to work with Blake, much as he detested the man. But he would have to keep an eye on him, because once a turncoat turns, you can never tell what he'll do next.

"What's your plan?" he asked.

"We must wait," Blake said, "until the ship is underway, until we are in Earth's sphere of influence."

"That makes no sense at all! They'll have a guard aboard. They'll be watching us, and watching extra-hard when we get near Point Bravo. Your people won't stand a chance. If we delay until that time, we'll all be killed without effecting anything."

Blake sat back in his command chair, found a small cigar, lit it. He smiled, a smile that Darfur found most exasperating.

"I can see that you don't know much about circus people," he said. "Especially circus people like us."

"What's there to know?"

"Have you ever wondered about why we're outcastes on all the humanoid worlds?"

"Probably because you smell bad."

Blake laughed. "Your humor is most infantile. I'll tell you later. You'd better get back to your quarters before the guard notices you're gone. And one more thing."

"What's that?"

"Get back into your clown suit. We don't want anyone suspecting you're not the ridiculous fellow we all know you to be."

Darfur went back to his quarters. He didn't trust Blake, but he had little choice in the matter.

One this was sure. When this was over, whatever way it went, he was going to settle up with the circus manager.

* * *

At last they were no more than a few hours from Point Bravo and contact with the League of Free Planets fleet. Usq-Usq-Tweed ordered Blake to his quarters. "Now, my friend, you are going to do a favor for both of us. You have probably already gathered that we are going to attack and destroy the fleet at Point Bravo."

Blake saw that a lot of new equipment had been installed. There was a bulky weapons-management system, with separate subsystems ready to display damage reports. The torpedo control center also occupied a prominent position.

"We're getting a signal from Bravo," Usq-Usq-Tweed said. "I want you to talk to them, tell them you're bringing the *Barnum* in as directed."

"All right," Blake said. He reached for the microphone.

"One thing first," Usq-Usq-Tweed said, a tentacle restraining Blake's hand. "You will do this correctly, Mr. Blake, and convincingly, or you will not live until the end of the transmission. And after we kill you, we'll snuff out all your people."

"That is not according to the protocols of interstellar warfare," Blake said. "You have no right to demand this of me, and no right to threaten. I have already shown you our papers. We are neutrals, noncombatants—"

"I have noted that," Usq-Usq-Tweed said. "I must tell you that in a struggle of this magnitude, there can be no neutrals. Either you are for us or against us."

Sensing the animosity in the Gerin commander's voice, his two squires came around either side of him, weapons ready, tentacles glowing an angry red. Blake shrank away from them.

"All right," Blake said. "What will you do to us if I do cooperate?"

"Then you are an ally," Usq-Usq-Tweed said. "An unwilling ally, but an ally nonetheless. If this goes as expected, I will recommend that you and your people be taken to the planet known to us as Gu'haorin, and to you as Gregor's World. There you will receive reindoctrination. When we think we can rely on you, you will be assigned to other duties. There can be fine rewards working for us, Blake. But death is certain if you go against us. Do you understand?''

"Of course," Blake said. Grimly he reached for the annunciator, pressed it on. "Blake to Fleet Navigation Control, Point Bravo."

"We've been waiting for you," a voice replied. "You took your own sweet time about getting here."

"Had to give our last performance on Rhea," Blake said. "Can't disappoint the paying customers, you understand."

"Don't you know there's a war on?"

"I think I heard something about it," Blake said, glancing at the huge alien standing beside him, holding a jagged-edged dagger—the sacred *khalifi*—poised at the back of his neck.

"You spot the Gerin or hear anything about them on Rhea?" the voice asked.

"Nothing at all," Blake said.

"We've got a lot of traffic just now," the voice said. "Can you hold station for a while?"

Usq-Usq-Tweed turned purple-red and waved a tentacle in an emphatic negative.

"Can't do that," Blake said. "We have several casualties aboard who need immediate attention. One of the trapeze setups collapsed."

"Just a minute." There was a short wait. Then the voice was back. "All right, I'm giving you an emergency clearance. You can come in right now." He gave a direction and bearing that would take them to the supply and hospital depots. Blake thanked him and signed off.

"You did well," Usq-Usq-Tweed said. "That was resourceful of you, to think up that emergency."

"You made it pretty clear that you wanted us to be taken in immediately."

"That is correct. Timing is everything. The main Gerin battlefleet in this sector is already in FTL space. They will be ready to downwarp and go into action against the League ships"—he glanced at a watch, incongruously strapped at the midpoint of one of his tentacles—"in just half an hour. By then we will be within range and already fighting. It will complete our surprise."

"Sounds good to me," Blake said.

"I shall note your excellent attitude in my report to headquarters. Now you may return to your people. You will all take your accustomed positions for in-flight routine, and stand ready to assist my men if need be."

"All right," Blake said. He went out of the bridge and into one of the corridors.

Commander Darfur was waiting for him in the main wardroom. "What's happening?" he demanded.

"They have established contact with the human forces," Blake told him. "We are starting in now."

"Damnation!" Darfur said, grinding his teeth. "What do we do?"

"I have been waiting for this," Blake said. "The Gerin are lulled now into a false sense of security. Or so I hope. They have already discounted us: we are noncombatants, less than vermin in their eyes. They expect us to do nothing but cower in the wardrooms and await the result."

"And that's about all you can do," Darfur said. "Your bunch of circus freaks won't stand a chance against trained Gerin warriors."

"We freaks may have a trick or two up our sleeves," Blake said. "You know all the stories about our special talents?"

"You told me they were all prejudiced lies."

"So I did. That's what we tell everybody. There's enough hatred of us anyhow without revealing the truth."

"Which is?"

"You will soon see. And then you must stand by, Commander, because you will have your part to play in all this, too."

"And that part is?"

Blake smiled grimly. "I'm not going to tell you yet. It might alarm you."

Darfur had to smile at that. This circus impresario was really crazy if he thought he had something that would frighten a commander in the forces in the League of Free Planets.

Time seemed to stand still as the *P.T. Barnum* crept toward the Point Bravo position. The circus people waited as the minutes ticked by. The Gerin soldiery stood to their weapons. A solemn silence reigned over the ship, broken only by the low throbbing of the engines. Tuning in on the ship's intercom system, Blake heard an alarm go off as long-range visual contact was established. Soon, in greatly magnified view, the ranks of League ships could be seen, and behind them, a yellowish world wrapped in mists, was the planet Bravo, which served as the supply depot and strongpoint for this sector.

"Damn you," Darfur said. "They're ready to begin hostilities against the League fleet. When are you going to pull this surprise of yours? Or was that just a bedtime story to keep me quiet?"

"You exaggerate the lengths I'd go to soothe your feelings, Commander," Blake said. "Unfortunately, my plan has no chance at all until hostilities begin. We need the distraction of battle for what I have in mind."

Just then the ship trembled from stem to stern and gave a slight sidewise heave. There was a noticeable pickup in acceleration, and then a din of screeching metal as the Gerin threw off the camouflaged shielding that hid the gun emplacements. Soon the ship was vibrating as the torpedoes and Gatlings opened up.

"Now!" Darfur said. "What are you going to do?"

"We are going to take over the ship," Blake replied.

"But you said yourself that was impossible! And what do your men know of hand-to-hand fighting?"

"You'd be surprised at what we have to contend with on some of the little worlds we visit," Blake said.

"All right, I'm for it," Darfur said. "But you said yourself this would be a suicidal undertaking. They'll pick us off one by one."

"Well, I see it's time I revealed our secret," Blake said. "We freaks do have one thing, you see. We share a telepathic linkage."

Darfur stared at him, then comprehension dawned on him. "So you can attack simultaneously!"

"Precisely."

"But after that . . . ?"

"I have plans," Blake said. "And now, Commander,

have the goodness to stand by while I put this plan into motion.''

Blake closed his eyes. Darfur could almost sense the effort the man was making, striving to contact by telepathy all his people no matter where they were on the ship. Blake knew that the plan must have been prearranged. Blake must have contacted his people via telepathy, telling them to be ready for this. But could he make that contact now? Telepathy was notoriously unreliable. . . .

A wail arose from somewhere down the corridor. An inhuman wail that was changed into a gurgle and then was cut short.

''We're on now,'' Blake said. He pulled a handblaster out of his belt, handed it to Darfur. ''Curtain time!''

The Gerin, alert at their posts, had, over the course of the last days, come to take the humanoid crew for granted. So apathetic did the circus people seem, so willing to obey orders, so little inclined to rebel, that the Gerin were caught completely by surprise. Suddenly, and within half a second of each other, several dozen fights burst out on the ship as the circus people turned simultaneously on their Gerin captors.

One moment everything was normal; the next, the Gerin were fighting for their lives. The circus people, using what weapons came to hand, or crude knives and clubs secreted in their clothing, struck suddenly, simultaneously, and with complete violence.

The circus freaks had received their orders telepathically from Blake, and on his signal they acted in concert. No sooner did a man kill his opponent than he rushed to assist the man nearest to him. The Gerin fought back savagely, but they had been caught by surprise, at a time when they were already in combat, and not expecting an attack from behind their own lines. Blood flowed over the deckplates, some of it the purple of Gerin, but mixed with the red of humanoid blood. Some of the Gerin crowded together to make a stand. Even then their individuality undid them: the Gerin warriors were all too ready to abandon their rallying points and sally forth each on his own, to be pulled down and hacked to bits by the furious circus folk.

Blake and Darfur raced to the bridge. There Usq-Usq-Tweed and his squire companions were trying to continue fighting the Point Bravo fleet and simultaneously put down the rebellion.

Usq-Usq-Tweed caught sight of Blake. "You dog!" he shouted. "You tricked me! For that you die!"

He aimed a handgun at Blake, who tried to dodge out of the way. But Darfur was already firing. A blaster was something never used aboard ship for fear of holing it. But Darfur had adjusted for range and was hoping for the best. He cut down the Gerin commander as he rushed at them. Blake had picked up another weapon, a laser projector, and was cutting around him with deadly effect.

"Careful with that!" Darfur shouted. The laser sliced through the remaining Gerin warrior. Darfur managed to switch the weapon off before Blake could pierce the hull.

"Good work!" Darfur cried. He rushed to the control console, pushing bits of chopped Gerin out of the way. "Now to signal the fleet and get out of here!"

"Actually," Blake said, "I think it's a little too late for that." He pointed to the rearview monitors.

Far away, but closing rapidly, Darfur could see dozens of Gerin globeships that had downwarped out of FTL space.

"What do you suggest now?" Darfur asked.

"They think we're still on their side," Blake said. "Retreat until we're in range, then open fire on them. With any luck, the Point Bravo flotilla will pull themselves together and follow."

Darfur laughed with glee when he realized how beautiful the scheme was. The Gerin were caught in their own trap! The Trojan Horse ship, which was supposed to open the way through Earth's defenses, would serve as a Trojan Horse for the other side, too.

"Great plan," Darfur said, his fingers dancing on the computer keys. "You've done it, Blake! Made them stick their neck out. Now we can get in there and really do some hitting."

He had the ship turned now and racing toward the Gerin

fleet, which held its fire, believing Usq-Usq-Tweed and his men were still in control. The intercom squabbled with questions directed to the dead Usq-Usq-Tweed.

Darfur said, ''We're coming into range. Tell your men to stand ready to fire.''

''There's only one thing,'' Blake said.

''What is it?''

''My men don't know anything about gunnery. They can swing a cudgel or use a dagger with the best of them, as you've seen. But as for laser cannon and plasma torpedoes, they haven't a clue.''

''Great,'' Darfur said. ''If we can't protect ourselves, those globeships will take us out before the Earth fleet can come to our aid.''

As he spoke, the viewplate showed the globe discharging small fighter craft.

''Oh, we're going to fight them,'' Blake said. ''We're going to use every weapon the enemy has so thoughtfully put at our disposal. The thing is, *you* are going to have to control it all.''

''But how can I? Even if I try to tell each man what he should do, it would take too long. We wouldn't stand a chance.''

''I think we can fix that,'' Blake said. ''With telepathy. You'll have to control all the guns, Darfur, via telepathic circuit. We can take you into the hookup—if you're willing.''

''No!'' Darfur said. Like many people, he had a deep-seated fear of mental control. The idea of Blake and these freaks sharing his mind . . . no, it was intolerable.

''You have to do it!'' Blake said. ''It's the only chance!''

''I can't do that!'' Darfur said.

''Commander,'' Blake said, ''you'd better give it a try.''

Darfur grimaced, then nodded glumly. ''All right. What do I do?''

''Just try to be receptive,'' Blake said. He closed his eyes. Darfur felt something tug at his mind, something huge and terrible. He resisted for a moment, then forced himself to give in to it.

There was a terrible moment of vertigo, in which Darfur thought he was going out of his mind. Then abruptly his vision cleared.

But he wasn't looking out of his own eyes anymore. He was in Blake's head, looking at himself.

"Good," Blake said. "Now try to move around. The crew has been warned. You can take over."

Darfur got control of himself and pushed out with his mind. He felt himself passing through darkness. Then all of a sudden he had a simultaneous view through many eyes. With the rapidity of thought he was in a dozen different heads at the same time. He tried to pump his knowledge of modern weaponry into the freaks, but it was faster finally to dart from mind to mind, taking over for a moment, sighting and shooting, adjusting, firing again as they bored into the Gerin fleet.

The Gerin hesitated, trying to figure out what had happened to Usq-Usq-Tweed's scheme. Then they started firing back. Darfur now had another task, not just to fire the weapons, but to continue adjusting the screens, which were threatening to go into overload. It became a mad dance for him, the finale of a circus of horror in which he was the one who gave the order to fire, the one who pushed the button, and also the missile itself, arcing out into space.

The ship's screens flickered and began to waver. Darfur had to forget about the weapons and put his full attention to maintaining the shields. He knew it would be a matter of moments before a voltage drop let the screens open long enough for a missile to come through. And what annoyed him was that he couldn't even hit back. But then he realized that he was hitting back, because plasma torpedoes were streaking past him, taking out fighters, trying to home in on the globeships.

Had his crew learned how to shoot from his example? Impossible. And anyhow, there was no accounting for the sheer number of torpedoes racing past him. Someone must have come to his aid.

He turned to his rear-vision viewplate and saw Admiral Van Dyne's flotilla coming up fast behind him. One globeship was gone and the others were trying to scramble back into FTL space.

"A classic Trojan Horse maneuver," Admiral Van Dyne said. "Only you turned it against them. Turned it into a Trojan hearse! I really must congratulate you, Commander Darfur. I've read of such things in the history of early space battles, but never thought I'd live to see one performed."

They were in the admiral's lounge aboard his command dreadnought, the *Saratoga*. Elements of the fleet were already out mopping up those elements of the Gerin fleet that had not been able to upwarp in time to escape destruction. The *Barnum* had survived, scorched and battered, leaking air from a dozen points, a quarter of her crew of circus people dead and another third suffering more or less serious injuries.

"Sir," Darfur said, "I have to tell you, I had very little to do with this fine victory. The credit belongs entirely to Blake. It was his scheme, and it was undertaken at great cost to his people. I only assisted in the final stage."

"The fighting against the Gerin, you mean?" Van Dyne asked.

"Yes, sir. I was able to assist with some of the more exotic weaponry they had brought aboard."

"I've been wondering about that," Van Dyne said. "How were those freaks able to operate that weaponry?"

Darfur was about to tell Van Dyne about the telepathic linkup, then stopped himself. He didn't want to do anything to jeopardize the circus people's precarious security. If it became generally known that they were indeed telepathic, it might go badly for them when they tried to bring their circus to different worlds.

"I ran around a lot, sir," Darfur said. "They really learned amazingly fast."

Van Dyne seemed about to say something, then thought better of it. He smiled—a rare sight on his grim battle-scarred old face.

"However it was done, it was well done."

"Thank you, sir. What will happen to the *Barnum* and Blake and his people now?"

"We've already taken his people into the infirmary. We'll save all we can. The ship will be repaired by our armorers. I offered Blake a commission in our forces."

"What did he say, sir?"

"Wasn't interested. That's the way it is with freaks. You can't tell what they'll do next."

"I suppose not, sir. I suppose he'll go back to circusing."

"All in good time," Van Dyne said. "Actually, he proposed that we refit his ship and turn him loose as a freebooter. A privateer. He could cause some merry hell in some of the neutral zones which the Gerin have been invading."

"Sounds like a good idea, sir," Darfur said. "He's a first class fighting man—as well as a pretty good circus man."

"You like him, don't you?"

"I didn't at first. But it's difficult not to like a man you've fought beside."

"That's what I thought. Blake pointed out that he would need a trained officer aboard to help maintain the weapons systems and train his crew."

"Good idea," Darfur said.

"He asked especially for you."

"Did he, sir?" Darfur flushed with pleasure. He could think of nothing better than ranging through space with Blake and his circus men in search of Gerin to kill. But then a thought struck him.

"This would be a first-class assignment, sir. But I'm afraid it ought to go to an officer with more seniority than I have."

"I discussed that point with Blake," Van Dyne said. "He was insistent that it be you. He said that you had another talent that was valuable to them, one not usually found in the armed forces."

"What was that, sir?" Darfur said.

"He said that you have the makings of a first-class clown. That ability will be important if the *Barnum* is to carry on secret missions on the fringes of Gerin-occupied territory.''

"He said I was a good clown, sir?" Darfur said.

"He said you had the makings of one," Van Dyne said. "Why? Does the occupation appeal to you?"

"Not at all, sir," Darfur said. "But I like to do whatever I do well. Can I go speak with Blake now?"

"Go ahead," Van Dyne said. "This assignment is going to be dangerous. But I'll tell you this—if I were a hundred years younger, I'd pull all the strings in creation to be assigned to the *Barnum* along with you. Dismissed!"

Darfur rushed off to find Blake. And so began the notable exploits of the privateer *P.T. Barnum*.

The League of Free Planets

Six months after the destruction of his home planet, Mac had gathered ships and troops from four worlds. After his victory at Gemini, this total tripled in a matter of weeks. Even so, the League of Free Planets, which comprised the largest, richest, and best-armed planets in the Far Stars region, stubbornly maintained their independence.

The raid on Klaremont was likely a reconnaissance in force by the Gerin. One of the greatest problems both sides faced was ferreting out the opposition worlds among the thousands of uninhabited planets in even this sparsely filled portion of the galaxy. At this point, it can be speculated that the main deterrent to Mac's leading those forces he had gathered in a revenge attack on the Gerin homeworld was that no one was sure of its exact location. Not that the humans and their allies weren't trying—they simply hadn't managed to be sure the location they had ascertained was correct. And there would be only one chance at this point, and at the cost of more worlds enslaved or destroyed.

Klaremont was a most unusual planet, even before the Gerin attack. On it had developed a wide range of avian life forms, to the virtual exclusion of all others. Most were brightly colored, and their calls, almost without exception, were melodious. Overhead, four most unusual moons, all tectonically active, filled every night's sky with new wonders. All this, when combined with a gentle equatorial climate, had enabled Klaremont to become a very successful resort world. Also found on this planet were the estates of the rich and powerful in the League of Free Planets.

The hostilities began when an orbital station spotted three Gerin globeships (roughly equivalent to light cruisers) entering the system. The planet's only intrinsic defense was a small force of planetary fighters manned by police and customs officers. Even so these rose in the hope that by sheer number or luck they could destroy the Gerin invaders. Vessels were then dispatched for aid, even though it would take almost a week to arrive. At great cost these lightly armed fighters disabled one ship, but were unable to prevent the escape of the other two Gerin vessels.

Request for aid had gone out to both the League navy and Mac's force, which was still orbiting Gemini. Apologists explain Mac's inaction by saying that he was still integrating the Gemini ships into his force and unprepared for battle. Most League historians assert that he was quite willing to sacrifice the two hundred thousand humans on Klaremont if their loss might compel the League to join in his crusade against the Gerin.

The League forces, spread over worlds varying from three days' to two weeks' flight apart, arrived separately and were forced uncoordinated into battle with the returning Gerin. The Gerin forces also grew in spurts, likely caused by their having been dispersed in the search for human worlds.

Where most space battles last no more than a few hours, the defense of Klaremont lasted over a week. It ended successfully only when Mac arrived at the head of his newly enlarged fleet. During that week Klaremont was changed from near paradise to a cratered hell. Most of the world's inhabitants died or were injured. This included the families of over half the League Council. Even then the League politicians were reluctant to join with Mac, whom they rightfully saw as a fanatic. In the weeks after the relief of Klaremont, Mac fought the war not with ships and marines, but with press releases and propaganda. Meanwhile, he personally toured every planet in the League, campaigning harder than any office seeker.

VOLUNTEERS
by Jody Lynn Nye

"C'MON, SMILE," the voice of Vinson, the trivideo cameraman, came over Sergeant Barlow's headset. "Look confident. You're going to bust those Gerin bastards. Show me you believe it."

What the hell am I doing here? Barlow mused, mustering a grimace that seemed to please Vinson. The sergeant was a stocky, muscular man with a heavy jaw like a bulldog's. He crouched in the bushes, overlooking what had to be the universe's most fetid swamp. *You volunteered, you dummy. When they asked for volunteers from all the marine detachments for a special mission, you stood in line, and let them go "You. You. And you."*

At least there were none of the usual precombat jitters among his men. No, what they seemed to be exhibiting was stage fright. Not exactly the best frame of mood for fighting men to be in. Barlow cursed Captain Avix for agreeing to such a boneheaded project as making a live combat video for the folks back home.

"We need the League of Free Planets to rally behind us," Avix explained apologetically to the ranks of men who had "volunteered" for the mission. "Support for this war is not as heavy as we would like—as we need. This will make good publicity, show that we're banding together to stamp out the Gerin Menace." The media types always seemed to speak in their own clichés.

It was more likely to stamp out the menace of Barlow and his men. Not only was the need for such a manned attack spurious, but the major difference between this and a real mission was the way the troop had been chosen. Captain Avix had gone down the line with a thin, languid civilian, who would nod or shake his head whenever the captain glanced at him. In the end they had the right number, but the wrong mix of specialities for a mission of this kind. Barlow knew it, and he knew Avix knew it. Hardly any of the regulars fanned out among the ferns behind him had ever worked with Barlow before. He had taken stock of them in the shuttle. They were good fighters. None of them had visible wounds or prosthetics. In fact, it seemed as if the producer who had reviewed the troops by Avix's side had chosen all the pretty boys and girls; the better for camera exposure, he guessed. In case that wasn't enough, not even the heavy squad was allowed any powered armor. Seems it didn't photograph well, hid the man inside too well.

Still, the sergeant's real concern was that lack of wounds likely meant lack of combat experience. Of course, a media man wouldn't care about that.

"Absolutely true," Vinson confirmed Barlow's thoughts in the shuttle on the drop to Skylark's surface. "He only wants the *shayna punim* for this film. He picked you for your looks, too, because you're the stereotypical gruff leader."

"For God's sake, don't they want us to come home again?"

Vinson lifted his hands helplessly. "They want to see a victory. It's better publicity than a loss. At least you haven't got a junior lieutenant in the way this time. The billet's all yours. If anyone can pull a diverse lot like this into a fighting unit in thirty minutes, it's you. Look, Sergeant, I'm a retired soldier myself. This is my job. Most of my equipment is incorporated into my suit, so there's no extra luggage to carry. I won't get in your way, and if I get hurt, I know where my medpak is. Just do what you've got to do, and I'll record the action for the folks back home.''

"I don't want this video to be the last thing my folks ever see of me,'' Private Hotchkiss grumbled into his helmet mike to his buddy Pete Omaya, standing at ready a meter away.

Vinson overheard the remark and smiled at him. His short, grizzled hair capped a weathered face that except for its finely lined texture could have been that of a man in his thirties. ''That's up to you, son. I don't make news. I just record it. You just do what the sergeant tells you, and you'll get home.'' Hotchkiss blushed, and Omaya grinned sheepishly into his collar.

Barlow was flattered by the snap judgment of his abilities, and wondered if Vinson had been soaping him just to make him calm down. He must have been a good officer when he was in the service.

Now Barlow was lying here in the mud smiling pretty for the cameras, and listening to the cameraman on the touchline muttering narration into his unit's audio pickup. He understood his men's resentment. If the mission wasn't balanced between specialties, their chances of getting out were lessened, and they knew it wasn't, no matter how gung ho and cooperative they were with one another. His best spotter was back on the transport ship. Not good-looking enough for the video, Barlow guessed. Well, that was likely true. Minkus had a face like a parrot, but he had a second sense about where Gerin ordnance and sensors were hidden. Barlow had had to make do with Corporal Scott, a much less experienced though prettier noncom.

Unseen, across fifteen yards of tropical greenery, Scott was combat-clicking to him via head mike. The squad had passed through the outer circle of defenses and were hiding in groups of three and four in the undergrowth. The spotter had determined how far it was from their position to the inner circle. She indicated via clicktalk that the Gerin had buried a wire in a ring attached to sensors instead of an outer line of defense and the churned-up ground on the topo map she sent him with a flick of her glove control meant deadfalls, both of which were more to scare off the indigenous animal life than safeguard a military entrenchment. They didn't seem to be expecting much in the way of an invading force. Then Barlow recognized the heat signature of unmanned laser weaponry far ahead.

Being water creatures, Gerin liked to hole up in the wettest, lowest ground possible. The troop was risking attack by holing up in the bushes, but Barlow didn't want to expose his position before he had to just to keep moving. The Gerin weren't stupid. Even if he put his men on the march, the Gerin would just count heads and wait until they stopped.

Barlow was quickly losing interest in penetrating the Gerin's perimeter. There was no one, not one single human, left alive on Skylark's surface after the Slime invaded. All that the fleet needed to do was drop neutron bombs on the swamp until nothing else moved. Scuttlebutt was that at HQ everyone hated the idea of this mission. Maybe that's why there were no officers in charge. Everyone, that is, except Ubiquitous Smith.

Barlow knew Corporal Smith's real first name, but Ubiquitous seemed to suit him so much better. There was never a man in his command who seemed to be in more places at once—especially ones he shouldn't be in. He was the original cadet who was known to have been out drinking in town when his boot camp sergeant would swear under oath at a disciplinary hearing that he'd seen Smith asleep in his bunk—and that two separate ladies on opposite ends of town each claimed to have him with her that night.

Smith was openly enjoying the presence of the videographer. He turned his faceplate toward the camera occasionally, showing a fierce, noble countenance or a confident smile. When Barlow gave the order to move in closer, Smith flung himself onto his belly and elbows right in front of Vinson, and scrambled. At least Barlow wasn't worrying about Smith's competence; the man was the veteran of numerous campaigns. It was his damned ego that was so annoying.

Jammers activated, they crossed the line of sensors. Scott indicated by a quick click that no transmission with their names on it had gone toward the Gerin camp. Inside the perimeter, the ambient humidity rose sharply, indicating that the water table was much higher here. The ground underfoot was saturated and spongy. In full combat gear, carrying heavy cargo nets and backpacks, the men left deep prints that became oval pools before the next boot toe or elbow hit the ground. Barlow's olfactory sensors gave him a clammy wave of swamp odors that curdled his nostrils. There was still no sign of occupied Gerin defenses, but they were still fifty feet from the inner ring. The slimeballs must be relying completely on whatever made up that defense line to protect them.

The marines lived by the motto "Do what is necessary and then get the hell out." Even if the mission was a turkey, they were carrying a new, powerful depth charge especially designed to be used against Gerin bases. These were small as a raise in pay and heavy as the burden of sin, but they packed a mean kick when exposed to the correct psi. Barlow was as interested as the brain trust back on board ship to see what kind of effect the charges had in the field. Anything that made it easier to get the job done was a plus. But he wondered about taking experimental ordnance on a publicity exercise. The charge's greatest drawback was that the pair of cylindrical charges rolled around in the cargo nets, unbalancing the troopers carrying them. Earlier, after nearly falling on a partially exposed land mine, one of the men complained about the awkwardness over their headset radios as they crawled. Barlow barked a quick order for radio silence.

Ubiquitous was also carrying a slugthrower loaded with cartridges he had filled with salt powder and alum. Some of the others had a few specials of their own, which normally they would not be allowed to carry, but this was a special occasion. Barlow figured that if they were going to die in a stupid cause, they might as well have fun doing it. Beside the regulation-issue firearms, sheath knife, and saber, he himself wore a razor knife which normally rested in a slit in the metal side of his personal locker.

They crept forward on their bellies through sodden

masses of rotting vegetation. The moist smells grew steadily worse as they approached the perimeter. Barlow finally had to turn off his smell sensors. They would tell him nothing he really needed to know. He heard gagging from more than one of the others in the company. The very atmosphere was attacking them. Even with the olfactory sensors deactivated, the filtered air still contained enough moisture to cloud up his faceplate. He nosed the dehumidifier control to dry it out, which also took care of a lot of the water-borne odors.

Dawn was breaking through the trees to planetary east, extending thin needles of light through the heavy foliage over their heads. An infrared trace of sunlight was beginning to interfere with the telemetry readings of his helmet's sensors. In response to a query, Scott clicked to Barlow that they were only five feet from the line of primary defense. Her readings were fixed from the time they had come over the horizon of the planet. The signature of hot laser weapons warming up in the treetops showed that the slimeballs knew they were coming but wouldn't trouble themselves to come out and make a personal attack. For a moment, the sergeant hoped that there were only a few in the base. It would give his men better odds of survival. The octopoidal Gerin always fought in threes. Two apprentices flanked and defended a warrior, who did most of the actual attacking. If the warrior was killed, the apprentices tended to lose their fighting edge and become easy victims.

Laser fire is silent and invisible to the naked eye. Unless one's helmet sensors are switched to infrared and facing toward the emplacement for the brief milliseconds when it fires, you can miss seeing the attack. Barlow's screen showed a red line etched momentarily on the green-black mass of hanging vines, just as Scott cried out, "Incoming!"

"Roll!" Barlow bellowed over the comlink. Before them, the ground erupted as vegetation caught fire and leaped into the air. The small screen inside his helmet below his faceplate was already showing suit telemetry from one of his men who had been scored down the back of his leg by the laser. The beam hadn't broken suit integrity, but the heat had fried the light armor's circuits, and had surely raised the temperature inside the suit.

"Retreat! Return fire! Any burns, Clarke?" he rapped, as the company hastily fell back. The lasers etched hissing lines in the muck in front of them, and then stopped when the company had backed up ten meters.

"Nossir," the marine replied, over the link. "Just hot, that's all."

"Injuries, report," Barlow requested, nudging the control with his chin to open his frequency to the whole company. A few men complained of burns on their suits, but only two had been wounded by the laser barrage. One couldn't feel his left hand, and the other had been burned where the laser had holed the suit on his back and wouldn't be much good in the near future. Fortunately, the crystalline fiber of the outer layer of the marine all-terrain uniform took much of the power out of laser attacks.

"Has that unit of yours got an infrared lens?" Ubiquitous asked the cameraman. "Otherwise you're going to miss all the action."

"Radio silence," the sergeant bellowed at his second. "All the laser units are still intact! Where are they?"

"I've got them, sir," Scott interjected. "Three laser emplacements in the immediate area. That fold of land to the west is protecting us from the laser in that quadrant. I'm getting no visual on them at all, just the heat signature." Scott's glove control gave him the map with hot spots high up in the trees.

"Too much spread to get a clear fix. Those units must be leaking power like nobody's business," Barlow complained. "Damned slimeballs must have a full-scale nuclear generator in their camp. Kalin, Smith, take them down before they hurt somebody. Blow up the trees."

"That won't make very good video," Vinson noted mildly as Smith wriggled into position, clutching his slugthrower.

"Did I ask you?" Barlow demanded over his shoulder, and then went redfaced as he realized that his outburst was now on disk for all the brass to see.

Vinson smiled through his faceplate, understanding the

sergeant's embarrassment, and touched the side of his helmet. "I've already erased that, Sergeant. Sorry. You only want to do this once, don't you?" Once again he hefted the small cylinder which was the hand-held component of the videocam.

Picturing an endless campaign of useless missions, Barlow was aghast. "They wouldn't dare send us out again for this kind of trivia!"

"We can make it more interesting," Smith offered, holding up his slugthrower. "Kalin and I have won medals for sharpshooting."

"Just get it over with," Barlow hissed. "I don't want to spend the rest of my life here."

From Scott's unit hidden in the brush to the left, Kalin appeared, crawling on his elbows and knees, carefully keeping his slugthrower up out of the mud. He was a slender, hatchet-faced man with black hair, and Barlow noticed that he was carrying one of the depth charges in his pack. He took his place beside Smith. "Now what are we supposed to do?" he asked with friendly interest. "I've never been on trivid before."

Vinson must have sensed Barlow's incipient outburst, and spoke quickly. "Nothing special. Take out the emplacements, just as if I wasn't here." Barlow counted ten and let his drawn breath out, and nodded to the two marines.

The heat traces showed the defense lasers had gone back to a ready state, but without targets weren't fully live. Kalin shrugged and took a lying-down firing stance beside Smith, who was already in perfect rifle-range form.

"At the word 'fire,' FIRE," commanded Barlow. The explosive rounds ripped through the foliage toward the center of two of the heat points, and detonated with a blast of flame.

"Oh, shit!" Kalin cried, as infrared showed the red lines of returned laser fire directly toward him, scoring a smoking line on his suit sleeve. "I thought we were out of swing range!" He beat at the laser score and sank the sleeve into the swamp ooze to cool it down.

"This must be the kind that fires back at the position

from which it was shot at,'' Smith speculated medita-
tively. "I guess you missed, Kalin. Move over about ten
meters behind that tree and fire at it again.''

Obediently, the other marine rolled to the tree and took
aim at the clump of brush they thought was a laser emplacement. He glanced toward Smith, who nodded, and
fired. Barlow could see on his screen that Kalin's shell
detonated millimeters below the center of the target. Almost as quickly as that information registered, the tree
was assaulted by lines of fiery red. Smith stood up and
fired from the shoulder toward the laser. Erupting at full
power, it exploded in a sky-high shower of sparks. No
more laser bolts came.

"Is that it?'' Barlow asked over his headset when the
last echoes of the blast died away. "There was a third
heat trace. Why isn't it firing at us?''

"I've analyzed it,'' Scott said, from behind the hanging curtains of broadleaf swamp vines. "Sir, it's not a
laser. It's a video pickup.''

"Well, I'll be damned. They're making a home movie,
too!'' Barlow exclaimed. "Come on, move out!''

From the point of the smoking line left behind by the
lasers, the land sloped downhill still farther. Barlow ordered every man, injured or not, to keep moving. Hidden
inside the rotten banks of leaves, thick vines caught unexpectedly on feet and cargo nets as they slithered toward
the Gerin stronghold. He led the way into a leaf-filled
gully that provided a fairly even 60-degree descent.

Morale was already slipping; Barlow could feel it. Not
only were they being put on disk, they were being
watched by the enemy. No action they had taken before
had ever been so redundantly observed. Scott identified
two or three other video units suspended from or between
trees along their path. Kalin destroyed them with skill-
fully aimed shots as he followed her. The unexpected
trickle of a small stream which crossed their path sufficiently saturated some of the wounded men's gear that
circuits shorted out with fat sparks, and headset contact
was intermittent.

"On your feet,'' Barlow ordered, and the company rose
and advanced, brushing away streamers and trailers of

sickly green which dripped over their faceplates and shoulders. The raucous cry of some creature rang through the silence, deafening in the amplified speakers inside each marine's helmet. As if it were a signal, the other marsh animals and birds set up their own outcry, drowning out the more subtle sounds which might help the company detect the approach of their enemy.

Abruptly, they broke through into a clearing.

"This is it, sir," Scott said, emerging next to him, holding her terrain map on her outstretched palms. Ubiquitous appeared next, followed by Vinson, whose lens was trained on the corporal.

"This is it? This is what?" Barlow asked incredulously.

"The base. The encampment."

"So where are the Gerin? I thought this place was full of them."

Scott shrugged. "This is where the telemetry places large life forms whose readings match those of the Gerin." The other marines crowded in behind them. Barlow gestured to them to stay partly hidden in the undergrowth while he took a quick look around.

He didn't think much of the clearing himself, as either a base, or a summer home, or a place in which he'd be caught dead. It looked like a junkyard for decayed office plants. The clearing was nearly waist-deep in narrow, pliable yellow reeds. Underneath them the ground was sodden, making footing uncertain. Huge, tonguelike leaves lay obscenely sprawled across moss-covered boulders and rotten stumps. Incongruously, lovely white flowers grew out of pools of bright green, which Barlow knew must be standing water underneath no more than a half inch of algae crust. Marsh insects with high-pitched whines buzzed annoyingly in his ears. An extruded-plastic building was all but hidden by fast-growing marsh plants. There was a low entrance through which one of them would have to crawl, provided they didn't decide to blow the thing up from where they stood. The power plant was a small boxlike unit which hummed quietly at the side of the building. Barlow looked up. For the first time he could see the sky, and decided he hadn't been missing anything. It was a grayish purple and mostly overcast. He tried to take a step forward and discovered that he had sunk knee deep into the bog.

"Treacherous footing throughout the clearing, sir," Scott noted helpfully.

"So where are they?" Barlow asked.

"In the pool, sir." The pool was a larger stagnant body of water covering more than half of the compound. Its surface was perfectly still, except for the tiny rippling rings made when one of the whining insects touched briefly down. From its center rose an irregular rocky promontory, like a reef. Scott consulted her table again, moved a wrist control under its translucent surface. "I count twenty-one Gerin. Yes, confirmed."

Twenty-one. The same number as the company. Barlow wondered if Captain Avix had known the exact count of the enemy when he chose his volunteers. One-on-one combat might look very pretty in the movies, but it would be sheer bloodshed to attack an entrenched foe with only equal numbers. Again, he cursed the brass for sending them on such a fool's mission.

"Kalin, prepare to launch depth charge," he commanded.

"Uh, sir," Kalin answered reluctantly, "they didn't supply any for us. The weapon's too new; they haven't designed a launcher yet."

"Then go and throw it in the water, soldier!" Barlow roared. Vinson threw himself to one knee and held the camera eye against his shoulder as Kalin squelched out unsteadily across the reeds. Hundreds of round-bodied marsh hoppers, disturbed by his passage, leaped crazily about, shrieking and chirping. Startled, he lost his balance and dropped the heavy charge into the grass. Everyone gasped and ducked, protecting their helmets. The charge didn't go off. As Barlow searched the cloudy heavens for strength, Kalin recovered the bomb and crossed the rest of the way to the pool, haloed by a cloud of marsh hoppers. The look backward he gave, waiting for the command, wasn't for Barlow, but for Vinson. "Throw it," the sergeant ordered, trying to ignore the trivid man at his feet.

Kalin drew back his arm and tossed the small canister overhand toward the water.

A mass of tentacles broke the brown surface of the pool. Some grabbed for the falling cylinder, curling closed too late as it slipped between them. Three sets, all clad in the sleeves of environmental suits, seized Kalin and dragged him under the water. More Gerin boiled out of the water and rolled purposefully toward the company. They didn't exactly roll, or walk, or crawl, but performed a combination of all three. There was no good way to express their form of ambulation in human terms.

"Kalin!" Barlow called, then switched to headset radio. "Kalin, respond! Is your rebreather circuit functioning?"

"Sergeant, a Gerin triad got me. I can breathe okay. I've got my knife and laser pistol, but the warrior I'm facing has the same, and two of his feet have iron claws fastened on to 'em. I can't back away far. The apprentices have got me flanked. Wait, I can see the depth charge down below. It's still falling—"

Kalin's voice cut off. Behind the emerging Gerin, the waters of the pool suddenly rose up in a cloudlike bubble with a roar like a launching rocket. Waves of fetid water dropped on the company and the enemy, knocking both forces off their feet and tentacles, respectively. Barlow rolled over but didn't rise, calling to his men to open fire on the Gerin triads moving toward them.

The company traded laser fire with the Gerin amid the falling water and pieces of rock. Barlow realized that he and his marines were at a disadvantage with the slope at their back. They hadn't taken the opportunity to choose an advantageous position, a mistake which could cost them all their lives. Under covering fire from two of the other triads, six Gerin, with the warriors well ahead of the smaller and less gaudily arrayed apprentices, closed in on them. Barlow ordered Hotchkiss, Omaya, Ivorsen, and three others to engage the first trio of Gerin.

The slimeballs undulated toward the humans in the same graceful, hypnotic way a tree sways in the wind. It could kill a soldier if he got caught looking and forgot what he was looking at. These were clad in heavy eight-legged environment suits made of a glistening brown rubbery compound. From the extra sway, Barlow suspected the suits were filled with water, to protect the Gerin's flesh from drying out in the air. It would also provide a second buffer layer between a slug or laser bolt. That meant a minimum of three shots to kill instead of two: one to pierce the suit and let the water out, one to wound, and one to finish.

The big goblin eyes stared out at Barlow's men through the round faceplates. All around the sergeant, the company were unpacking their special armaments. Weapons that had been outlawed by the Jupiter Convention were turned out of rucksacks and cargo nets. Barlow swept a swift, astonished glance over his shoulder, then returned his attention to the fighting. A tall woman named Ricci slipped out of the clearing and vanished into the perimeter with a coil of synthfiber.

Hotchkiss was nervous. He missed his first shot with the slugthrower. His buddy opened fire with a laser rifle and scored across the ''neck'' of the first Gerin warrior's environment suit. The material was tougher than Barlow's first estimation of it. Water dripped slowly down the creature's knees and into the reeds, but no major breach had been cut. Hotchkiss cocked and fired again, but the triad were already on top of them. The warrior pushed him out of the way and into the arms of his assistants. An iron-tipped tentacle pierced through the body of Omaya's suit and withdrew, leaving a trail of blood down the front. The private looked down in astonishment and slowly folded up. Hotchkiss let out a bellow and blew a large hole in the head of the assistant holding him. He struggled free of the flailing arms and tried to kick his way to his friend's body.

''Private Hotchkiss, pay goddam attention to what you're doing!'' Barlow called. He aimed his own slugthrower and fired, propelling an explosive charge squarely into the faceplate of the second assistant, who was about to spit Hotchkiss on a tentacle as his friend had been. There was a horrible squelching, tearing noise, and the Gerin dropped like a sack of laundry with most of its head blown away. The marine staggered away into the reeds and sat down, obviously in shock, as the other four attacked the now-unprotected warrior. Barlow and the rest provided return covering fire for them and for Hotchkiss, invisible in the marshweeds. The fight was only beginning. And behind them, Vinson was recording it all.

Barlow detailed another group of men to attack the second triad, now advancing on the company. Scott had folded up her telemetry equipment and was firing on the leftmost trio of armed Gerin with a narrow-barreled rifle. Her slugthrower shot hypodermic-shaped bullets which caught and pierced softer materials, like rubber, or insulation, or flesh, and exploded on contact. One of the Gerin showed the characteristic wound on its body immediately below its eyeplate. Its exposed flesh color alternated with the purple of fury and the sickly green of pain. Two of its tentacles applied a white dressing to the wound while two more fired an energy weapon erratically toward the group.

"See, in one-on-one combat, a human has little chance of defeating a Gerin—you know, hand-to-hand-to-hand-to-hand-to-hand-to-hand . . ." Ubiqutous explained cheerfully to the cameraman as he put two shells into his slugthrower, one small and one large. "But you can knock them off their feet with the right combination. Like this." He put the weapon to his shoulder, aimed, and pulled the trigger. The small shell impacted in the top of a Gerin's rubbery hood. It stopped shooting at the marines and put two of its arms up to search the bullet hole, and exposed a span of its underside to Smith. With a crow of triumph, Smith fired. The larger shell took the Gerin full in the bottom and propelled it into the air. All eight legs stretched out to their tips, then curled up as the slime fell to the ground and lay still.

"Smith, save it for target practice," Barlow said wearily. His ears were still ringing with the death cries of two marines, pulled out of their suits and strangled by the second Gerin warrior. His gunmen cut the warrior nearly in half with a barrage of slugs, and mowed down the confused apprentices left suddenly leaderless. More wounded moved back from the fighting line, to be replaced by fresh men, but Barlow knew that his roster was dwindling quickly. He wanted to finish and get out.

"Could you turn this way slightly, Sergeant?" Vinson asked. "I'd like to get your reaction shot to Smith's success. Sorry to intrude."

Barlow turned, wishing all wise-asses and cameramen buried fifty feet deep in peat, but careful to keep his thoughts off his face. Smith did his trick on another Gerin sharpshooter, this one the warrior on the right side of the field. The sergeant had to admit that it was an impressive move. He'd have to make the corporal teach it to the other marksmen at practice on shipboard. The remaining marines tripped and crawled over the reeds to attack its apprentices, whose flesh through their eyeplates was light pink with fear. Barlow led the attack on the left-hand nest, which still contained the warrior and one apprentice. His feet sank into the ground a good six inches with every step, making the going next to impossible. Disgusted, he undid the strap holding on his cargo net with one hand as he ran, and thew the heavy bag onto the ground. It flattened the grasses and floated, buoyant on the hollow reeds.

Cries of triumph from across the field announced that the other squad had dispatched the remaining assistant of the right-hand triad. Ten Gerin were dead so far, but five humans had died, too.

The warrior was more heavily armed than any of the other three. It kept the marines dodging laser and slug fire.

"Hey, Sarge!" yelled a voice over the head mikes. "No, up!" From his position facedown in the reeds, Barlow looked up. Private Ricci was five meters high in a tree, waving a loop of her rope, which was anchored to a branch above her. She gave him thumbs up.

"Good, Ricci! Drop it on that damned warrior. We can't get near him." Barlow made a gesture with the flat of his hand.

Two more of his men went down under slug fire before the loop fell. Before the Gerin could do more than look up, Ricci jerked the rope tight and hauled down on the loose end. The warrior was lifted into the air, its face red with fury, tentacles waving like a barroom wagon-wheel chandelier. Though it kept hold of the laser pistol, its furious shots hit no one but some inoffensive trees. The heavier slugthrower fell from its grasp.

Unfortunately, the Gerin had a pretty good reach even suspended six feet in the air. It continued to stab at everyone with the two iron-tipped tentacles. The human marksmen peppered it with slugs, which it ignored, even though water and ichor dripped from holes in the rubbery suit. The apprentice got in everyone's way, swinging hysterical blows at the soldiers with a few of its legs while trying to pull its master down. Barlow heard a wild scream over the headsets as the warrior's iron claw penetrated the joint between Ivorsen's helmet and suit. The metal must have pierced the jugular vein. In only seconds Ivorsen's vitals slowed to zero, and the man collapsed.

"Higher, Ricci!" Barlow called, sloshing forward to catch the body.

"All right, Sarge, but it's only five feet from me now!" With an effort, the woman hauled on the rope hand over hand. The warrior's flailing arms went slack as the jerk of the rope caught it by surprise. It was not caught off guard for long. As soon as it was in reach, it attacked Ricci with all its resources, stabbing and lasing the private, who did her best to hang on to the rope and keep steady. Blood from half a dozen wounds seeped in shimmering ribbons down the front of her environment suit.

"Smith!" the sergeant shouted.

"I see him, Sarge," came the cheerful voice of Smith. Just as it seemed Ricci was about to let go, the hiss of a shell from a slugthrower barrel whizzed overhead. The Gerin exploded from within, and ceased its attacks on Ricci, just as her hands went slack. She collapsed against the bole of the tree and her head fell back. The rope, released from her grip, shot upward, and the limp body of the warrior fell heavily to the ground, in front of its apprentice.

Squealing, the surviving Gerin broke free of the marines and rolled hastily to the pool. It dove in under a hail of bullets, and vanished, leaving a greasy trace of ichor on top of the water.

"Coward!" Barlow crowed. "Good shot, Smith. Ricci, are you all right?"

"I'm alive, Sarge," her voice came weakly over the comlink. "If you don't need me, I'd better stay up here . . . for a while."

Her vital signs showed that she was probably in shock. Barlow ordered her to program a relaxant from her med-kit, and turned back to the field of battle. There were no more Gerin alive on the surface.

"There should be ten left alive down there, sir," Scott replied to a query. "Three trios, and the apprentice we just saw."

"Those'll probably be the high-rankers, the administrators, at the bottom," Barlow speculated. "They'd wait until most of us were killed, and then come out to knock off the rest and claim the victory for themselves." Officers, he reflected, were all alike, no matter what they looked like.

"But I'm not getting the readings of body heat any more," Scott said. "Either they've escaped through an underground stream, or they have some sort of cooling mechanism in those suits to disguise them."

"How can we detect them, then?"

The spotter considered the question. "Movement?"

"Chuck the second grenade at them," Smith suggested. "Hotchkiss has it." The private had recovered from his friend's death and was eager to get revenge on the slimeballs. He flourished the heavy little canister.

"No," the sergeant said, forestalling them. "I don't want to waste it if there are no Gerin down there to blast." His eye fell on the trivid man and his camera unit. "Say, Vinson, you want to get a really good shot? Come here."

He dragged the protesting cameraman through the threshed-down grasses to the pool's edge and pulled him to his knees. "There, take a look down through there." He pulled the lens unit out of the man's hands and thrust it into the water.

"I don't see anything, Sergeant," Vinson said. "The water's too murky."

"They recognized the shape, sir. They're moving

away," Scott announced joyously, transmitting the images to her CO's screen. "They're down there. All ten are on the north edge of the pool."

"Hotchkiss! Prepare to deploy depth charge!"

With a toothy, feral smile, the young marine dashed to the far end and heaved the bomb into the water with both hands. He watched, sinking knee deep in mud, as the charge detonated, carrying most of the murky pool water high into the air. It fell on him like a wave breaking. When the air cleared, Barlow could see that the rocky promontory in the middle was gone. But Hotchkiss was still standing on the bank.

"No life forms left in the water, sir," Scott announced through the cheers of her fellows. "We got 'em all."

"A bang-up ending, if I may say so," Vinson complimented them. "This is going to look terrific on video."

The cheering died away, and the surviving marines glanced at each other warily. Many of them had forgotten the cameraman's presence, and eyed him as if he were one of the slime. Even Smith was looking askance at his pet videographer now that the reality had struck him.

"Real people, men and women, died today," Barlow said, and knew that every marine there felt the same way. "Friends of mine. Kids, some of them. Those weren't actors. I'll throw you and that camera in the pool myself with a brick sinker before I let their deaths go for a lousy exploitation vidisk."

"The folks back home need to know the ugly realities of the Gerin war," Vinson explained apologetically, crossing a protective arm across his camera unit. "We need their support to fight this war and win. Yes, those were real men and women, with interests and hopes beyond their service in the LFP, just as you are. Maybe you don't know how much a fantasy this war seems to the people on the more distant planets, who have never seen a Gerin and don't know anyone who has. This disk is for them."

"It still stinks," croaked Ricci grimly, limping up to join them. The blood on her suit had been washed away by Hotchkiss's geyser, but her face was pasty.

As they made their way back up the hill to pickup point,

Barlow considered. He agreed with a lot of what Vinson was saying, though he didn't like any of it. There was nothing worse than having units shortchanged on money or gear because the finance committees back home didn't understand the threat out on the front line. It didn't affect them, therefore it didn't exist. The kids in the service tried so hard. This company, even as an untried, scratch unit, had done pretty well. He would be proud to lead them as a special squad. He wanted to throw the disk into the pool and refuse to let the brass make another video until the big men up top came down in person to pose with the Gerin.

Most of the marines were wounded, some beyond the abilities of the medical service to cure completely. They tried to make themselves and their buddies comfortable without too much bitching while they waited for the transport ship to retrieve them from the top of the slope. A few would wear their disfigurements openly, though prosthetics would replace severed limbs. As usual, Ubiquitous Smith had come out of it without a mark on him, but he was almost the only one. Barlow resented him and resented Vinson, but most of all, he hated the brass-hatted fools who had put a company of strangers down on a planet where they never needed to be.

Barlow was still trying to make up his mind whether or not to lase a hole in the cameraman's storage disk when the transport ship picked them up.

Mac

War has many effects. It can make cowards out of otherwise reasonable men, and heroes out of the least likely candidates. During a war, science seems to surge ahead, and business booms. More than for anyone else, the Far

Stars War was a personal quest for revenge for Chu Lee Macdonald. Born and raised on Castleman's, Mac, as he was almost universally referred to, commanded the remnants of the fleet that tried to defend her. It is an indication of the man that he ordered his ships to remain in combat, outnumbered ten to one, until there was no hope of evacuating survivors. It is a further indication of his leadership, and the temper of those manning the ships, that his orders were obeyed at such a high cost.

Physically, Mac was not exceptional. He stood slightly taller than average and had a slight frame that masked his height. Mac had inherited from his mother hair of a particularly rich, glossy black. His features were regular, and those who knew him before Castleman's said a smile once came easily to them. The admiral's eyes were such a deep blue as to be almost black. Even on trivid recordings there is a riveting quality to those eyes, and a pool of sorrow that was never to drain away.

In the dark weeks after Castleman's fell, Mac was an officer. He reorganized the surviving ships and used them to intimidate other worlds into contributing to his force. He drove the men, though no harder than he drove himself. The last survivors of their world, the men carried ghosts with them, and it was best that they fell exhausted into their hammocks.

Mac had once had a family, though after the fall their picture disappeared from his desk. Even after the victories at Gemini and Klaremont, Mac would drive himself until he collapsed from exhaustion. War demands an exceptional leader; amazingly often one appears. In the past there had been Churchill, then Wainford and Ben Aleef, and Fleisher, who saved Earth at the beginning of man's expansion. The Far Stars War created Mac, and in many ways Mac made the war his own—needed its all-encompassing cause to fill the emptiness inside himself.

Mankind needed a diplomat, and a trivid hero, to rally behind. Mac supplied this requirement with careful calculation. After his first victories, the need to unify humanity became as great an obsession as destroying the Gerin. Once he had wooed and coerced the League of Free Planets into joining forces with him, there was never any question who would really be in control: the homeless admiral became more ruthless in his insistence that every human world join his crusade. Sometimes his tactics were questioned; more often they were ignored by men more concerned with surviving the next Gerin assault. Even when he destroyed thousands of colonists on Goldsack, the destruction was forgotten in the fury of the Battle of Ten Moons and the euphoria of that hard-fought victory.

EDGE

by Steve Perry

THERE was a planet, only I don't remember the name. It had to be in a system somewhere, but I can't recall that, either. The scum who inhabited it were rebels, humans, some kind of religious cult, I can manage that much. They refused to join the fight against the Gerin, they told Admiral Chu Lin MacDonald to take his League and jam it, they were rogues, they were traitors, and they would die to the last man before they would send one soldier to an immoral war, they said.

I can remember that much.

And there are other parts of it I remember.

I think.

We were hidden in the sawbush, watching the soldiers in the clearing. Human soldiers. The air was hot and wet and the insects kept trying to get past the chem I wore to keep them off. They didn't bite but they buzzed. I didn't much like jungle work.

The four guards weren't armored but they all had Stein 2mm carbines with drums. The drums each held five hundred rounds of ultra-velocity explosive caseless and the weapons had a high cycle rate, quick enough so that a casual wave on full auto would chop a man in half as fast as you could blink. Our softsuits wouldn't even slow them down.

I pulled four shocktox arrows from my clip and arranged them on the warm ground next to me in a fast-fan pattern. Even if the wounds weren't fatal, the shocktox would slap a man senseless in half a second and keep him that way long enough so that if I wanted him dead, I could stroll up and finish him. I took a deep breath and let it out slowly.

"No," Razor said. "They're mine."

I put my stacked-graphite recurve bow down. "All right. It's your show."

That was true enough. I was last-over-the-fence, the newest member of the hex, so fresh I still had a real name. You had to earn your hexnom, and I hadn't been in it long enough. This was my first mission. I was replacing a woman called Fish. All I knew about her was that she'd 'gotten careless" with a trio of aliens.

"Stay here, Peel," he said. "I'll wave you up when I'm done."

I nodded.

Razor pulled his tanto from the delrin sheath where it snugged the cro-patch on his left hip. He rose from his crouch. The rosette softsuit's refractors started to alter, but slowly as always. With his shock of short black hair and thick eyebrows, he looked like some ancient Japanese demon. He kissed the knife the way a man kisses a lover. The weapon's blade was a mottled gray, from the hand-folding and hammering and tempering used to forge the steel into something that would hold a sharp edge and yet remain flexible. The knife was twenty centimeters long, thick across the spine, the point angled up from the angle-ground edge and sharp all the way to the tip. It was a Damascus pattern, and the technology of it was more than two thousand years old. The handle was tightly wound black silkwire. Razor had made the knife himself.

The four guards were alert and well armed, and had a clear field of fire for twenty meters around them. To try to take them with nothing more than a knife in daylight ought to be suicide.

Razor started toward the four. His trick was that he could see the future. That's what he said, though the brainboys couldn't find it. Only a few seconds, he said, maybe ten, tops. If he could or not, who could say? *He* believed it, and that was his edge. I had never seen him work, but I had heard the stories. He never carried any weapon other than his knife; he was the deadliest of the deadly and he liked killing. He had once taken out a pair of fully armed Gerin warriors and their four drones by himself. That said something.

The word "mute" can cut different ways. It can mean silent. It can also be short for "mutant." Either way, most regular JTs start looking for a place to spit after they say it. Mutes are six-person teams, technically named Detached Advanced Hexes. They work under two imperatives: FEUB and IMKI—"Fuck 'Em Up Bad," and "If It Moves, Kill It." No, not "they." We. I was one of them now. Me and my bow. We're supposed to be able to walk on water, to fly, to vanish into thin air, and our purpose is to scare the shit out of the enemy. Mutes eat regular jump troopers for breakfast, have marines for dessert, and use shippies to pick their teeth. *Our* teeth.

The first guard went down from a thrust to the heart.

The second caught the tanto through the left eye.

The third guard, a woman, swung her weapon around but never got a chance to trigger it before she died from a powerful stab under the chin.

The fourth guard was so stunned that he just stood there like an animal waiting for slaughter. He didn't even try to move as Razor cut his throat.

It took maybe nine seconds from the time Razor stood until the last man fell. I've seen some of the very best martial artists move, and none of them could touch Razor for sheer speed. He was a freak.

Yes, Razor enjoyed it. He grinned at me and waved with the bloody knife. According to Glass, Razor had special lubes he used to wipe the weapon each time he used it. He supposedly went through a lot of those cloths—alien blood was bad on untreated steel.

I had left the arrows out, just in case. I reclipped them save for one, and moved out from the cover of the jungle

into the clearing. It was early morning but already hot.
If nobody found the bodies, they'd be bloating by dark.
And when they did find them, it would have to be fright-
ening. Four dead soldiers, one cut each, in the middle of
a clearing, not a shot fired. *How?*

It's war, I thought, looking at the three dead men and
the dead woman. They weren't real people, they were
just broken dolls, oozing red machine oil, no before and,
now, no after. Besides, it could just as easily be me lying
there. They'd have shot me without a second thought if
I'd strolled into their ken. It's war. People get killed.
They should have thought about that before they turned
traitor.

I had something to prove. I suspected everybody in the
hex did, but Razor did like it too much.

"Come on," he said. "We've got to get to our TBR
coordinates. We're late and Tilt will have our balls."

Tilt, our hexleader, was a man who never smiled. He
was small, thin, almost innocuous to look at, hair
cropped close, pale green eyes. Everybody in the hex was
terrified of him, even Razor; I hadn't figured out why
yet, but he scared me, too. I felt it on a level way below
conscious thought, a racial memory from the time when
we lived in caves and *some*thing prowled out there in the
dark and stirred the hairs on our necks. Something too
horrible to face with spear or fire, especially in the dark.
That was Tilt's trick, his edge.

We moved through the bush carefully. This sector was
supposed to be clear, except for the guard post Razor had
just eliminated, but you never could be sure of what *MI*
told you. We both wore confounders, but as electronic
scramblers, the devices make good paperweights. A
properly tuned confounder might fool a particularly stupid simadam running a heatscope or a motion sensor one
time in five; not odds a trooper in the field cared for
much when they ran in the enemy's favor. Confounder
technology had a way to go.

We got to our assigned coordinates with an hour to
spare; we were the first to arrive. The rest of the hex
showed during the next half hour.

First were Tilt, the HxL, and Glass. Glass was Arnie

Average, nothing special about him, the kind of face you can forget a second after turning away. But turn back and you'd have trouble finding him again. According the stories I'd heard in the JTs, Glass could hide in bright sunlight in the middle of an open field without any camo gear, and he could make the best ninja who ever lived look conspicuous. He was the one who had taken me under his wing and talked to me about the others. He'd rather be killing octopods, he said, but you went where they sent you and did what they paid you to do.

The final two members of our hex were Lout and Asp. Lout walked into the clearing as if he owned the planet, and Asp suddenly appeared behind us. She might give Glass a good run for invisible, but that was not her main trick. Asp could throw a poison pencil fifty meters and hit a man-sized target ninety times out of a hundred at that range. She carried a 6mm flechette pistol, a silenced chatterbox, as backup, but nobody in the hex had ever seen her use it. So I'd been told.

My recurve bow has a pull of thirty-five kilos, no compound pulleys, an honest draw. I was trained to use it with either hand and alternate frequently enough so that I work both sides more or less equally. Years of work with the bow have given me a fair amount of muscle in the arms and shoulders, and across the upper back. I'm not a weakling.

Compared to Lout, I might as well be a skeleton. The man has obviously moved some serious weights more than a little distance, and if somebody wanted to bet that he could pick himself up with one hand, I wouldn't take the bet. One story said he'd wrestled a Gerin warrior hand to hand and had broken the thing's back. The aliens are *strong*.

Lout bore an 8mm Rand caseless rifle. The entire barrel is essentially a silencer. Low-velocity, subsonic. He also carried a drop-forged one-piece hatchet made of black anodized 660-Diamond-grade duralum.

Tilt's main weapon was an Immelhof 6mm spring darter.

Glass wore a pair of 10mm DW subsonic rocket pistols.

Mutes aren't issued weapons. The QM gives us each a softsuit, a TBR, distill-can, medkit, 8/gen NV goggles, and a confounder. That's it. If we want to eat, we can draw Q-rats or find local produce. We furnish our own hardware for fighting, and there are only two criteria: the weapons must be deadly and they can't make much noise. If it spikes an audiometer higher than aud 20 at two meters' distance, it's too loud for a mute to carry. That's where the nickname ostensibly comes from. If you hear an explosion and the trooper next to you drops dead, you can deal with that. But if the soldier talking to you quietly keels over with a dart or pencil or arrow in him and you don't see it, it can surprise the hell out of you. Maybe it's contagious. I don't know if the fucking rubbery aliens think that way, but men do. And the Gerin bleed and die like the rest of us, so maybe they get scared, too.

The other gear is standard military-issue and useful only sometimes, although it made what the local rebobs were using look like dark-age antiques. Our softsuits are supposed to be proof against medium-to-high-velocity nonexplosive projectile weapons in the 5mm-10mm range, but nobody with half a brain risks his life on that. The refract camo mostly works, but it is slow. The tight-beam radio is okay when the operators on both ends know what they are doing. The distill-can will give you potable water from any oxy atmosphere where the humidity is 10 percent or higher. The medkit runs a stupecomp that is pretty good on wounds and common infections, but it's fragile. The spookeyes work best under a medium star-field or less, but point them at any suddenly bright light source and they will temporary blind the wearer. The confounder might be used to smash a bug in an emergency, or maybe you could throw it to distract an enemy. If I had to limit myself to one item, I'd take the distill-can. Drinkable H_2O is worth a lot in the field. But even so, we were technical miracles on this planet and we knew it. Between that and our personal skills we might be excused for feeling a little arrogant. We ought to be able to go through the locals like a laser through smoke. Even as a newboy I was confident.

Tilt said, "Okay, here's the scope." He squatted and

pulled a one-time holoproj unit from his belt and lit the timer. He set the unit on the ground. The rest of us crouched down to watch. We had a real mission this time, not just normal FEUB stuff. A major piece of work.

The air warbled at Tilt's feet and a threedee colored itself into life over the projector. From where I was, the holgram looked like a four-building business complex. Two were multistory, the other two single-levels. The scale and compass built into the edge of the holo gave me an idea of the size and layout.

"You can see the place is disguised," Tilt said. "Not a speck of military visible anywhere. This is from a spysat we have footprinting the area, and the resolution is good enough so you can read the numbers on the vehicles. You can bet there are troops stashed and some kind of defensive perimeter buried or camoed good enough to fool the sky eye."

None of us said anything. If this was what it was supposed to be, there'd have to be some safeguards; anything else would be foolish, and the enemy couldn't all be fools.

Tilt pointed at one of the smaller buildings. "This is what MI thinks is the Target's sleeping quarters."

"Isn't that an oxymoron?" Lout said. " 'MI' and 'thinks' in the same sentence?"

Glass laughed, and I added my own chuckle.

Asp didn't crack a smile. Neither did Razor.

"Vacuum it, Lout," Tilt said. "It's our job to hit the Target and either bring him back or bury him."

"He's some kind of holy man, isn't he?" Asp said.

"Does it matter?" Tilt said.

"No, it doesn't matter," Razor put in.

Asp and Razor glared at each other. They'd been lovers once, according to Glass. It hadn't ended well.

"Asp?"

She looked at Tilt. "No. It doesn't matter."

"Yeah, he's the head holy man. And he's ours."

Tilt finished the briefing. He had allowed us time enough to memorize the layout before the clock flashed the holoproj. The thick plastic oozed as the acid inside did its work. Tilt kicked dirt and brush over the dead holoproj. By the time anybody found it, we'd have finished our mission or we'd be dead, and either way it wouldn't matter—the unit would tell no tales.

"It gets full dark at around twenty hours," Tilt said. "We move then. It's an hour-and-a-half walk. Flake out and get some rest. Rotate watch by twos—Glass and I will take it first, Lout and Asp next, Razor and newboy last."

Tilt and Glass moved out of the clearing. Razor stretched out, leaned back against a clump of brush, and fell asleep. Lout stripped his Rand and began cleaning and oiling it. Asp sat a couple of meters away from me and stared at the dirt between her knees.

I was new to the hex and I didn't know as much as I wanted to know, so I said to Asp, "Can I ask you something?"

She was an attractive woman, dark hair cut in a military buzz and even features, but she wore a scar from the corner of her left eye to the edge of her jaw under the ear. Plastics could have smoothed that out easily, so she wanted it there for a reason. I couldn't tell about the body under the softsuit, but if she had survived more than a couple of missions as a mute, her body would be fit and hard.

She looked at me as a woman might look at a pet that had just pissed on a rare carpet. "I don't know you," she said. "Fish was my friend and she was good and one of the amphibians killed her. Show me something."

I knew what she wanted. If she was going to risk anything on me, a word or her life, she wanted to know if I had what it took to be in the hex. If I had an edge. MI had sent me, but that didn't mean anything. Tilt had signed my orders and taken me in, but that was Tilt. This was personal. She knew she was one of the Chosen, but was I?

I glanced up and saw a wrist-thick vine that wound around a tree trunk twenty meters away. "The vine, over there," I said. "Two meters up."

I pulled an arrow from my clip and picked up my bow.

It doesn't matter if you are shooting formal *daikyu* or a short recurve field bow, the kyu technique is essentially the same. There are several basic movements to be observed: stance, breathing, notching the arrow, raising and drawing, lowering, extension, sighting, release, and zan-shin pause. With the long bow this sequence can take some time. It can also be speeded up. I already knew where the target was, and I was going to shoot sitting down. I kept looking at Asp for the second it took to fastrun the moves and loose the arrow. I heard the arrow hit solidly, but I didn't look. She watched me, then her gaze flicked away from mine for a second before it flicked back.

"Ask your question," she said.

"Why are you here?" I meant why the mutes, not why here doing this pick-up scuzz work instead of fighting in the real war against the aliens.

She knew what I meant. She looked away, at the vine. "Because it doesn't matter. One enemy is as good as another; man, or Gerin. It's technique that's important."

I nodded. I could understand that. That was peak bushido, to do it right above all. "Okay. Thanks."

She looked back at me. "What about you?"

"Because I want to see if *kyudo* can be *kyujutsu.*"

"The theoretical into the practical," she said. It was not a question.

"Yes."

Well. That was that. If you wound up in the mutes, it was because something was seriously wrong with the way your mind worked. Here was where they dumped the psych cases, the laughing sociopaths and those men and women who didn't care if they lived or died. IMKI freaks and those with a thirst for blood. Mutes were jokingly rumored to eat their own dead, and regular JTs laughed when they said that, but I'd heard rumors of cannibalism that didn't seem so funny. Roast octopod was supposed to be a delicacy in some hexes. But you also had to have more going for you than just being crazy to get into the mutes. You had to be *good* at something, something the military could use. You had to have an edge.

I had spent twelve years learning all there was to know about my Art. I'd run out of teachers who were better at it. I didn't have to look to know where my arrow had gone, I could skewer targets all day long, it was like a kind of magic. There wasn't anything to psi, they said, like Razor's claim of chronopathic ability. The brainboys couldn't find it, they said it was all in his mind, but there was a lot they didn't know. Whatever it was, it was my trick. I almost always hit what I aimed at. But that was *do*, the Way, and it was practice. The *jutsu* aspect needed to be tested. What I needed was to *see* if a two-thousand-year-old art could compete in a modern war; that was my flaw. It was crazy. But I had to know. I was the best there was and I needed the test. If you have a talent, you have to exercise it.

I had done my first tour on DuQuesne, I had killed Gerin, but that had been with guns. That I knew I could do. Could I survive with nothing but my Art?

The mutes was the place to find out.

The military isn't the most efficient machine ever designed, but it knows about some things. We might all be locked up back in civilization, but they had a use for us out here. Scare an enemy bad enough and he stops working the way he should. Teams of armed crazies could get real scary, especially if they had some kind of martial skill going for them, something you couldn't explain, something akin to magic.

We were our side's magic. Its edge.

We wore the spookeyes for night travel, until we were within ten minutes of the complex. Tilt made us pull them off then. He didn't want us going blind if somebody had rigged any heat-sensing flares.

Glass was riding scout, and when we were almost to the area, he came back and did a jive that froze us. *Troops ahead*, the hand signal said.

We backed off half a klick to hear Glass's story.

"Two tens," he said, "plus an officer. Issue gear, near as I can tell, sixteen Stein carbines, two grenadiers, two medics with sidearms. The officer is wearing a class-III hardsuit with helmet and shield." Glass snickered. "But *leather* boots."

I shook my head. Some of these backrocket planets lost big points for logic. Class-III armor would stop anything we were carrying, though I might get an arrow through if I hit a seam just right. But unarmored boots wouldn't stop anything, and a guy with his feet chopped off was a piss-poor soldier. Stupid. Why'd we want these guys on our side?

"Where are they?" Tilt produced a small flatscreen and handed it to Glass. Without being asked, everybody pulled in tight to form a circle that would block the glowing screen from outside view.

Glass tapped the controls. After a couple of minutes, the pale gray lines appeared in the air over the screen, a dim light in the darkness.

Glass had outlined the shape of the defensive perimeter, complete with positions of trees, heavy brush, and twenty-one troopers. A crosshatch grid wrapped the image and grid numbers sparkled along the edges. The twenty-one were strung out in a long quarter circle a couple hundred meters long.

"Okay, that's three each, with three left over." Tilt looked at me. "How fast are you with that bow?"

"I can get three in six seconds," I said.

"Okay. You get three. These." He pointed at the grid and I nodded.

"Lout, you take these four. The officer is yours—do him first, he's got the communications pod."

"That's a xerox, Tilt."

"Asp, these three here—"

"I can do four."

Tilt looked away from the holoproj and at the woman. The moment stretched. "Okay, these four, here and here."

She nodded once.

"Glass, you take the four on this end. I'll get these three. Razor, the three by the big tree."

"I can get four. I can get five," Razor said.

"Too slow. If these guys start chopping shrubs with those Steins it's gonna get real noisy out here. We don't want to announce to the Target that we're on our way."

"Listen, Tilt—" Razor began.

"It's not open for discussion." He stared at Razor and I saw fear light the man's eyes. Krishna, it was scary to watch even from where I was, and Razor was facing it dead on. I wondered what he saw.

"Okay, okay," Razor said quickly.

"Set your timers. I want it to start in exactly twelve minutes from . . . now. Let's get there before any of them move. Go. Don't fuck it up."

I didn't opt for my spookeyes even though Glass said there were no flares around. I didn't like the sickly green light they provided, plus if anybody was running a scope they might spot the power-up.

The troops evidently weren't expecting trouble. I got into position, locked my clip next to me so I could get to all sixty arrows in a hurry if need be, and nocked the first shaft. The arrow was match-grade aluminum with a shocktox armor-piercing head, fletched with *ari* feathers, the best in the known galaxy. I could shoot this arrow through a steel plate and the feathers would lie flat and not be damaged.

My three were almost exactly where they were supposed to be, only I had a slight problem: a fourth had wandered over into my grid, and it looked like it was the officer, checking on his troops.

I couldn't see Lout, couldn't see or hear any of the other mutes, and I didn't know if I should take the officer or not. He was Lout's assignment, but the big man might not be in a position to see him now. The other soldiers might be wearing dentcoms in back teeth to talk among themselves, but those were short-range units. If the officer triggered his compod and called for help, we might be down the tubes.

Coming up on time, I had fifteen seconds to decide.

As I watched the seconds blink off on my timer, I took a cleansing breath and concentrated on my technique.

At eight seconds to go, the officer turned and started back toward Lout's grid. I recalled that the S-shaped line of sawbush was where my grid ended and Lout's began. I figured that if he was in my grid when the time expired, then he was mine. I could do four.

Three seconds. Two. Still on my side of the line, no more than ten meters away—one—

I sent the first arrow toward the officer's ankle, at the leather boot.

The trick to speedshooting, whether it's a bow or a gun, is to keep going and not to watch the targets you've already shot to see if you've hit them. As soon as I loosed the first arrow, I reached for the second, nocked it, and sent it toward the second trooper. The zanshin pause was only there in spirit and not in real time. I let fly the third, saw that the last man had become aware of danger, and drew the fourth arrow to my ear as he unshouldered his slung carbine. Before he could level his weapon, the shocktox hit him and he arched backward and collapsed.

Seven seconds had passed from the first shot until the last. I reviewed my technique. Four hits. Left ankle, right thigh, left shoulder, right hip. Not a killing wound among them, just as I intended. Any competent bowman could have killed them. Somebody with my skill had to take a handicap. At a hundred and fifty meters, I could not have been so choosy, but this close killing them would have been the same as missing, a failure.

I was aware of the silenced spring guns going off and of the bodies thumping to the jungle floor, and I listened for the half-expected sound of a Stein going full auto and wrecking the night's quiet. It didn't happen.

I shifted carefully toward Lout's position, and saw him coming up from hiding, his Rand held ready. Twenty meters beyond Lout, Asp was already moving into the clearing.

In another minute, it was apparent that our attack had been a complete surprise; all twenty-one of the enemy were down.

Lout said to me, "Thanks for getting the officer. I couldn't see him where I was."

Tilt gathered us past the clearing, under cover.

"Hell, that was easy," Razor said. "I could do that all day long. These guys are sticks." He wiped at his tanto, cleaning it. "Nothing compared to the 'pods."

Tilt shook his head. "It shouldn't have been that easy. Somebody should have gotten off a few loud rounds."

"So we're lucky," Glass said. "You going to fault that?"

"Depends on whether it's good luck or bad," Tilt said. "Well, whatever it is, it's done. Take the scout, Glass."

I didn't share Tilt's worry. We were the best there were, doing our jobs as they were supposed to be done. We all had our own edges, and the enemy didn't really have a chance, not ordinary men. How could we not feel secure in our superior talent and higher technology? It was going to go by the numbers, no sweat.

We were almost there. The compound was quiet, well lighted but not obsessively so, and there were no signs of any more troops.

Glass came back and confirmed that. "Nobody else is out there."

We squatted in the brush and considered it.

"That's crazy," Tilt said. "You are telling me that that one double-ten was it? Bunched up on one side in a ragged-ass quarter circle? There's nobody on the rest of the perimeter?"

"That's what I said."

"It doesn't make any sense."

"Listen, I know about hiding, Tilt. I can feel them. Have I ever been wrong?"

Tilt shook his head.

"Automatics, maybe?" Lout said. "Trip plates, laser lines, heatproxies. Anybody gets past the troops and they get fried when they try to stroll across the grounds, that'd make sense."

We all nodded. That's how we might do it ourselves.

"Yeah, it would make sense," Glass said, "only it ain't happening. I went to the far end and back and there aren't any automatics on these grounds."

"Maybe they're just stupid," Razor said. "Remember the leather boots."

"I don't think so," Asp said.

"Or maybe they're overconfident," I said. "The ground war here is mostly a hemisphere away. This place is in the middle of nowhere—maybe they don't think we can find it."

Tilt nodded at that. "Yeah, maybe. Like sending valuable pharmaceuticals in an old transport instead of an armored convoy to keep from drawing attention to it. That might be it.''

We all looked at the HxL.

''Guess we'd better go see,'' he said. It was his job to worry, but I knew he really wasn't afraid. None of us was.

All I knew about the Target was that he was the top leader in a local religion. A holy man, as Asp had said. The drill was, if we could snatch him, we'd have a major pawn for the diplocrats to use. If not, we were supposed to bury him, because according to the local religious jive, the leader was invulnerable. A gift from the local god, apparently, bestowed on the head priest for services rendered or somesuch. Razor had laughed when he'd told me that part, but I tried to keep an open mind about it. The universe is full of things we don't know about. These people were off the beaten path; they could have gotten real inbred. Maybe the priest had some kind of supereficient metabolism, he didn't get sick or he could heal fast or something. Who could say? It wouldn't matter, of course. There were six of us and only one of him and he'd have to heal damned fast if we chose to bury him.

Anyway, if we made the priest dead, that would pull the locals up short. Maybe they'd think God was on our side and not theirs. Good psychology to have going for you.

We spread out and went for the smallest of the buildings, broken-hex-style, each of us on his or her own track.

I reached the door behind Lout, with Asp right behind me. The portal was a standard prefab plastic with a lock that wouldn't keep out anybody larger than a child.

Lout grabbed the handle and prepared to shoulder the door open. ''There'll probably be alarms,'' he said. ''Get ready.''

Asp and I nodded. I glanced at my timer. Thirty seconds.

Glass, Razor, and Tilt circled around to a second entrance.

As the time ran down, Lout took a firmer grip on the door's handle. It moved.

"Krishna, the damned thing's not even locked!" he said.

"Go," Asp said.

Lout shoved the door open and jumped inside, going left. I went in and right, with Asp covering the center.

No alarms blared, no lights flashed, nobody yelled or started blasting at us. Nothing.

The place was like a warehouse, it was one huge room. The lighting was dim, enough for us to see each other but hardly bright. Toward the middle of the big enclosed space was a bluish glow that seemed to pulse.

"I don't like this at all," Lout said.

I calmed my own breathing and fought to keep my heartbeat slow. I itched all over suddenly.

"Biologicals?" I said. "Chem?"

"Maybe. Too late now if there are."

It didn't feel right, whatever was going on here. I had a sudden urge to turn and run from this place as fast as I could, to not look back as I fled.

"Company!" Lout said. "Over there." He pointed with his rifle.

I raised the bow for a draw. Next to me, Asp pulled two pencils and cocked both hands for a double throw.

"Welcome," a soft male voice said. "I am Nobiki, Father of the Faith." He was a short, roundish man, wearing some kind of silky shirt and split skirt. Both looked maroon-colored in the dim light. His feet were bare, and he was bald. Probably pushing sixty or seventy TS years old, I guessed, at least twice my age. A harmless old man.

"It's him, the Target," I said.

I scanned the room as best I could, looking for guards. Asp and Lout did the same.

"We'll have to ask you to come with us," Lout said. "You are now a prisoner."

"I think not," Nobiki said.

And vanished.

It had been all ours until now, but it got woo-woo; just like that, the madness began.

I mean, he blinked out like a hologram with the power cut.

"Holy shit!" I said.

"It's a trick," Asp said, mirroring my thought. "Some kind of projection."

"Spread out," Lout ordered. "Watch the door, Peel."

Asp and Lout moved off, and I lost them in the low light. The blue glow I'd noticed before had vanished, too.

I put my back against the wall near the door and kept my bow ready for a fast draw. Nobody was leaving here while I could help it.

"Nobody wants to leave," came that soft voice again.

As I jerked around to locate the speaker, a section of the warehouse lit up suddenly, like a diorama in a museum, and I saw Nobiki standing there in his red pajamas, smiling. Facing him about ten meters away was Lout. The big man lifted his rifle and pointed it at the priest. I couldn't hear what Lout said, but I was sure it was an order to surrender. The smaller man did not move, just continued to smile, his arms down by his sides.

Lout raised his rifle and aimed. Since we were supposed to take the Target alive if possible, I guessed that Lout intended to clap a round to scare the priest.

Lout held his aim for a moment, and then lowered the weapon. He stared at it, and I knew somehow that the rifle had misfired. Lout ejected the magazine and reloaded another, aimed again, but nothing happened, it didn't fire. He put the gun down and drew his hatchet. All the while, the smiling priest never moved.

Lout shuffled in carefully.

The priest stood still until the bigger man reached out to grip his shirt, then he dodged to the left a few centimeters. Lout tried again, and Nobiki shifted again. As fast as Lout moved, the smaller man was faster.

I guessed that Lout must have realized that the little man knew some fighting skill and that he wasn't going to be able to catch him. And if we couldn't capture him, there was the other option.

Lout raised the hatchet and leaped, cutting at the priest's skull.

Nobiki snapped his left arm up and blocked the strike. Just stopped it cold.

Nothing I'd seen in here so far impressed me as much as that block. Lout's arm could have hit a ferrofoam wall and not stopped so short. He maintained his grip on the hatchet for an instant, then he snarled and tossed the cutting weapon away and grabbed at the priest.

Nobiki brought his own hands up, and the two men interlaced fingers. I could see the strain on Lout's face.

Incredibly, Lout dropped to his knees, his wrists bent back by the force of Nobiki's grip.

I couldn't believe it.

Lout rolled to one side, breaking contact, and came up. He charged Nobiki. The smaller man leaped to meet him. They came together like two sumo wrestlers, silently, but I could see the power. Lout was knocked aside.

Impossible!

Lout sprawled on his back, looking stunned.

I lifted my bow and arrow and made ready to punch Nobiki's heart out.

No. Not yet. I heard a voice say inside my head.

I lowered the bow. It didn't occur to me to question the command. Maybe the air *was* drugged. I couldn't care less.

Lout came up, and from whatever made him what he was, he pulled forth his reserves. I could see it, I knew that everything he had went into his attack. He slammed into the smaller man, lifted his hands to encircle Nobiki's throat, and started to choke him. The priest caught Lout's neck in the same grip.

They stood there for what seemed like a long time.

Finally, the priest sagged, went limp, and fell. Lout's chest rose and fell with his rapid breathing, but it was obvious that Nobiki was dead. I felt a surge of relief at that knowledge.

The light went out and Lout vanished. What—?

Another section of the warehouse lit suddenly, and I saw Asp, facing a resurrected Nobiki. She threw a poison pencil, but he ducked it and pulled from his clothing an identical weapon, hurling it back at her. Asp dove, came up from the roll, and slung a pair of darts backhanded—

And in the end, after much effort, she killed him.

And then Glass killed him.

And then Razor.

And Tilt.

I killed him, too.

I was sweating and afraid as I shifted to my left and he drew his bow back, aiming for me, and I bent my own bow and I was a quarter second faster, and I sent my arrow to his heart and he fell—

But only after I realized that he was as good as I was, *exactly* as good, and that I had to go to my very center, to dig up every last bit of myself that I had, so that it wasn't skill against skill, but my essence that saved me. I stood there breathing hard, staring at the body with the arrow in its chest.

I had to draw upon my edge, the thing that made me different from other men, the core of who I was. Only then, full out, was I able to win, and then only just barely.

It was the ultimate test, and my triumph was unbounded when I passed it. I had met the best there was, no doubt of that whatsoever, I had challenged him and I had won! All my adult life I had been searching for an equal, and finally I'd found one.

It was the peak moment of my life. I wanted to hold on to it forever, or failing that, I was ready to die right now, either way was fine. I had climbed the mountain and met the gods and nothing was ever going to top it. I knew, in that moment, peace.

Then the warehouse light clicked on and I found myself standing in a bright room, empty except for the other five members of the mute hex. We all stared at each other in wonder.

It only took a few minutes for us to realize we'd all had the same experience. It had to be some kind of induced hallucination, but it *felt* real to all of us. What did it mean? What was the point?

We stood outside the building. Morning was coming; false dawn was already past, and the black sky was going gray. We were all shaken.

"Hey," Glass said. "Trouble."

We looked. More than two dozen figures came from the trees across the compound.

We looked at Tilt. If everybody felt the way I did, we were caught. I'd fight if he wanted, but my heart wasn't in it. It didn't matter.

Tilt shook his head. He put his dartgun down. The rest of us did the same thing with our weapons.

The troopers got closer.

"It's them," Razor said. "The guys we killed. The ones at the perimeter and the four I did yesterday morning." His voice was absolutely calm.

I saw that it was true, and oddly enough, it didn't bother me, either. The troopers showed no signs of any wounds, and they were smiling as they came toward us. We had killed them, they were dead, but there they were. It had to be an illusion. Had we really slaughtered them and was this a lie? Or had we only *thought* we'd killed them before and were they alive? Which way did the truth lie?

"Oh, man," Lout said. "What does it mean?"

Tilt sighed. "It means we're going to lose this war."

"No, not really," came a voice from behind me. I didn't need to turn to know it was Nobiki, but I looked anyway.

"You're going to forget this war," he said.

I stared at him.

"I'm going back with you," he said. He smiled.

I got it, then.

Nobiki was their edge. Somehow, he could give us what we wanted most. What our hearts most desired. We were the best our side had at killing, and he'd turned us into children. We'd come rolling in full of arrogance and technology, but we'd never had a chance. Was it from some chemical or biological agent? Some kind of radiopathic broadcast? Telepathy?

It didn't matter. If he could do that to us, the best, what could he do to anybody less?

His edge was sharper than any of our own. How can you fight a man who will give you exactly what you want the most, and in so doing, will learn exactly who you are, and what buttons to push to control you? How can you fight that?

We must have all understood the danger, for we killed

him again. And again and again. But it didn't matter, because he kept coming back. And that was not the worst of it.

None of us can remember the name of the planet. Nobody remembers sending us there. Maybe it never even happened, but I think it did. I think there is a world out there we were made to forget, only I can remember part of what happened there.

I think I remember it.

Gerin Tactics
by Elizabeth Moon and Bill Fawcett

The Gerin are octopoid amphibians with a very hierarchical society, one with very strong ideas of warrior honor, but a demonstrated lack of compunction about killing off civilian populations. As amphibians they are especially good at 3-D warfare, and have therefore a natural advantage in air and space combat. Like most amphibians, they are territorial and fiercely defend their breeding grounds, though instinctively they are otherwise limited in their aggressive defense to the bottoms of whatever body of water they're in. This is again shown by the suicidal attacks of the Gerin civilians and the few marines who actually landed on Gerin Prime.

The Gerin tend to attack defended positions, and are surprisingly inept at mobile land warfare. They see the defended position as a challenge to their authority and hence a threat, whereas a land force in motion is considered to be composed of inferiors and so a lesser threat. Human ground forces quickly learned that if you want the Gerin to attack, simply stop and dig in.

The Gerin's aquatic origins are also reflected by their preference for concussive artillery and explosive shells. Shrapnel slows rapidly in water and was never extensively used. While they use laser and other beam weapons in space battles, their weapon of preference is the missile.

The Gerin response to an invasion from space is highly peculiar to human notions of tactics. As long as the shuttles are in the air, the Gerin attack them viciously. A grounded shuttle disgorging troops gives a confusing picture. They are "down" with respect to the space and air ships, meaning they have a high status, making them hesitate to attack. To the Gerin ground forces, which instinctively gravitate to lower elevations, the marines are above and so have a lower status. In this same way the Gerin tend to retreat *down*, rather than *away*, whenever there is an option. The status of a landed shuttle is undetermined until the troops take up a position, offering a definite challenge, or move slowly away from the Gerin, thus forfeiting the right to a challenge, and so they are often left unmolested.

Two-dimensional tactics are not a Gerin strong point. Again, while much of their combat is ruled by the instincts, they have little programming for handling a situation with an up or down dimension. Often they fail to see opportunities that are apparent to humans. For an amphibian, the higher you go, the farther you are from a defensible position and the more desirable water. Even though military logic may state that the higher ground gives an advantage, the Gerin tend to send lower-status forces up first.

POLITICS

by Elizabeth Moon

POLITICS is always lousy in these things. Some guy with rank wants something done, and whether it makes any sense or not, some poor slob with no high-powered friends gets pushed out front to do it. Like Mac . . . he wants a fuzzball spit-polished, some guy like me will have to shave it bare naked and work it to a shine. Not that all his ideas are stupid, you understand, but there's this thing about admirals—and maybe especially *that* admiral: no one tells 'em when their ideas have gone off the screen. That landing on Caedmon was right out of somebody's old tape files, and whoever thought it up, Mac or somebody more local, should've had to be there. In person. In the shuttles, for instance.

You know why we didn't use tanks downside . . . right. No shields. Nothing short of a cruiser could generate 'em, and tanks are big enough to make good targets for anyone toting a tank-bashing missile. Some dumb ass should have thought of shuttles and thought again, but the idea was the cruisers have to stay aloft. No risking their precious tails downside, stuck in a gravity well if something pops up. Tradition, you know? Marines have been landed in landing craft since somebody had to row the boat ashore. Marines have died that way just about as long.

Now on Caedmon, the Gerin knew we were coming. Had to know. The easy way would've been to blast their base from orbit, but that wouldn't do. Brass said we needed it, or something. I thought myself it was just because humans had had it first, and lost it; a propaganda move, something like that. There was some kind of garbage about how we had this new stealth technology that let the cruisers get in real close, and we'd drop and be groundside before they knew we were there, but we'd heard that before, and I don't suppose anyone but the last wetears in from training believed it. I didn't, and the captain for sure didn't.

He didn't say so, being the hardnosed old bastard he is, but we knew it anyway, from the expression in his eyes, and that fold of his lip. He read us what we had to know—not much—and then we got loaded into the shuttles like so many cubes of cargo. This fussy little squirt from the cruiser pushed and prodded and damn nearly got his head taken off at the shoulders, 'cept I knew we'd need all that rage later. Rolly even grinned at me, his crooked eyebrows disappearing into the scars he carries, and made a rude sign behind the sailor's back. We'd been in the same unit long enough to trust each other at everything but poker and women. Maybe even women. Jammed in like we were, packs scraping the bulkheads and helmets smack onto the overhead, we had to listen to another little speech—this one from the cruiser captain, who should ought to've known better, only them naval officers always think they got to give marines a hard time. Rolly puckered his face up, then grinned again, and this time I made a couple of rude gestures that couldn't be confused with comsign, but we didn't say anything. The navy puts audio pickups in the shuttles, and frowns on marines saying what they think of a cruiser captain's speechifying.

So then they dropped us, and the shuttle pilot hit the retros, taking us in on the fast lane. 'Course he didn't care that he had us crammed flat against each other, hardly breath room, and if it'd worked I'd have said fine, that's the way to go. Better a little squashing in the shuttle than taking fire. Only it didn't work.

Nobody thinks dumb marines need to know anything, so of course the shuttles don't have viewports. Not even the computer-generated videos that commercial shuttles have, with a map-marker tracing the drop. All we knew was that the shuttle suddenly went ass over teakettle not anything like normal reentry vibration or kickup, and stuff started ringing on the hull, like somebody'd dropped a toolshed on us.

Pilot's voice came over the com, then, just "Hostile fire." Rolly said, "Shut up and fly, stupid; I could figure out that much." The pilot wouldn't hear, but that's how we all felt. We ended up in some kind of stable attitude, or at least we weren't being thrown every which way, and another minute or two passed in silence. If you call the massed breathing of a hundred-man drop team silence. I craned my neck until I could see the captain. He was staring at nothing in particular, absolutely still, listening to whatever came through his comm unit. It gave me the shivers. Our lieutenant was a wetears, a butterbar from some planet I never heard of, and all I could see was the back of his head anyway.

Now we felt reentry vibration, and the troop compartment squeaked and trembled like it was being tickled. We've all seen the pictures; we know the outer hull gets hot, and in some atmospheres bright hot, glowing. You can't feel it, really, but you always think you can. One of the wetears gulped, audible even over the noise, and I heard Cashin, his corporal, growl at him. We don't get motion sickness; that's cause for selection out. If you toss your lunch on a drop, it's fear and nothing else. And fear is only worthwhile when it does you some good—when it dredges up that last bit of strength or speed that we mostly can't touch without it. The rest of the time fear's useless, or harmful, and you have to learn to ignore it. That's what you can't teach the wetears. They have to learn for themselves. Those that don't learn mostly don't live to disagree with me.

We were well into the atmosphere, and dropping faster than my stomach liked, when the shuttle bucked again. Not a direct hit, but something transmitted by the atmosphere outside into a walloping thump that knocked us sideways and half over. The pilot corrected—and I will say this about the navy shuttle pilots, that while they're arrogant bastards and impossible to live with, they can pretty well fly these shuttles into hell and back. This time he didn't give us a progress report, and he didn't say anything after the next two, either.

What he did say, a minute or so later, was "Landing zone compromised."

"Landing zone compromised" can mean any of several things, none of them good. If someone's nuked the site, say, or someone's got recognizable artillery sitting around pointing at the strip, or someone's captured it whole (not common, but it does happen) and hostile aircraft are using it. What "landing zone compromised" means to us is that we're going to lose a lot of marines. We're going to be landing on an unimproved or improvised strip, or we're going to be jumping at low level and high speed. I looked for the captain again. This time he was linked to the shuttle com system, probably talking to whatever idiot designed this mission. I hoped. We might abort—we'd aborted a landing once before—but even that didn't look good, not with whatever it was shooting at us all the way back up. The best we could hope for was an alternate designated landing zone—which meant someone had at least looked at it on the upside scanners. The worst—

"Listen up, marines!" The captain sounded angry, but then he always did before a landing. "We're landing at alternate Alpha, that's Alpha, six minutes from now. Sergeants, pop your alt codes." That meant me, and I thumbed the control that dropped a screen from my helmet and turned on the display. Alternate Alpha was, to put it plainly, a bitch of a site. A short strip, partly overgrown with whatever scraggly green stuff grew on this planet, down in a little valley between hills that looked like the perfect place for the Gerin to have artillery set up. Little colored lines scrawled across the display, pointing out where some jackass in the cruiser thought we ought to assemble, which hill we were supposed to take command of (that's what it *said*), and all the details that delight someone playing sandbox war instead of getting his guts shot out for real. I looked twice at the contour lines and values. Ten-meter contours, not five . . . those weren't just little-bitty hills, those were going to give us trouble. Right there where the lines were packed together was just about an eighty-meter cliff, too much for a backpack booster to hop us over. Easy enough for someone on top to toss any old kind of explosive back down.

And no site preparation. On a stealth assault, there's minimal site preparation even on the main landing zones—just a fast first-wave flyover dropping screamers and gas canisters (supposed to make the Gerin itch all over, and not affect us). Alternate strips didn't get any prep at all. If the Gerin guessed where alternate Alpha was, they'd be meeting us without having to duck from any preparatory fire. That's what alternate landing sites were like: you take what you get and are grateful it doesn't mean trailing a chute out a shuttle hatch. That's the worst. We aren't really paratroops, and the shuttle sure as hell aren't paratroop carriers. Although maybe the worst is being blown up in the shuttle, and about then the shuttle lurched again, then bounced violently as something blew entirely too close.

Then we went down. I suppose it was a controlled landing, sort of, or none of us would have made it. But it felt, with all the pitching and yawing, like we were on our way to a crash. We could hear the tires blow on contact, and then the gear folded, and the shuttle pitched forward one last time to plow along the strip with its heatshield nose. We were all in one tangled pile against the forward bulkhead by then, making almost as much noise as the shuttle itself until the captain bellowed over it. With one final lurch, the craft was motionless, and for an instant, silent.

"Pop that hatch, Gunny." The captain's voice held that tone that no one argues with—no one smart, anyway— and Rolly and I started undogging the main hatch. The men were untangling themselves now, with muttered curses. One of the wetears hadn't stayed up, and had a broken ankle; he bleated once and then fell silent when he realized no one cared. I yanked on the last locking lever, which had jammed in the crash, just as we heard the first explosions outside. I glanced at the captain. He shrugged. What else could we do? We sure didn't have a chance in this nicely marked coffin we were in. Rolly put his shoulders into it, and the hatch slid aside to let in a cool, damp breath of local air.

Later I decided that Caedmon didn't smell as bad as most planets, but right then all I noticed was the exhaust trails of a couple of Gerin fighters who had left their calling cards on the runway. A lucky wind blew the dust away from us, but the craters were impressive. I looked at the radiation counter on the display—nothing more than background, so it hadn't been nukes. Now all we had to do was get out before the fighters came back.

Normally we unload down ramps, four abreast—but with the shuttle sitting on its nose and the port wing, the starboard landing ramp was useless. The portside hatch wouldn't open at all. This, of course, is why we carry those old-fashioned cargo nets everyone teases us about.

We had those deployed in seconds (we *practice* that, in the cruisers' docking bays, and that's why the sailorboys laugh at us). Unloading the shuttle—all men and materiel, including the pilot (who had a broken arm) and the wetear with the bad ankle—went faster than I'd have thought. Our lieutenant, Pascoe, had the forward team, and had already pushed into the scraggly stuff that passed for brush at the base of the nearest hill. At least he seemed to know how to do that. Then Courtney climbed back and placed the charges, wired them up, and came out. When he cleared the red zone, the captain pushed the button. The shuttle went up in a roiling storm of light, and we all blinked. That shuttle wasn't going anywhere, but even so I felt bad when we blew it . . . it was our ticket home. Not to mention the announcement the explosion made. We had to have had survivors to blow it that long after the crash.

What everyone sees, in the videos of marine landings, is the frontline stuff—the helmeted troops with the best weapons, the bright bars of laser fire—or some asshole reporter's idea of a human-interest shot (a marine looking pensively at a dead dog, or something). But there's the practical stuff, which sergeants always have to deal with. Food, for instance. Medical supplies, not to mention the medics, who half the time don't have the sense to keep their fool heads out of someone's sights. Water, weapons, ammunition, spare parts comm units, satellite comm bases, spare socks . . . whatever we use has to come with us. On a good op, we're resupplied inside twenty-four hours, but that's about as common as an honest dockside joint. So the shuttle had supplies for a standard week (navy week: Old Terra standard—it doesn't matter what the local rotational day or year is), and every damn kilo had to be off-loaded and hauled off. By hand. When the regular ground troops get here, they'll have floaters and trucks, and their enlisted mess will get fresh veggies and homemade pies . . . and that's another thing that's gone all the way back, near as I can tell. Marines slog through the mud, hump their stuff uphill and down, eat compressed bricks commonly called—well, you can imagine. And the next folks in, whoever they are, have the choppers and all-terrain vehicles and then make bad jokes about us. But not in the same joint, or not for long.

What bothered me, and I could see it bothered the captain, was that the fighters didn't come back and blow us all to shreds while all this unloading went on. We weren't slow about it; we were humping stuff into cover as fast as we could. But it wasn't natural for those fighters to make that one pass over the strip and then leave a downed shuttle alone. They had to know they'd missed— that the shuttle was intact and might have live marines inside. All they'd done was blow a couple of holes in the strip, making it tough for anyone else to land there until it was fixed. They had to be either stupid or overconfident, and no one yet had accused the Gerin of being stupid. Or of going out of their way to save human lives. I had to wonder what else they had ready for us.

Whatever it was, they let us alone for the next couple of standard hours, and we got everything moved away from the strip, into a little sort of cleft between two of the hills. I wasn't there: I was working my way to the summit, as quietly as possible, with a five-man team.

We'd been told the air was breathable, which probably meant the green stuff was photosynthetic, although it was hard to tell stems from leaves on the scrub. I remember wondering why anything a soldier has to squirm through is full of thorns, or stings on contact, or has sharp edges . . . a biological rule no one yet has published a book on, I'll bet. Caedmon's scrub ran to man-high rounded mounds, densely covered with prickly stiff leaves that rustled loudly if we brushed against them. Bigger stuff sprouted from some of the mounds, treelike shapes with a crown of dense foliage and smooth blackish bark. Between the mounds a fine, gray-green fuzz covered the rocky soil, not quite as lush as grass but more linear than lichens. It made my nose itch and my eyes run, and I'd *had* my shots. I popped a broad-spectrum anti-allergen pill and hoped I wouldn't sneeze.

Some people say hills are the same size all the time, but anyone who's ever gone up a hill with hostiles at the top of it knows better. It's twice as high going uphill into trouble. If I hadn't had the time readout, I'd have sworn we crawled through that miserable prickly stuff for hours. Actually it was less than half a standard when I heard something click, metal on stone, *ahead* of us. Above and ahead, invisible through the scrub, but definitely something metallic, and therefore—in this situation—hostile. Besides, after DuQuesne, we knew the Gerin would've wiped out any humans from the colony. I tongued the comcontrol and clicked a warning signal to my squad. They say a click sounds less human—maybe. We relied on it, anyhow, in that sort of situation. I heard answering clicks in my earplug. Lonnie had heard the noise, too (double-click, then one is his response), which figured. Lonnie had the longest ears in our company.

This is where your average civilian would either panic and go dashing downhill through the brush to tell the captain there were nasties up there or get all video-hero and run screaming at the Gerin, right into a beam or a slug. What else is there to do? you ask. Well, for one thing you can lie there quietly and think for a moment. If they've seen you, they've shot you—the Gerin aren't given to patience—and if they haven't shot you they don't know you're there. Usually.

It was already strange that the Gerin fighters hadn't come back. And if Gerin held the top of this hill—which seemed reasonable even before we went up it, and downright likely at the moment—they'd have to know we got out, and how many, and roughly where we were. And since Gerin aren't stupid, at least at war, they'd guess someone was coming up to check out the hilltop. So they'd have some way to detect us on the way up, and they'd have held off blowing us away because they didn't think we were a threat. Neither of those thoughts made me feel comfortable.

Detection systems, though . . . detection systems are a bitch. Some things work anywhere: motion detectors, for instance, or optical beams that you can interrupt and it sets off a signal somewhere. But that stuff's easy enough to counter. If you know what you're doing, if you've got any sort of counterhunt tech yourself, you'll spot it and disarm it. The really good detection systems are hard to spot, very specific, and also—being that good—very likely to misbehave in combat situations.

The first thing was to let the captain know we'd spotted something. I did that with another set of tongue-flicks and clicks, switching to his channel and clicking my message. He didn't reply; he didn't need to. Then I had us all switch on our own counterhunt units. I hate the things, once a fight actually starts: they weigh an extra kilo, and unless you need them it's a useless extra kilo. But watching the flicking needles on the dials, the blips of light on the readouts, I was glad enough then. Two meters uphill, for instance a fine wire carried an electrical current. Could have been any of several kinds of detectors, but my unit located its controls and identified them. And countered them: we could crawl right over that wire, and its readout boxes wouldn't show a thing. That wasn't all, naturally: the Gerin aren't stupid. But none of it was new to our units, and all of it could fail—and would fail, with a little help from us.

Which left the Gerin. I lay there a moment longer wondering how many Gerin triads we were facing. Vain as they are, it might be just one warrior and his helpers, or whatever you want to call them. Gerin think they're the best fighters in the universe, and they can be snookered into a fight that way. Admiral Mac did it once, and probably will again. It would be just like their warrior pride to assign a single Gerin triad to each summit. Then again, the Gerin don't think like humans, and they could have a regiment up there. One triad we might take out; two would be iffy, and any more than that we wouldn't have a chance against.

Whatever it was, though, we needed high ground, and we needed it damn fast. I clicked again, leaned into the nearest bush, and saw Lonnie's hand beyond the next one. He flicked me a hand signal, caught mine, and inched forward.

We were, in one sense, lucky. It was a single triad, and all they had was the Gerin equivalent of our infantry weapons: single-beam lasers and something a lot like a rifle. We got the boss, the warrior, with several rounds of rifle fire. I don't care what they say, there's a place for slugthrowers, and downside combat is that place. You can hit what you can't see, which lasers can't, and the power's already in the ammo. No worry about a discharged powerpack, or those mirrored shields some of the Gerin have used. Some navy types keep wanting to switch all marine forces away from slug weapons, because they're afraid we'll go bonkers and put a hole in a cruiser hull, but the day they take my good old Belter special away from me, I'm gone. I've done my twenty already; there's no way they can hold me.

Davies took a burn from one of the warrior's helpers, but they weren't too aggressive with the big number one writhing on the ground, and we dropped them without any more trouble. Some noise, but no real trouble. Lonnie got a coldpak on Davies, which might limit the damage. It wasn't that bad a burn, anyway. If he died down here, it wouldn't be from that, though without some time in a good hospital, he might lose the use of those fingers. Davies being Davies, he'd probably skin-graft himself as soon as the painkiller cut in . . . he made a religion out of being tough. I called back to our command post to report, as I took a look around to see what we'd bought.

From up here, maybe seventy meters above the strip, the scattered remains of the shuttle glittered in the sun. I could see the two craters, one about halfway along, and another maybe a third of the way from the far end. Across the little valley, less than a klick, the hills rose slightly higher than the one we lay on. The cliffs on one were just as impressive as I'd thought. The others rose more gently from the valley floor. All were covered with the same green scrub, thick enough to hide an army. Either army.

I told the captain all this, and nodded when Skip held up the control box the Gerin had used with their detectors. We could use the stuff once we figured out the controls, and if they were dumb enough to give us an hour, we'd have no problems. No problems other than being a single drop team sitting beside a useless strip, with the Gerin perfectly aware of our location and identity.

Brightness bloomed in the zenith, and I glanced up. Something big had taken a hit—another shuttle? We were supposed to have two hundred shuttle flights on this mission, coming out of five cruisers—a full-scale assault landing, straight onto a defended planet. If that sounds impossibly stupid, you haven't read much military history—there are some commanders that have this thing about butting heads with an enemy strength, and all too many of them have political connections. Thunder fell out of the sky, and I added up the seconds I'd been counting. Ten thousand meters when they'd been blown—no one was going to float down from that one.

"What kind of an *idiot* . . . ?" Lonnie began; I waved him to silence. Things were bad enough without starting that—we could place the blame later. With a knife blade, if necessary.

"Vargas . . ." The captain's voice in my earplug drowned out the whisper of the breeze through stiff leaves. I pushed the subvoc microphone against my throat and barely murmured an answer. "Drop command says we lost thirty cents on the dollar. Beta-site took in four shuttles before it was shut out." Double normal losses on a hostile landing, then, and it sounded like we didn't have a secure strip. I tried to remember exactly where Beta site was. "We're supposed to clear this strip, get it ready for the next wave—"

I must have made some sound, without meaning to, because there was a long pause before he went on. If the original idea had been stupid, this one was stupid plus. Even a lowly enlisted man knows it's stupid to reinforce failure; why can't the brass learn it? We weren't engineers; we didn't have the machinery to fill those craters, or the manpower to clear the surrounding hills of Gerin and keep the fighters off.

"They're gonna do a flyby drop of machinery," he went on. I knew better than to say what I thought. No way I could stop them, if they wanted to mash their machinery on these hills. "We're going to put up the flyspy—you got a good view from there?"

"Yessir." I looked across the valley, around at all the green-clad slopes. The flyspy was another one of those things that you hated having to take care of until it saved your life. "By wire, or by remote?"

"Wire first." That was smart; that way they wouldn't have a radio source to lock on to. "I'm sending up the flyspy team, and some rockers. Send Davies back down." Rockers: rocket men, who could take out those Gerin fighters, always assuming they saw them in time, which they would if we got our detection set up.

Soon I could heard them crashing through the scrub, enough noise to alert anyone within half a klick. The rockers made it up first, four of them. I had two of them drag the Gerin corpses over to the edge and bounce 'em over, then they took up positions around the summit. Now we could knock off the Gerin fighters, if they came back: whatever's wrong with the rest of Supply, those little ground-air missiles we've got can do the job. Then the flyspy crew arrived, with the critter's wing folded back along its body. When they got to the clearing, they snapped the wings back into place, checked that the control wire was coiled ready to release without snagging, and turned on the scanners.

The flyspy is really nothing but a toy airplane, wings spanning about a meter, powered by a very quiet little motor. It can hold an amazing amount of spygear, and when it's designed for stealth use it's almost impossible to see in the air. On wire control, it'll go up maybe a hundred meters, circle around, and send us video and IR scans of anything it can see; on remote, we can fly it anywhere within line-of-sight, limited only by its fuel capacity.

Soon it was circling above us, its soft drone hardly audible even on our hilltop, certainly too quiet to be heard down on the strip. We didn't know whether the Gerin *did* hear, the way we hear, but we had to think about that. We know they hear big noises, explosions, but I've heard a theory that they can't hear high-pitched noises in atmosphere. The videos we were getting back looked surprisingly peaceful. Nothing seemed to be moving, and there was only one overgrown road leading away from the strip. Garrond punched a channel selector, and the normal-color view turned into a mosaic of brilliant false colors: sulfur yellow, turquoise, magenta, orange. He pointed to the orange. "That's vegetation, like this scrub.

Yellow is rock outcrops.'' The cliff across from us was a broad splash of yellow that even I could pick out. "Turquoise is disturbed soil: compacted or torn up, either one.'' The strip was turquoise, speckled with orange where plants had encroached on it. So was the nearly invisible road winding away from the strip between the hills. So also the summit of the hill which ended in cliffs above the strip . . . and the summit of our own hill. Another outpost, certainly.

But nothing moved, in the broad daylight of Caedmon's sun. According to briefing, we'd have another nine standard hours of light. None of our scanners showed motion, heat, anything that could be a Gerin force coming to take us out. And why not?

It bothered the captain, I could see, when he came up to look for himself. Our butterbars was clearly relieved, far too trusting an attitude if you want to survive very long. Things aren't *supposed* to go smoothly; any time an enemy isn't shooting at you, he's up to something even worse.

"An hour to the equipment drop,'' said the captain. "They're sending a squad of engineers, too.'' Great. Somebody else to look after, a bunch of dirtpushers. I didn't say it aloud; I didn't have to. Back before he saved Admiral Mac's life and got that chance at OCS, the captain and me were close, real buddies. Fact is, it was my fault he joined up—back then they didn't have the draft. Wasn't till he started running with me, Tinker Vargas, what everyone called gypsy boy—gambler and horsethief and general hothead—that Carl Dietz the farmer's son got into any trouble bigger than spilled milk. He was innocent as cornsilk back then, didn't even know when I was setting him up—and then we both got caught, and had the choice between joining the offworld marines or going to prison. Yet he's never said a word of blame, and he's still the straightest man I know, after all these years. He's one I *would* trust at poker, unlike Rolly, who can't seem to remember friendship when the cards come out.

And no, I'm not jealous. It hasn't been easy for him, a mustang brought up from the ranks, knowing he'll never make promotions like the fast-track boys that went to the

Academy or some fancy-pants university. He's had enough trouble, some of it when I was around to carefully not hear what the other guy said. So never mind the pay, and the commission: I'm happy with my life, and I'm still his friend. We both know the rules, and we play a fair game with the hand dealt us—no politics, just friends.

In that hour, we had things laid out more like they should be. Thanks to the flyspy, we knew that no Gerin triads lurked on the nearest two hilltops, and we got dug in well on all three hills that faced the strip on the near side. There was still that patch of turquoise to worry about on the facing hill, above the cliffs, but the flyspy showed no movement there, just the clear trace of disturbed soil. Our lieutenant had learned something in OCS after all; he'd picked a very good spot in a sort of ravine between the hills, out of sight beneath taller growth, for the headquarters dugout, meds, and so on.

Then the equipment carrier lumbered into view. I know, it's a shuttle same as the troop shuttle, but that's a term for anything that goes from cruiser to ground. Equipment carriers are fatter, squatty, with huge cargo doors aft, and they have all the graceful ease of a grand piano dumped off a clifftop. This one had all engines howling loudly, and the flaps and stuff hanging down from the wings, trying to be slow and steady as it dropped its load. First ten little parachutes (little at that distance), then a dark blob—it had to be really big if I could see it from here—trailing two chutes, and then a couple more, and a final large lumpy mass with one parachute.

"I don't believe it!" said the captain, stung for once into commentary. But it was—a netful of spare tires for the vehicles, wrapped around a huge flexible fuel pod. Relieved of all this load, the shuttle retracted its flaps and soared away, its engines returning to their normal roar.

Already the lieutenant had a squad moving, in cover, toward the landing parachutists. I watched the equipment itself come down, cushioned somewhat by airbags that inflated as it hit. Still nothing moved on the hilltop across from us. I felt the back of my neck prickle. It simply isn't natural for an enemy to chase you down, shooting all the while, then ignore you once you've landed. We know Gerin use air attack on ground forces: that's how they cleaned up those colonists on DuQuesne.

Yet ignore us they did, all the rest of that day, as the engineers got themselves down to the strip from where they'd landed, and got their equipment unstowed from its drop configuration and ready for use. One grader, what we called back on my homeworld a maintainer, and two earthmovers. The whole time the engineers were out there getting them ready, I was sure some Gerin fighter was going to do a low pass and blow us all away . . . but it didn't happen. I'd thought it was crazy, dropping equipment that had to be prepped and then used in the open, but for once high command had guessed right.

By late afternoon, the engineers had their machines ready to work. They started pushing stuff around at the far end of the strip, gouging long scars in the dirt and making mounds of gravelly dirt. The captain sent Kittrick and one platoon over to take a hill on the far side; they got up it with no trouble, and I began to think there weren't any Gerin left there at all. Half that group climbed the hill with the cliff, and found evidence that someone had had an outpost there, but no recent occupation.

We were spread out pretty thin by this time, maybe thirty on the far side of the strip, the rest on the near side, but stretched out. We'd rigged our own detection systems and had both flyspys up, high up, where they could see over the hills behind us. What they saw was more of the same, just like on the topo maps: lots of hills covered with thick green scrub, some creeks winding among the hills, traces of the road that began at the landing strip. Some klicks east of us (east is whatever direction the sun rises, on any world), the tumbled hills subsided into a broad river basin. The higher flyspy showed the edge of the hills, but no real detail on the plain.

Meanwhile the engineers went to work on that strip just as if they *were* being shot at. Dust went up in clouds, blown away from our side of the strip by a light breeze. Under that dust, the craters and humps and leftover chunks of our troop shuttle disappeared, and a smooth, level landing strip emerged. There's nothing engineers like better than pushing dirt around, and these guys pushed it fast.

By dark they had it roughed in pretty well, and showed us another surprise. Lights. Those tires we'd laughed at each held a couple of lamps and reflectors, and the coiled wiring that connected them all into a set of proper landing lights controlled by a masterboard and powered from an earthmover engine. By the time everyone had had chow, the first replacement shuttle was coming in, easing down to the lighted strip as if this were practice on a safe, peaceful planet far from the war.

None of us veterans could relax and enjoy it, though. The new arrivals had heard the same thing I had—30 percent losses on the initial drop, sixty shuttles blown. No report from anyone on what we'd done to the Gerin, which meant that the navy hadn't done a damn thing . . . they tripled their figures when they did, but triple zilch is still zilch. So how come we weren't being overrun by Gerin infantry? Or bombed by their fighters? What were the miserable Slime up to? They sure weren't beat, and they don't surrender.

During the night, five more shuttles landed, unloaded, and took off again. Besides the additional troops and supplies, we also had a new commanding officer, a mean-looking freckle-faced major named Sewell. I know it's not fair to judge someone by his looks, but he had one of those narrow faces set in a permanent scowl, with tight-bunched muscles along his jaw. He probably looked angry sound asleep, and I'd bet his wife (he had a wide gold ring on the correct finger) had learned to hop on cue. His voice fit the rest of him, edged and ready to bite deep at any resistance. The captain had a wary look; I'd never served with Sewell, or known anyone who had, but evidently the captain knew something.

Major Sewell seemed to know what he was doing, though, and his first orders made sense, in a textbook way. If you wanted to try something as impossible as defending a shuttle strip without enough troops or supplies, his way was better than most. Soon we had established a perimeter that was secure enough, dug into each of the main hills around the strip, each with its own supply of ammo, food, and water. Besides the original headquarters and med dugout, he'd established another on the far side of the strip. All this looked pretty good, with no Gerin actually challenging it, but I wasn't convinced. It takes more than a few hundred marines to secure an airstrip if the enemy has a lot of troops.

Shortly after sundown, one of the squads from the first replacement shuttle found ruins of a human settlement at the base of a hill near the end of the strip, and had to get their noses slapped on the comm for making so much noise about it. Not long after, the squad up on that clifftop put two and two together and made their own find. Having heard the first ruckus, they didn't go on the comm with it, but sent a runner down to Major Sewell.

There's a certain art to getting information, another version of politics, you might call it. It so happened that someone I knew had a buddy who knew someone, and so on, and I knew the details before the runner got to Major Sewell.

We'd known the strip itself was human-made, from the beginning. What we hadn't known was that it had been privately owned, adjacent to the owner's private residence. It takes a fair bit of money to build a shuttle strip, though not as much as it takes to have a shuttle and *need* a shuttle strip. The same class of money can take a chunk of rock looking out over a little valley and carve into it a luxurious residence and personal fortress. It can afford to install the best-quality automated strip electronics to make landing its fancy little shuttle easier, and disguise all the installations as chunks of native stone or trees or whatever. The Gerin had missed it, being unfamiliar with both the world and the way that humans think of disguise. But to a bored squad sitting up on a hilltop with no enemy in sight, and the knowledge that someone might have hidden something . . . to them it was easy. Easy to find, that is, not easy to get into, at least not without blasting a way in . . . which, of course, they were immediately and firmly told not to do.

Think for a little what it takes to do something like

this. We're not talking here about ordinary dress-up-in-silk-everyday rich, you understand, not the kind of rich that satisfies your every whim for enough booze and fancy food. I can't even imagine the sort of sum that would own a whole world, hollow out a cliff for a home, operate a private shuttle, and still have enough clout left to bribe the navy in the middle of a desperate war. This was the sort of wealth that people thought the military-industrial complex had, the kind that the big commercial consortia do have (whether the military get any or not), the kind where one man's whim, barely expressed, sends ten thousand other men into a death-filled sky.

Or that's the way I read it. We were here to protect—to get back—some rich man's estate, his private playground, that the Gerin had taken away. Not because of colonists (did I see any colonists? Did anyone see any evidence of colonists?) but because of a rich old fart who had kept this whole world to himself, and then couldn't protect it. That's why we couldn't do the safe, reasonable thing and bomb the Gerin into dust, why we hadn't had adequate site preparation, why we hadn't brought down the tactical nukes. Politics.

I did sort of wonder why the Gerin wanted it. Maybe they had their own politics? I also wondered if anyone was hiding out in there, safe behind the disguising rock, watching us fight . . . lounging at ease, maybe, with a drink in his hand, enjoying the show. We could take care of that later, too. If we were here.

Sometime before dawn—still dark, but over half the night gone—the higher flyspy reported distant activity. Lights and non visible heat sources over at the edge of the hills, moving slowly but steadily toward us. They didn't follow the old road trace, but kept to the low ground. According to the best guess of the instruments, the wettest low ground. I guess that makes sense, if you're an amphib. It still didn't make sense that they moved so slow, and that they hadn't come to hit us while we were setting up.

The next bad news came from above. Whatever the navy had thought they'd done to get the Gerin ships out of the way, it hadn't held, and the next thing we knew our guys boosted out of orbit and told us to hold the fort while they fought off the Gerin. Sure. The way things were going, they weren't coming back, and we wouldn't be here if they did. Nobody *said* that, which made it all the clearer that we were all thinking it. During that long day we made radio contact with the survivors at Beta site. They were about eighty klicks away to our north, trying to move our way through the broken hills and thick scrub. Nobody'd bothered them yet, and they hadn't found any sign of human habitation. Surprise. The major didn't tell them what we'd found, seeing as it wouldn't do them any good. Neither would linking up with us, probably.

The smart thing to do, if anyone had asked me, was for us to boogie on out of there and link with the Beta-site survivors, and see what we could do as a mobile strike force. Nobody asked me, at least nobody up top, where the orders came from. We were supposed to hold the strip, so there we stuck, berries on a branch ready for picking. I know a lot of the guys thought the same way I did, but hardly anyone mentioned it, seeing it would do no good and we'd have a lot more to bitch about later.

Slow as the Gerin were moving, we had time to set up several surprises, fill every available container with water, all that sort of thing. They ignored our flyspy, so we could tell where they were, what they had with them, estimate when they'd arrive. It was spooky . . . but then they didn't need to bother shooting down our toy; they only outnumbered us maybe a hundred to one. If everyone of our ambushes worked, we might cut it down to ninety to one.

Gerin ground troops might be slow to arrive, but once they were there you had no doubt about it. Just out of range of our knuckleknockers, the column paused and set up some tubing that had to be artillery of some sort. Sure enough, we heard a sort of warbling whoosh, and then a vast *whump* as the first shells burst over our heads and spat shards of steel down on us. After a couple or three shots, fairly well separated, they sent up a whole tanker load, and the concussion shuddered the hills themselves.

We watched them advance through the smoke and haze of their initial barrage. They were in easy missile range, but we had to save the missiles for their air support. Everyone's seen the news clips—that strange, undulating way they move. They may be true amphibians, but they're clearly more at home in water or space than walking around on the ground. Not that it's walking, really. Their weapons fire slower on automatic than ours, but they can carry two of them—an advantage of having all those extra appendages. And in close, hand-to-hand combat, their two metal-tipped tentacles are lethal.

They came closer, advancing in little bobbing runs that were similar to our own tactics, but not the same. It's hard to explain, but watching them come I felt how alien they were—they could not have been humans in alien suits, for instance. The very fact that I had trouble picking out the logic of their movements—why they chose to go *this* way up a draw, and not that—emphasized the differences.

Now they were passing the first marker. Rolly tapped me on the shoulder, and I nodded. He hit the switch, and a storm cloud rolled under them, tumbling them in the explosion. Those in the first rank let off a burst, virtually unaimed; the smack of their slugs on the rocks was drowned in the roar and clatter of the explosion, and the dust of it rolled forward to hide them all. Chunks of rock splattered all around; a secondary roar had to mean that the blast had triggered a rock slide, just as we'd hoped. When the dust cleared a little, we couldn't see any of the live ones, only a few wet messes just beyond a mound of broken stone and uprooted brush.

One of the wetears down at the far end of the trench stood up to peer out. Before anyone could yank him back, Gerin slugs took his face and the back of his head, and he toppled over. Then a storm of fire rang along the rocks nearby while we all ducked. Stupid kid should have known they wouldn't all be dead: we'd told them and told them. Our flyspy crew concentrated on their screens; at the moment the critter was reading infrared, and the enemy fire showed clearly. Garrond gave us the coordinates; our return fire got a few more (or so the flyspy showed—we didn't stand up to see).

But that was only the first wave. All too soon we could see the next Gerin working their way past the rockslide toward our positions. And although I'd been listening for it, I hadn't heard an explosion from the other side of the strip. Had they been overrun, or had the Gerin failed to attempt an envelopment?

Suddenly the sky was full of light and noise: the Gerin had launched another barrage. Oddly, the weapons seemed to be intended to cause noise as much as actual damage. And they were noisy: my ears rang painfully and I saw others shaking their heads. Under cover of that noise, Gerin leaped out, hardly ten meters away. Someone to my left screamed; their slugs slammed all around us. We fired back, and saw their protective suits ripple and split, their innards gushing out to stain the ground. But there were too many, and some of them made it to us, stabbing wildly with those metal-tipped tentacles. One of them smashed into Rolly's chest; his eyes bulged, and pink froth erupted from his mouth. I fired point-blank at that one. It collapsed with a gasping wheeze, but it was too late for Rolly.

Even in all the noise, I was aware that the Gerin themselves fought almost silently. I'd heard they had speech, of a sort—audible sounds, that is—but they didn't yell at each other, or cry out when injured. It was almost like fighting machines. And like machines, they kept coming. Even in the dark.

It was sometime in that first night when I heard the row between the captain and the major. I don't know when it started, maybe in private before the Gerin even got to us, but in the noise of combat, they'd both raised their voices. I was going along, checking ammo levels, making sure everyone had water, and passed them just close enough to hear.

"—You can't do that," Major Sewell was saying. "They said, hold the strip."

"Because it's that bastard Ifleta's," said the captain. He'd figured it out too, of course; he didn't turn stupid when he got his promotion. I should have gone on, but

instead I hunkered down a little and listened. If he talked
the major around, I'd need to know. "So no heavy artillery, no tactical nukes, no damage to his art collection
or whatever he thinks it is. And it's crazy. . . . Listen,
the Gerin are amphibs, they even have swim tanks in their
ships—"

"So? Dammit, Carl, it's the middle of a battle, not a
lecture room—"

"So they're territorial." I could hear the expletive he
didn't say at the end of that . . . Sewell was a senior
officer, however dense. "It's part of that honor stuff:
where you are determines your role in the dominance
hierarchy. If we move, we're no threat; if we stay in one
place they'll attack—"

"They *are* attacking, in case you hadn't noticed, *Captain*. We're dug in here; if we move they can take us
easily. Or were you suggesting that we just run for it?"
The contempt in Sewell's voice was audible, even through
the gunfire.

The captain made one more try. I knew, from our years
together, what it took for him to hold his temper at the
major's tone; the effort came through in his voice. "Sir,
with all due respect, after the massacre on DuQuesne,
there was a study of Gerin psychology in the *Military
Topics Review*—and that study indicated that the Gerin
would choose to assault stationary, defended positions
over a force in movement. Something about defending
certain rock formations in the tidal zone, important for
amphibians—"

"Yeah, well, what some egghead scientist thinks the
Slime do and what the Slime out here in combat do are
two different things. And our orders, Captain, say stand
and defend this shuttle strip. It doesn't matter a truckful
of chickenshit whether the strip is Ifleta's personal private
hideaway or was built by the Gerin: I was told to defend
it, and I'm going to defend it. Is that clear?"

"Sir." I heard boots scrape on the broken rock and
got myself out of there in a hurry. Another time that I'd
heard more than I should have, at least more than it would
be comfortable to admit. Not long after, the captain met
me as I worked my way back down the line. He leaned

over and said in my ear, "I know you heard that, Gunny. Keep it to yourself."

"You got eyes in the dark?" I asked. It meant more than that; we'd used it as a code a long time ago. I didn't think he'd choose that way, but I'd let him decide.

"No," he said. A shell burst nearby, deafening us both for a moment; I could see, in the brief glare, his unshaken determination. "No," he said again after we could hear. "It's too late anyway."

"Ifleta's the owner?" I asked.

"Yeah. Senior counselor—like a president—in Hamny's Consortium, and boss of Sigma Combine. This is his little hideaway—should have been a colony, but he got here first. What I figure is this is his price for bringing Hamny's in free: three human-settled worlds, two of 'em industrial. Worth it, that's one way of looking at it. Trade a couple thousand marines for three allied planets, populations to draft, industrial plants in place, and probably a good chunk of money as well."

I grunted, because there's nothing to say to that kind of argument. Not in words, anyway. Then I asked, "Does the major know?"

The captain shrugged. "You heard me—I told him. I told him yesterday, when they found the house. He doesn't care. Rich man wants the aliens out of his property, that's just fine—treat marines like mercs, he doesn't give a damn, and *that*, Tinker, is what they call an officer and a gentleman. *His* father's a retired admiral; he's looking for stars of his own." It was a measure of his resentment that he called me by that old nickname . . . the others that had used it were all dead. I wondered if he resented his own lost patrimony . . . the rich bottomland farm that would have been his, the wife and many children. He had been a farmer's son, in a long line of farmers, as proud of their heritage as any admiral.

"Best watch him, Captain," I said, certain that I would. "He's likely to use your advice all wrong."

"I know. He backstabbed Tio, got him shipped over to the Second with a bad rep—" He stopped suddenly, and his voice changed. "Well, Gunny, let me know how that number-three post is loaded.'' I took that hint, and went on; we'd talked too long as it was.

So now I knew the whole story—for one thing about Captain Carl Dietz, he never in his life made accusations without the information to back them up. He hadn't accused me when it might have got him a lighter sentence, all those years ago. If he said it was Ifleta's place, if he was sure that our losses bought Ifleta's support, and three planets, then I was sure. I didn't like it, but I believed it.

The pressure was constant. We had no time to think, no time to rest, taking only the briefest catnaps one by one, with the others alert. We knew we were inflicting heavy losses, but the Gerin kept coming. Again and again, singly and in triads and larger groups, they appeared, struggling up the hills, firing steadily until they were cut down to ooze violet fluid on the scarred slopes. Our losses were less, but irreparable.

It was dawn again—which dawn, how many days since landing, I wasn't at all sure. I glanced at the rising sun, irrationally angry because it hurt my eyes. What I could see of the others looked as bad as I felt: filthy, stinking, their eyes sunken in drawn faces, dirty bandages on too many wounds. The line of motionless mounds behind our position was longer, again. No time for burial, no time to drag the dead farther away: they were here, with us, and they stank in their own way. We had covered their faces; that was all we could do.

Major Sewell crawled along our line, doing his best to be encouraging, but everyone was too tired and too depressed to be cheered. When he got to me, I could tell that he didn't feel much better. One thing about him, he hadn't been taking it easy or hiding out.

''We've got a problem,'' he said. I just nodded. Speech took too much energy, and besides it was obvious. ''There's only one thing to do and that's hit 'em with a mobile unit. I've been in contact with the Beta-site survivors, but they don't have a flyspy or good linkage to ours—and besides, their only officer is a kid just out of OCS. The others died at the drop. They're about four hours away now. I'm gonna take a squad, find 'em, and go after the Gerin commander.''

I still didn't say anything. That might have made sense, before the Gerin arrived. Now it looked to me like more politics—Sewell figured to leave the captain holding an indefensible position, while he took his chance at the Gerin commander. He might get killed, but if he didn't he'd get his medals . . . and staying here was going to get us all killed. Some of that must have shown in my face, because his darkened.

"Dammit, Gunny—I know what Captain Dietz said made sense, but our *orders* said defend this strip. The last flyspy image gave me a lock on what may be the Gerin commander's module, and that unit from Beta site may give me the firepower I need. Now you find me—'' My mind filled in "a few good men" but he actually asked for a squad of unwounded. We had that many, barely, and I got them back to the cleft between the first and second hills just in time to see that last confrontation with the captain.

If I hadn't known him that long, I'd have thought he didn't care. Sewell had a good excuse, as if he needed one, for leaving the captain behind: Dietz had been hit, though that wound wouldn't kill him. He couldn't have moved fast for long, not without a trip through med or some stim-tabs. But they both knew that had nothing to do with it. The captain got his orders from Sewell in terse phrases; he merely nodded in reply. Then his eyes met mine.

I'd planned to duck away once we were beyond the Gerin lines—assuming we made it that far, and since the other side of the strip hadn't been so heavily attacked, we probably would. I had better things to do than baby-sit a major playing politics with the captain's life. But the captain's gaze had the same wide-blue-sky openness it had always had, barring a few times he was whacked out on bootleg whiskey.

"I'm glad you've got Gunny Vargas with you," the captain said. "He's got eyes in the dark."

"If it takes us that long, we're in trouble again," said the major gruffly. I smiled at the captain, and followed

Sewell away down the trail, thinking of the years since
I'd been in that stuffy little courtroom back on that miserable backwater colony planet. The captain played fair,
on the whole; he never asked for more than his due, and
usually got less. If he wanted me to baby-sit the major,
I would. It was the least I could do for him.

We lost only three on the way to meet the Beta-site
survivors, and I saved the major's life twice. The second
time, the Gerin tentacle I stopped shattered my arm just
as thoroughly as a bullet. The major thanked me, in the
way that officers are taught to do, but the thought behind
his narrow forehead was that my heroism didn't do him
a bit of good unless he could win something. The medic
we had along slapped a field splint on the arm and shot
me up with something that took all the sharp edges off.
That worried me, but I knew it would wear off in a few
hours. I'd have time enough.

Then we walked on, and on, and damn near ran head-
long into our own people. They looked a lot better than
we did, not having been shot up by Gerin for several
days; in fact, they looked downright smart. The butterbar
had an expression somewhere between serious and
smug—he figured he'd done a better than decent job with
his people, and the glance I got from his senior sergeant
said the kid was okay. Sewell took over without explaining much, except that we'd been attacked and were now
going to counterattack; I was glad he didn't go further.
It could have created a problem for me.

Caedmon's an official record, now. You've seen the
tapes, maybe, or the famous shot of the final Gerin assault up the hills above the shuttle strip, the one that
survived in someone's personal vicam to be stripped later
by naval intelligence after we took the hills back, and
had time to retrieve personal effects. You know that our
cruisers came back, launched fighters that tore the Gerin
fighters out of the sky, and then more shuttles, with more
troops, enough to finish the job on the surface. You know
that the "gallant forces" of the first landing (yeah, I heard
that speech too) are credited with *almost* winning against
fearful odds, even wiping out the Gerin commander and
its staff, thanks to the brilliant tactic of one marine cap-

tain unfortunately himself a casualty of that last day of battle. You've seen his picture, with those summer-sky-blue eyes and that steadfast expression, a stranger to envy and fear alike.

But I know what happened to Major Sewell, who is listed simply as "killed in action." I know how come the captain got his posthumous medals and promotion, something for his family back home to put up on their wall. I know exactly how the Gerin commander died, and who died of Gerin weapons and who of human steel. And I don't think I have to tell you every little detail, do I? It all comes down to politics, after all. An honest politician, as the saying goes, is the one who stays bought. I was bought a long time ago, with the only coin that buys any gypsy's soul, and with that death (you know which death) I was freed.

Ships of War

The warships used in the Far Stars War were all of the same basic configuration. Whether the tapered cylinders of the humans, the saucers of the D'Tarth, or the spherical ships the Gerin fly, all are limited by two engineering factors.

The first limitation is size. The drive universally used for FTL travel is quite bulky. The smallest FTL drives weigh in the range of three tons. For this reason no fighter is capable of FTL travel. Up to 20 percent of the mass of most warships is devoted to their warp drives. The necessity that the entire ship be contained within the warp field also serves as an upper limit to size. The larger the ship, the greater the proportion of the ship that has to be devoted to housing warp engines capable of producing a field that will contain it. The construction of dreadnoughts, favored before the war, was soon shown to be impractical and wasteful of resources.

Developed only a few decades before the Far Stars War, the energy shield is capable of deflecting most beam weapons and radiation. The early screen generators required immense power. Enough power was needed that when functioning none remained for the warp drives. As a result, when a ship was prepared for combat, it was unable to flee. Conversely, should a captain choose to flee into warp drive, he had to do so when his ship was not under fire.

Fighters and most merchant ships are incapable of powering defensive screens. Fighters have no option except to use their speed and agility to avoid enemy fire. Merchants either escape or are destroyed. A functioning screen provides ten times the protection of ten inches of durasteel. One of the side effects of even the early defensive screens was to render obsolete the armored hulls of the larger ships. Most of these heavy cruisers and dreadnoughts were scrapped or converted into orbiting platforms. A few were used in other ways.

MUSEUM PIECE
by William C. Dietz

"ADMIRAL KYRO is an old fart." Commodore H. L. Heath, Sector Commander for the Nargo Star Cluster, let the words roll off his tongue. Heath was a big man with a face to match. His high forehead, thick lips, and heavy jowls gave him the look of a Buddha, though few thought of him as especially enlightened.

His aide, Captain George Sokolof, nodded sagely and tapped some ash from the end of his cigar. Like the man, the cigar was slim and elegant.

"True, true. But Kyro pulls some heavy gees. He

served with the admiral back when Mac was *Lieutenant* Chu Lin MacDonald, and he's a war hero to boot. Battle of Gemini, Legion of Merit, and all that.''

Heath nodded, remembering Kyro's last visit. Somehow he always felt nervous and a little bit ashamed as the metal box whirred and hummed its way into the room, sensors swiveling this way and that, fans stirring the expensive nap of his rug, all of it reminding Heath of the other man's sacrifice.

It was no way for a man to live, if you could call Kyro a man. "A brain in a box," someone had said. Ugly words but true nevertheless.

Everyone knew the story. How the Gerin globeships cut him off from the rest of the fleet. How Kyro fought to the last man, never dreaming that the last man would be himself, and how the medics had brought him back to life.

Well, a sort of half-life anyhow . . . because these days Kyro was little more than brain tissue in a nutrient bath. Had the medics been able to save some spinal cord they could've given him a bionic body and something approaching normal life.

But such was not the case, so Kyro was forever imprisoned in a metal box. And then, goddam his soul, the miserable old bastard retired to Gloria, where he would live out his days making Heath's life miserable.

Sokolof raised an eyebrow and smiled, as if reading Heath's thoughts.

The commodore scowled and swiveled his chair a few degrees right. His office occupied the entire top floor of the League Tower and afforded him an unobstructed view of Felson Prime, Gloria's largest city.

It was pretty, completely untouched by the war which raged a few hundred light-years away, all spires and soaring conifers.

There were factories, of course, hundreds of square miles of them, but they were miles away, where their smoke and pollution wouldn't bother the citizens of Felson Prime.

Ah, Gloria! A plum, actually, and well deserved, too, considering Heath's many accomplishments. After all, wars are fought by factories when you boil it all down. Factories which make the guns, body armor, hull plating, medical kits, bombs, coffee cups, and the million other things it takes to kill the enemy. Factories run by unsung heroes.

"Yes," Heath told himself, "if it weren't for men like me, the navy would be throwing rocks instead of torpedoes. Maybe we don't lead ships into battle, but we *do* turn factories into engines of war, and transform planets into fortified arsenals."

Yes, Gloria was a reward for services rendered. But could he enjoy it? Hell no. He had Gerin raiders nibbling along the edges of his sector, a daughter who was completely unreasonable, and a retired admiral who insisted on a war museum.

More specifically, Kyro wanted the *Hebe*, a dreadnought almost as ancient as her name. Decommissioned in orbit six years before, the *Hebe* had since served as a platform for weather studies and as a lab for zero gee experiments. She was presently unused and scheduled for salvage.

And like all other military property in the Nargo Cluster, the *Hebe* came under Heath's authority. Twice Kyro had requested use of the ship as a museum, and twice Heath had refused. Then the letter arrived.

It came via official message torp and was rushed to Heath's office. The letter was typed on admiralty stationery and bore the signature of Admiral Chu Lin MacDonald himself. Heath picked it up and read it again.

> Dear Herbert,
> Kyro tells me he could use some help creating an orbital war museum for Gloria. Sounds like a good idea to me. It'll keep the old bastard out of your hair! I'd appreciate any help you could provide.
> Thanks, Mac

Heath ran a hand through his thinning hair and wondered if Mac had cracked a bald joke at his expense.

A war museum indeed! What did the people of Gloria

need with a war museum? Many were like Kyro himself . . . used-up has-beens sent to a backwater planet to nurse broken bodies and shattered minds. The rest were good citizens, working round the clock to make weapons for the navy, blissfully ignorant of real war.

Yes, Heath decided, the people might be ready for war memorials in another twenty-five or thirty years, but not yet. Right now they needed encouragement to work extra shifts, to make their quotas, to win the war of production.

Still, the meaning of Admiral MacDonald's letter was quite clear: "Help my old friend or pay with your ass."

Heath shifted that rather large piece of his anatomy and turned back toward his aide. "Damm it . . . why did Kyro have to retire to my sector?"

Sokolof blew a long thin streamer of smoke toward the nearest vent and smiled. "Some people are just lucky, I guess."

Though not comparable to the small lake which occupies the center of Gerin command ships, the *Sea Storm*'s battle center did boast a rather comfortable pool, and La'seek took comfort from it. He used four of his eight arms to shift himself into a more comfortable position, and felt the water move behind him as Nu'rech and Is'amik did likewise.

Each of his warrior apprentices would rather self-kill than be one garik out of position. Always behind him, Nu'rech and Is'amik made a perfect triangle, and protected his back. That's how it was and how it would always be.

Having seen to his own comfort, La'seek turned his attention to the level-three subordinate across from him. As befitted his lower rank, Wa'neck had draped himself over a slightly higher rock, signifying his determination to protect La'seek from any dangers which might lurk above, and ceding first rights to whatever bottom food might be handy. A bit old-fashioned, perhaps, but laudable nonetheless. So too the seemly green color of the other warrior's skin. It signified peace and cooperation.

La'seek waved a tentacle in Wa'neck's direction. When

he spoke, his words came out as a series of ultrasonic squeaks and twitters. "You may proceed."

Wa'neck squeezed a small remote, and a holo popped into existence between them. It shimmered slightly with the movement of the water but not enough to trouble their double-lidded eyes. It was a battle map complete with pulsing yellow disks to symbolize stars and brown squares to represent their planets.

"We are here," Wa'neck intoned, and a red diamond popped into existence just off the star Iba S-8.

"I recommend a surprise raid deep into human-held space." Another diamond popped into existence, this one a brilliant blue. It pulsated next to a star identified as Nargo S-2. A human descriptor, lacking in elegance, but sufficient for military purposes.

"This star has four planets," Wa'neck continued, "and two of them are infested with humans. One is of little importance, but the other produces vast quantities of armaments, and is ripe for the plucking."

The battle map disappeared and was replaced by real video. What La'seek saw was beautiful, a rotating blue jewel blessed with equal parts water and land, the very embodiment of the Gerin ideal.

Seeing his superior's skin turn pink with excitement, Wa'neck took full advantage. "The humans call it Gloria, which is a word of worship."

"And worship they should," La'seek replied. "The planet is very beautiful. Tell me, Wa'neck, how did we come by such images? How many warriors life-gave to bring them here?"

"None," Wa'neck answered. "We received the pictures from a human spy, a former prisoner who has agreed to do our work, and profit in the process."

"How extraordinary," La'seek said. "How very extraordinary." Human spies were extremely rare, partly because of loyalty to their own species, but also because the Gerin form seemed to tap xenophobic fears buried deep in their psyches.

"And what of their defenses?"

The holo changed. Now La'seek looked at a detailed listing of the planet's defenses. He found them rather weak by wartime standards. The local naval contingent boasted seven cruisers and a deactivated dreadnought. A "useless hulk," according to Wa'neck's annotation.

The planet's single moon was only lightly fortified. There were no orbital defense platforms to speak of, and nothing much on the ground. A rather tempting target.

"A raid you say. Details, please."

La'seek was interested! Inside Wa'neck rejoiced, but outside he was careful to maintain the same subservient skin color. He made a bold move by slithering down to a lower rock only gariks higher than La'seek himself. Behind Wa'neck his two apprentices did likewise.

The battle map reappeared as Wa'neck spoke. "It would work like this. Two of our ships will attack Dusa, Nargo S-2's second planet, and draw off the naval contingent. Then, when the human warships are out of position, a strike force of ten globeships will attack Gloria, and eradicate the population."

The battle map vanished and was replaced by what appeared to be a detailed receipt for naval stores, printed on League stationery and signed by a human named Heath. La'seek wondered if he was the spy.

"Time permitting," Wa'neck continued, "we will also load our ships with human weapons. If not, our warriors will destroy them. That accomplished, our ships will up-warp and return here. Should the humans follow they will downwarp into a well-prepared trap."

La'seek turned light blue in approval. It was classic Gerin strategy, and with any luck at all, would bring great honor on both of them. Expelling air from his main vent, La'seek rose to entwine tool tentacles with Warrior Wa'neck. "Well said, war brother. Death to humans!"

Gil used his remaining eye to scan the cavernous interior of the League supply depot. Huge storage racks rose on every side and disappeared into the darkness above. Their shelves were loaded with everything imaginable: electronic components, chemical toilets, energy weapons, holo tanks, control consoles, live ammo, aircraft engines, and more. The air was heavy with the odor of sealers, lubricants, and new plastic.

A grin spread across Gil's face. "Damn, Chiefy, lookit this stuff! This'll be more fun than three days in a class-one pleasure dome!"

Gil was short and squat, much like the drives he'd once served, his open features a map to a very simple soul. A soul completely untroubled by the fact that a Gerin beam weapon had taken his left eye and right leg. And why should it be? Though not especially pretty, the bionic replacements worked better than the originals, and were much easier to maintain.

Gil was retired now, mustered out as a power tech first class, and damned tired of it. For months his thick fingers had ached for something to do, something to fix.

Oh, there were jobs, all right, like working in a munitions factory, or maintaining the big robo miners which bored their way through Gloria's mountains. But that was child's play compared to working on a ship's monster drives. The *Hebe* was like a dream come true.

Yup, Gil thought to himself, *thanks to Admiral Kyro, I've got a ship again. An old rust bucket to be sure, but a ship nonetheless, and that's a helluva lot better than nothing.* Gil smiled and waited for some instructions from Chiefy.

Chiefy was a small man with small needs and small dreams. Patches of bright blue marked the spot on each sleeve where missing chevrons had once identified him as a chief petty officer, setting him above the other enlisted personnel and providing his nickname.

Servos whined as he looked down at the translucent key card, then up at the rows of storage racks which marched away in every direction. Gil was right. This *would* be more fun than three days in a class-one pleasure dome! Thanks to Admiral Kyro they could take anything they needed.

For thirty-six years Chiefy had fought for supplies. Even during the best of times there'd never been enough, and in the worst of times, well, he'd been forced to misappropriate, liberate, and just plain steal what he needed. What his *ship* needed.

Because for Chiefy ships were alive, having souls and personalities, which it was his job to understand and cater to. This was his mission, his purpose, his only reason for existence. And because of that the *Hebe* took on special meaning. Chiefy was going to resurrect a goddess, restore her to working order, and spend the rest of his life paying homage.

Light reflected off Chiefy's arms as he pulled a mini-comp out of his breast pocket and tapped the keys. It made a whirring noise as it printed out the list of the supplies the ship would need.

Chiefy never said "museum," not even to himself. A ship's a ship, not a museum. Chiefy tore the printout off and grinned. "Come on, Gil . . . we've got work to do."

" 'Work' is not a dirty word, Daddy," Carolyn Heath pleaded. "I'm good with computers, you said so yourself. Besides, it's boring sitting around the house all day."

Commodore Heath looked across the dining table and into his daughter's eyes. Sometimes, when the light hit her face just so, Carolyn looked so much like his dead wife it brought a lump to his throat.

Dark brown hair, worn long so it brushed her shoulders, wide-set eyes, a straight nose, only a tiny bit too large, his fault probably, and full red lips, presently set in a hard, determined line. He tried to sound angry, but she looked so much like Lydia that his heart wasn't in it.

"Bored?" Heath gestured expansively to the elegant dining room and the veranda beyond. "You have this, plus a two-seater, plus a skimmer, and you're bored? Yes, you're good at computers, but that doesn't mean you should take a job like some settler's daughter. My God! They'll think we need the money!"

Heath's family were landed nobility in Cathgart, where they still passed titles down the male side, and women occupied themselves in ways which befitted their station.

Carolyn crossed her legs impatiently. "Daddy, you're such a snob. Besides, Deputy Administrator of the Felson Prime Mainframe is more than just a job. Lots of people would give their left nut, or ovary as the case may be, for my position."

Heath frowned as he took a sip of his drink. His daughter was starting to sound like Admiral Kyro. "I wish you wouldn't talk like that, Carolyn. Your mother wouldn't like it."

Carolyn sighed. She hated to manipulate her father, but sometimes he left her no choice. Plastering what she hoped was a contrite look on her face, she switched to the little-girl voice, and gave it another try.

"I'm sorry, Daddy. Here, let me freshen up your drink. I'll think about quitting if that's what you want. But first I need your help on something."

Commodore Heath smiled. "Name it, honey, and it's yours."

"I need to borrow someone from your intelligence section."

The frown returned. "Whatever for?"

Carolyn was silent for a moment, the serious set of her eyes reminding him of the way Lydia used to look when working a problem. "I think there's a drain on the main-frame."

"A what?"

"A drain. I think someone's stealing data from the mainframe, draining it from a subroutine, and dumping it God knows where. But I can't be sure, because the subroutines are protected by naval codes, and I don't have access."

Carolyn smiled her most winning smile. "So that's why I need someone from your intelligence section, someone who really is, intelligent I mean, and knows computers."

Heath choked off the words before they could slip out. Carolyn had always been rather dramatic, like the time she'd been on a camping trip, and reported seeing a Gerin scout ship land in the mountains. Security had searched for two days making sure she was wrong. Of course, she'd been younger then, but still, this computer thing sounded like another false alarm. He'd pretended to take her seriously nevertheless. What with the Gerin and Admiral Kyro he had problems enough already without a war at home. Heath forced a smile.

"I'll call Commander Paulitz. I'm sure she'll find someone to help you."

* * *

Someone was screaming deep in Kyro's dreams. Was it his exec? A tech? Or the ship itself? Dying a little more as still another bolt of energy sliced through its hull. Pieces. There were pieces of him all over the place. His arms, his legs, they'd come off somehow, each one sealed inside a section of suit. "Oh God, it hurts! Please, Mommy, make it stop!"

Kyro jerked awake. As he did the vision of dying ships and men disappeared, replaced by Felson Prime at night, a sea of twinkling lights. He'd fallen asleep on the veranda. An empty extension of an empty house.

Outside of his metal box the night had grown cold. It made little difference to Kyro. He could sleep wherever he chose. Beds were irrelevant now, and so was he. Kyro willed his optical scanners up toward the sky, toward the stars among which he yearned to roam, and wished that he were dead.

The battle klaxon bleated in the background as Marlo bent over to kiss her children. What if she never saw them again? What if the Gerin killed her and Jax too? It didn't bear thinking about. She forced a smile.

"Erica, take care of your little brother, and Pol, do what Erica says. You promise?"

They said, "Yes, Mommy," and stood on tiptoes to give her one last kiss. Then Marlo gave them over to a matronly-looking warden and turned her back. They'd be deep underground in a few minutes, safe from everything but a direct hit, and the possibility of losing both their parents in battle.

Marlo's combat boots made a loud thumping sound as she strode down the hall to the door. It swung open at her touch and allowed the heat to hit her face.

Marlo squinted into bright sunlight. Beyond the whitewashed adobe walls of the settlement, yellow desert stretched off in every direction. Way out there, shimmering in the heat, she could see the house that she and Jax were building. It would be square, with a central courtyard, a little waterfall, and lots of room for the kids. Was this the last time she'd see it?

"Come on!"

The voice belonged to Jax. He and about fifteen or twenty others were packed into the back of Chang's flatbed hovertruck. They waved and yelled friendly insults. All wore flight gear and were members of the Fighting Fifteenth. A reserve unit, but a good one.

Marlo ran down the path and allowed Jax to pull her aboard. He was a big man with kinky black hair, a handsome face, and gleaming white teeth. His arm felt strong and warm behind her back. She wanted to touch him, to feel him, to remember what he was like.

Chang hit the gas and everyone was thrown backward as the truck roared down the main street and toward the west end of town. Beyond it lay the spaceport and Dusa's tiny naval base.

People came out to cheer and wave as the truck passed by, their confidence out of synch with the feeling in Marlo's stomach and the nervous chatter of those around her.

"Is this for real?" Marlo had to yell in order to be heard over the roar of the truck's dual engines.

"'Fraid so," her husband yelled back. "Two Gerin globeships downwarped about fifteen minutes ago. They're headed this way. How're the kids?"

"Scared," Marlo replied, looking into his brown eyes. "And so am I."

Jax nodded. "Me too. Everybody is, but what the hey, chances are we'll wax their ass!"

"I'm not sure the Gerin have asses," Marlo yelled. "Besides, it could go the other way."

"Anything's possible," Jax agreed, "but we'll give it our best shot."

Marlo gave him a twisted smile. "Yes sir, Captain sir. But why would the Gerin attack Dusa? It's practically all desert. Besides, Gloria has a huge supply dump and makes a better target."

Jax shrugged. "Beats the hell outta me, hon. Maybe the creeps want a suntan. But whatever it is they want, they ain't a-gonna get it."

Marlo nodded, but deep inside she wasn't so sure.

"It won't be easy," Koop said grimly, "But if you're willing to put in the time we can beat 'em."

Carolyn Heath nodded her agreement. She was willing to put in weeks if necessary. Lieutenant Koop was everything she'd hoped for and more. Koop was not only knowledgeable about computers, he was charming, and good-looking to boot.

Koop stood about six-two, wore his hair in the modified Mohawk favored by the navy, and filled his uniform quite nicely. Though he was handsome, a scar ran down across his right cheek, and saved him from being too pretty.

"So you agree that someone's stealing data?"

Koop nodded vigorously. "Damned right I do. And you were right. Someone's stealing data from a major subroutine. The one that handles supplies is my guess. What I don't understand is *why* your computer tracks naval supplies. I thought our computers handled that."

Carolyn smiled agreeably and hoped that he'd ask her out. If not, she'd ask him.

"You're right, Lieutenant. But *your* supplies are moved in and out of the depot by civilians working on contract through the port authority. We don't track your inventory, but we *do* track everything that comes and goes."

Koop frowned, his green eyes locking with her brown ones. "I fail to see the difference."

Suddenly it hit her. There *wasn't* any difference. If you knew every item that came and went you could easily figure out what stayed. And given the fact that the Felson Prime Mainframe was a good deal less secure than its military counterparts, it was an obvious target.

Carolyn felt something heavy drop into the pit of her stomach. Someone knew right down to the last pair of pliers what was stored in the League's supply depot. The question was, who? And why?

"You've got one on your tail!" Marlo rolled her fighter right and dumped hot chaff. The Gerin fell for it, fired his single plasma torpedo, and saw it explode in a flash of blinding light.

Marlo gritted her teeth, pulled back on the stick, and performed an Immelmann turn. As the Gerin fighter appeared in Marlo's sights she pressed the red button on top of the stick. The Gatling laser spat coherent energy and the alien ship came apart. Dark smoke and chunks of debris blew by as she passed through the space where the Gerin ship had been.

A quick check of her heads-up display showed a clean tail. Marlo looked for friendlies and bit her lip when she saw that only six were left. The battle had started in space, but bit by bit the Gerin had pushed the humans down into Dusa's atmosphere, and were winning the battle of attrition. Another ten or fifteen minutes and the contest would be over.

"Shit, Jax! I've got two of the bastards on my tail! Get 'em off! Get 'em off!"

"On the way, Norm . . . hang tight."

The sound of her husband's calm voice made Marlo's throat constrict as she pulled back on the stick and blasted upward. If Marlo was going to die, she'd do it with Jax at her side, and take some slimeballs with her. Up above she saw white contrails intertwine and connect in a flash of light.

"Got 'em!" Jax was jubilant as one alien fighter exploded and the other went down trailing smoke.

Then as Marlo pulled up beside him a woman's voice crackled over the radio. It was Kathi, or maybe her twin sister, Kate; Marlo couldn't tell the two of them apart. "Heads up, folks, it's raining slimeballs."

One glance told Marlo that the other woman was right. Another fifty or sixty Gerin fighters were on the way down. There were so many they filled her heads-up display.

"Form on me," Jax ordered gruffly. "You did a good job, everybody. Let's grease a few more on the way out."

As the five fighters obeyed, Marlo placed herself just off her husband's starboard wing, and bit back the tears as Jax gave her one last thumbs-up. She didn't want to die. She didn't want her children to die. The whole thing was so stupid.

Down below a long row of white mushroom clouds marched across Dusa's deserts. The bombing had started. The Gerin had won.

* * *

"That's a roger, we have full power on the board, with indicators in the green." Chiefy stood in front of *Hebe*'s main power control panel. All the indicator lights had just flickered from red to green. Gil might be a bit rough around the edges, but that sonovabitch sure knew his stuff!

All around him the ship came to life. Power pulsed through massive cables, light leaped down hair-thin fiberoptic filaments, air whispered through miles of ducts, and the deck began to vibrate beneath his feet. Weeks of work had paid off. *He* had a ship once more. *They* had a ship once more. Chiefy knew that somewhere, miles below, a man in a metal box would be extremely pleased.

Meanwhile, a thousand yards away, deep in the mechanical maze of *Hebe*'s drive room, Gil retrieved a half bottle of booze from his tool box. Grabbing a pair of dirty mugs, Gil poured a healthy dollop of whiskey into each, and handed one to Molly. She was his assistant, a onetime power tech herself, and to Gil's eye pleasingly plump.

Molly grinned as she held the mug aloft. "To the *Hebe*! May she outlive us all!"

"Dusa? The Gerin attacked Dusa? Whatever for?" Commodore Heath asked in disbelief. "The planet's nothing but sand."

"More like radioactive glass," Captain Sokolof corrected him. "The slimeballs were busy nuking the place as the message torp was launched."

"Damn!" Heath slammed his fist down so hard that his com set jumped. "Are they coming this way?"

"Not so far, sir . . . not according to our scouts."

"It figures," Heath said heavily. "Dusa was easy pickings, a couple of beat-up ships, and two or three flights of ground-based interceptors. They're afraid to tackle Gloria. They know we'd have 'em for lunch."

Sokolof wasn't so sure but nodded anyway. "Will we respond, sir?"

"Respond?" Heath demanded. "Hell yes, we'll respond! We'll find the slimy bastards and cancel their goddam ticket! What've we got?"

Sokolof leaned over Heath's desk and tapped a series of commands into the commodore's terminal. A color-coded list flooded the screen.

Heath mumbled as he read it. "Let's see . . . two transports . . . forget them . . . seven cruisers . . . and Kyro's orbiting mausoleum." Heath looked up from the screen and grinned. "Well, George, it isn't much, but it'll have to do. I'll leave you three cruisers to protect Gloria and take the rest with me."

Sokolof frowned. "With you, sir? With all due respect, your combat experience is, ah, somewhat limited, and—"

"That's enough!" Heath snapped, getting to his feet. "I may be lacking in experience, but my officers aren't and I'll be damned if I'll stay. Besides, if I can run entire planets, I can command a battle group."

"Yes, sir." Sokolof was careful to empty his face of all expression.

Heath came around the desk and put a hand on Sokolof's shoulder. "Don't take it so hard, George. Someday it'll be your turn to have all the fun."

"Yes, sir. Good hunting, sir."

Heath was halfway to the door when he stopped. "Oh, and send my apologies to Admiral Kryo. I'm afraid I'll miss the rechristening of his flying museum."

Sokolof noticed that his commanding officer looked anything but sorry. "I'm sure he'll understand, sir."

Commodore Heath waved and disappeared through the door.

Sokolof shook his head in amusement and lit a cigar. Once it was drawing to his satisfaction, he walked around the desk and sat in Heath's chair. *His* chair now that the commodore was gone.

Sokolof pulled the computer keyboard a little closer, frowned in concentration, and tapped in a series of numbers. A menu appeared. He requested a routine activity scan. The menu disappeared and a screenful of information came up to replace it.

His heart froze. There shouldn't be more than a line or two. Someone was tracing his way back to him through the subroutines!

Working quickly, Sokolof tapped in another code. This
brought up a new mask which demanded a new code.
This process was repeated three more times before the
last mask disappeared, and words PROGRAM RUN-
NING flashed on the screen.

Sokolof tapped some ash onto the immaculate surface
of the commodore's desk and leaned back in Heath's
chair. He felt mixed emotions. The trail was gone and
with it any chance of being caught. But someone had
been extremely close. Who?

Kyro didn't need eyes to know he was back in space.
He would've known without his sensors, without being
told, without any external information at all. The feeling
came from somewhere deep inside. A feeling of rightness
and completion which came only in space.

So as the shuttle rose through Gloria's atmosphere,
Kyro's spirits rose with it, and he was happier than he'd
been in a long, long time. He looked forward to the day
ahead.

Later there would be a formal rechristening, complete
with Heath and a bargeload of other dignitaries, but first
there would be a private party for those who had brought
the *Hebe* back to life.

As the shuttle approached, Kyro watched the main
screen. *Hebe* was about two miles long. A little tubbier
than the latest ships of her class, but less vulnerable, too,
thanks to a thicker hull. True, her nav comp, tac tank,
and electronic warfare systems were almost primitive by
modern standards, but in an all-out close-in brawl Kyro
would take the *Hebe* over younger ships.

The outer surface of the vessel's hull was covered with
antennas, cooling fins, weapons blisters, and countless
other installations. They gave the ship a rough, functional look.

But to Kyro the *Hebe* was a thing of beauty. Over the
years he'd approached sixteen other naval vessels in much
the same way, ultimately taking a part of the ship with
him, and leaving a part of himself behind. It was good
to meet a new friend.

The shuttle entered the ship's massive launching bay,

hovered for a moment, and dropped gently to the deck. The pilot, Lieutenant Commander Kathi Forney, League Navy retired, grandmother of three, twice decorated for valor, cut power and renewed her makeup.

Massive doors slid closed as atmosphere was pumped into the bay. During combat no such luxury would be allowed, but this was a ceremonial occasion, and everyone wanted to greet Kyro in the proper way.

When the bay was pressurized the crew entered and formed three ranks. The youngest were middle-aged and the oldest were pushing a hundred. Some uniforms were tight, some were loose, and some were brand-new. Boots shuffled, light gleamed off metal limbs, and servos whined as they dressed the ranks. But when Chiefy called them to attention, they stood ramrod-straight, proud of who they were, and what they'd done.

The shuttle's hatch whirred open, and as Admiral Kyro floated down the ramp, Chiefy piped him aboard. The high keening notes of his bosun's pipe sent a chill down Gil's spine as they bounced from one bulkhead to another. Then Chiefy stepped forward and snapped to attention. "Welcome aboard, sir."

"Welcome aboard, sir." As Heath stepped through the lock, Captain Janice Yakamura was there to greet him. She hardly reached his shoulder, but her doll-like face was hard and determined. Heath was well acquainted with her quick mind and aggressive attitude. In fact, Yakamura was the reason he'd chosen to put his flag aboard her cruiser. She'd make up for his inexperience, and if something happened to him, then God help anything that got in her way.

As they headed for the bridge, Heath said, "Thank you for your quick response, Captain. We haven't got much time. You read the intelligence summary?"

Yakamura nodded. Her shorter legs were taking two steps for every one of his. "Yes, sir. The slimeballs waxed our ass."

Heath smiled, suddenly reminded of Carolyn. She'd be furious when she found out that he'd gone into space. "A colorful way to put it . . . but essentially correct. Get us there in a hurry.''

"Yes, sir. We'll be in hyperspace fifteen minutes from now. A few hours after that we'll downwarp off Dusa, find the greasy bastards, and send 'em to hell.''

True to Yakamura's word, the battle group broke orbit five minutes later, entered the acceleration phase eight minutes after that, and upwarped right on time.

"Hyperspace. I said your father's in hyperspace." The voice belonged to Miss Woods, her father's administrative assistant.

Carolyn swore, causing Miss Woods to gasp and Lieutenant Koop to grin. He knew Carolyn rather well by now, and nothing would surprise him, least of all a little swearing.

"All right, Miss Woods, thank you." Carolyn pushed a button and turned to Koop.

"The Gerin attacked Dusa and Daddy went after them. I'm worried. Daddy's a reserve officer and doesn't have the faintest idea how to fight a space battle."

"Well, his officers do," Koop replied. "Besides, I'll be surprised if the Gerin are still there when your father arrives."

Carolyn raised an eyebrow.

Koop shrugged. "I wouldn't be."

"So what now?"

Koop smiled in the lazy sort of way which led some people to underestimate his abilities. "So now we handle the problem ourselves."

"Report." La'seek wore a pressure suit, and along with his two warrior apprentices was pacing back and forth across the now empty conference pool. The water had been vacuumed up and stored in preparation for the coming battle. Dry now, the rocks looked like those which lined the beaches of La'seek's native planet.

"Most of the humans are on their way to Dusa," Wa'neck replied carefully. "The way is clear."

La'seek believed him but was nervous nevertheless. The strike force was a long way from home and the possibility of reinforcements. What if the spy had lied? What if Gloria was a well-prepared trap?

"How many ships?" La'seek inquired, hoping Wa'neck would miss the stiffness of his movements.

"Three cruisers, the decommissioned dreadnought, two transports, and a variety of small craft."

Inside his pressure suit La'seek turned green with relief. His strike force of ten globeships would eradicate the vermin and he would gain command of an entire fleet! He waved a talk tentacle in the other Gerin's direction. "Well done, Warrior Wa'neck. You may attack."

"Information," Koop said calmly. "Information which you've been stealing. That's what this is all about, Captain Sokolof. Miss Heath here found a data drain in the Felson Prime Mainframe. And guess what? We had just run into a huge dead end when you came on-line, detected our presence, and scrubbed the program.

"Once we realized what you were doing it was easy to put a tracer on your activity and follow it back to the commodore's terminal."

Koop nodded toward Carolyn. "Miss Heath here had a bad moment when it looked like her father was to blame, but a quick check showed that *he* was on his way to the spaceport at the critical moment, and *you* were sitting at his desk. Captain Sokolof, you are under arrest."

Sokolof lounged behind his desk, a smile on his face, apparently unconcerned. "I'm afraid you're mistaken, Lieutenant. And while I usually have time for misguided junior officers and hysterical young women, I'm a bit rushed at the moment. It seems that some errant slimeballs are coming our way. Lieutenant Koop, I strongly suggest that you report to your planetary defense station, and Miss Heath, I think you'd be better off in a shelter."

Moving casually, Sokolof opened a desk drawer and reached toward the box of cigars prominently displayed within. Instead, Sokolof's hand went for the small hand blaster hidden toward the back of the drawer, and got it halfway out before Koop's slugs smashed through his chest and into his chair. Sokolof slumped forward, and his head hit the desk with a loud thump. The chair's hydraulics sighed and adjusted to his new position.

"Position three, grid four, sector fourteen, I have six, make that seven, make that seven plus unidentified ships dropping hyper. Standard query brings no code. Repeat, no code. I have a nine point nine match to Gerin formations and tactics. Recommend scramble all units. Repeat, scramble—"

"And that's where the transmission ended, Admiral," Chiefy said, addressing the metal cube. "We think the message came from a courier ship which was in the wrong place at the wrong time. Our long-range detectors confirm ten globeships headed this way."

Kyro was silent for a moment. "You say most of the fleet's gone?"

"Yes, sir. We didn't think much of it at the time, but Sparks, he likes to listen in, heard a lot of code, and all of a sudden four cruisers broke orbit. They went hyper a few minutes later."

"What's left?"

"Three cruisers, two transports, and a few odds and ends."

"Give me the senior captain."

Because he was retired, Kyro had less authority than the lowest enlisted personnel, but he hoped they'd talk with him at the very least.

"Aye, aye, sir." A moment passed and Chiefy was back. "I've got the *Mandela*'s commanding officer on the horn, sir—she just broke orbit. Morgan's her name."

Kyro turned an optical pickup toward the comm screen. He saw a middle-aged woman who wore the comets of a commander and a rather grim expression. She spoke first.

"No offense, Admiral, but there's big trouble on the way, so I hope this is something more than a social call."

Kyro laughed, the sound strangely metallic as it came out of his speech synthesizer. "No, Captain, it isn't social. We wondered if we could help."

"You've got some functional weapons aboard that tub?"

Kyro swiveled a pickup toward Chiefy. He nodded in the affirmative.

Kyro looked back to the comm set. "Yes. The *Hebe* has the normal complement of weapons for a ship of her type."

This was not strictly true, since they were still waiting for some spare parts, but Chiefy had no intention of correcting him. The *Hebe*'s weapons systems were an 87 percent "go," and that's more than a lot of line ships could boast.

Morgan shook her head in amazement. "All right, Admiral. We can use all the help we can get. We're all going. Scouts, a minelayer, even a tug. We'll do our best to slow 'em down and break up their formation. You keep 'em off the planet."

"I understand and will obey," Kyro replied formally. "Good luck, Captain. *Hebe* out."

Kyro was already turning to Chiefy as the comm screen snapped to black. "Sound action stations, Chief."

"Aye, aye, sir!" Chiefy replied with a grin. His hand hit a large red disk and a klaxon went off.

Down on the messdeck two hundred heads looked up all at once. They'd been sitting there enjoying the refreshments and talking about old times. The klaxon was a mistake or someone's idea of a joke. They looked at each other and laughed.

Then Chiefy's voice came over the intercom. "This is *not* a drill. I repeat, this is *not* a drill. We have incoming Gerin globeships. All crew members report to battle stations. Repeat, all crew members report to battle stations."

Someone said, "Oh, shit," and they all started to run. And as they ran, the klaxon continued to sound, pumping adrenaline into aging minds and bodies.

Most didn't think, they didn't have to, they just responded to a lifetime of drills, heading for whatever duty station they knew best. And if that one was manned, they sought another, until they found an open position.

Visiting dignitaries were herded into empty slots, where they were instructed to "shut up, sit down, and for gawdsakes don't touch anything."

Up on the bridge Lieutenant Commander Kathi Forney had the con. Her seat was extended and almost horizontal. Wires ran from her helmet and command gauntlet into the ship's nav comp and gave her control of the ship.

Forney's mind was everywhere, darting through long strings of numbers, gliding over drive readouts, and caressing the ship's weapons systems. She'd been a stone-cold killer once, a brilliant pilot, a fierce competitor. And under the white hair and wrinkled skin she still was. She had grandchildren down below, and if the slimeballs wanted Gloria, they'd have to kill her to get it.

"Report." Kyro snapped the word out and listened as section leaders reported in.

Gil's voice was strong and clear. "Power section closed up and ready, sir."

Kyro recognized the next voice as that of Gunny Norvus. Like his own the Gunny's voice was synthesized. "Weapons section closed up and ready, sir. We're eighty-seven percent on weapons, eighty percent on personnel, and ready to kick some ass."

Kyro smiled inside himself. "Thank you, Gunny. Medical?"

"Medical closed up and ready, sir."

And so it went until all departments were accounted for. Kyro thought about what these men and women had given before, and what they were ready to give again, and he felt a tremendous sense of pride.

"Thank you, everyone. If the Gerin think Gloria's a pushover, they'll soon know differently. Chiefy, plug me in."

Having been warned a few minutes before, Chiefy was ready. He had already connected two cables to the ship's tac comp, so it was a simple matter to plug them into Kyro's life-support box.

As Chiefy made the connections, Kyro suddenly understood why cyborg pilots are considered the very, very best. Suddenly he and the ship were a single entity. He felt himself expand to fill every circuit in the ship's vast network of electronics.

It was like having a body again, only better. Every sensor was his, every readout an additional source of information for his brain, every crew member a subprocessor on which he could depend.

He sensed which weapons were manned and which were on automatic, he left Forney gliding in and around him as she pulled the ship out of orbit, he knew that Gil's pulse was 120, and he winced when one of Morgan's ships vanished in a flash of light.

The light was just disappearing off the main screen when La'seek began to wonder if something was wrong. He pointed a talk tantacle at the green dot in *Sea Storm*'s tac tank, the one which was just breaking orbit. "What's that?"

Wa'neck wished that La'seek would shut up and allow him to carry out his duties, but knew such hopes were in vain, and felt his skin turn an angry red. Fortunately La'seek couldn't see through Wa'neck's spacesuit and take offense.

"Probably just a transport trying to run."

"Oh, really?" La'Seek asked. "Then why is it coming *toward* us, rather than running away?"

Wa'neck took a closer look. He forced himself to be civil. "You are right, of course. It's the dreadnought our spy spoke of."

"A dreadnought which was decommissioned, 'little more than a hulk,' you said. Why would a hulk come straight at us?"

"Perhaps they intend to ram," Wa'neck said defensively. "Who cares? We will destroy them long before they are close enough to do any damage."

"I'm pleased to hear it," La'seek answered coldly, "But remember, it is written that in the tentacles of warriors, worn out tools have accomplished many things."

Like a blade. That's how Commander Morgan cut through the Gerin formation, splitting them in two, and forcing them out and away from the planet.

All three of her cruisers launched fighters, the Gerin did likewise, and before long a complicated dogfight developed with both sides giving and taking death. The humans were terribly outnumbered, but they had fewer cruisers to defend, and were driven by desperation. All of them know what *had* happened to Dusa and *would* happen to Gloria if the Gerin got through.

Meanwhile the larger ships had gone straight for the heart of the Gerin strike force. The tug had vanished almost immediately, quickly followed by the minelayer, and a cruiser. The cruiser had done well, taking two globeships with her, but that still left eight of the alien ships to Morgan's two.

Morgan fought like a demon, ignoring conventional strategy, twisting and turning through an intricate maze of lethal energy, taking hit after hit as she fought the globeships.

She watched with a lump in her throat as a small scout ship made its way through a rainbow of energy beams and hurled itself against a globeship's force field. It vanished in a flower of light and left the alien vessel untouched.

Then Morgan saw it, the Gerin command vessel, no larger than the rest but conspicuous by its location at the center of their formation.

She gritted her teeth as her second cruiser was snuffed from existence and gave the order to attack. All around her lights flashed red and orange, systems went down, and people screamed.

Morgan smelled smoke, and suddenly realized there was something wrong with her legs. They wouldn't move. Maybe it had something to do with all that blood.

There was an atmosphere leak around someplace, but it must be a small one, because Morgan's suit was holed and she could still breathe. Someone was talking, asking her questions, making demands.

Morgan looked at her pilot, and found that *he* was looking at *her*. "Where to, skipper?"

Morgan gave him a lopsided grin. "Straight down their throats, Lieutenant. Straight down their throats."

Kyro watched Morgan's ship go in. For a while it looked as though she would hit the Gerin command vessel, but at the last moment another globeship moved in to block the way, and together they made a sun.

"Well done, Captain Morgan, well done," Kyro said within the vast complexity of his expanded mind. Four of the alien ships remained, and they were his.

Kyro left the piloting to Forney, using his interface with the ship to plot strategy and devise tactics. He had little time to do either, because with Morgan gone, the enemy ships had arrived, and were throwing everything they had in the *Hebe*'s direction.

The dreadnought's screens flared under the massive bombardment, but held. Energy weapons spit bolts of blue destruction, plasma torpedoes whispered through tubes, and smaller missiles flashed outward seeking warmth.

First one, then another Gerin ship flashed incandescent, and disappeared from *Hebe*'s screens.

Then two Gerin plasma torpedoes hit within seconds of each other. The resulting explosion pushed the *Hebe*'s defensive screens in so far that they almost touched the hull. Everything more than six inches high was suddenly exposed.

That's when the Gerin fighters moved in for the kill. They came in overwhelming numbers, energy weapons spitting lethal light, torpedoes accelerating inward at awesome speeds.

Unprotected by defensive screens, a section of *Hebe*'s weapons blisters vanished in the twinkling of an eye, while a row of cooling fins sagged into molten slag.

Down in the drive room Gil swore as red lights began to flash and klaxons began to hoot. The Gerin had destroyed 30 percent of the ship's cooling capacity! He and Molly were already stripped to the waist, but sweat was pouring off their bodies. In a little while they'd start losing people to heat prostration.

Molly touched the tiny receiver to her ear. It was hard to hear over the klaxons. "The Admiral wants more power to the screens! The slimeballs are breaking through!"

Gil's stubby fingers tapped a quick tattoo on his keyboard. Power which had been going to *Hebe*'s drives and energy weapons went to the ship's defensive screens. The screens flared outward and a cheer went up over the intercom.

The cheer was little more than distant static to Kyro. His mind was full of interception vectors, tac ratios, ship readouts, and enemy intelligence. One of 132 different weapons counters began to flash on and off in a corner of his mind. The *Hebe* was running out of torpedoes.

"It's time to withdraw," La'seek said sadly. "The battle is over. Even if we beat this museum piece we don't have enough ships left to destroy the ground defenses. 'Ripe for the plucking' I think you said, Wa'neck? The fruit is somewhat stubborn, is it not?"

Wa'neck didn't answer. His spirit was heavy with shame and his mind full of death.

La'seek turned violet in resignation. He turned to the pilot. "Warn the others. We upwarp in fifteen breathings."

Gunny Norvus died when an overloaded junction box exploded and hurled hot schrapnel all over the fire control center. A large piece of metal casing took his head off and splattered the room with blood.

Weapons Tech Sonny Baktu wiped the blood off his face, murmured a short prayer, and took control of the automated weapons systems. It was a complicated version of the computer games he'd played as a kid.

Choose an unmanned weapon, take it off auto, and pick a target. Wait for a delta-shaped fighter to enter the screen like so, line up the cross grid, and pulse the weapon. Presto! Cooked slimeball! Baktu grinned. "Hang around for a while, Gunny, and I'll send you some more!"

"Now!" On Kyro's command the last of the torpedoes and a host of smaller missiles left their tubes and accelerated toward the command ship.

Many exploded harmlessly as they were intercepted by fighters or antimissile missiles, but three, a plasma torpedo and two missiles, got through and exploded against the other ship's forcefield.

By chance all three went off at the same time. The

combined explosion drove that section of the globeship's forcefield into overload and created a small hole.

The hole existed for only a fraction of a second, but that was long enough for an energy beam to slip through and punch a hole in the vessel's hull. As luck would have it the hole was centered over the command and control compartment. There was a moment of intense heat followed by explosive decompression. La'seek and Wa'neck never knew what hit them.

Seconds later the last globeship disappeared into hyperspace, and in spite of the fact that fully a third of the dreadnought's crew were dead or wounded, there was cheering on the *Hebe*'s intercom.

Kyro sounded tired as he said, "The Gerin left a lot of their fighters behind. Watch 'em, and check for casualties. Well done, everyone."

Twenty-six hours later the ship was empty—empty, that is, except for Admiral Kyro. By then Heath had returned with enough ships to protect the planet, the last of the Gerin fighters had been rounded up, and the casualties had been taken dirtside.

At his own request Kyro had stayed behind. He was still plugged in, still aware of the ship, still in command. If the Gerin returned he would know and give the alarm. In the meantime he snuggled deeper into the warmth of his metal flesh and gave a sigh of satisfaction. He was whole again.

The Battle of the Rift Nebula

Hundreds of minor skirmishes continued as the Gerin were gradually driven back into their own systems. In the open reaches of space you fight only if both sides wish to. Normally this means that battles occur in systems where one of the combatants is forced to fight. The Battle of Olympus was such a situation. League forces managed to subject the attacking Gerin ships to severe losses, at the cost of fifty thousand civilian casualties, a major supply dump, and an orbital fleet repair station.

An exception to the pattern was the Battle of the Rift Nebula. Bowing to pressure to minimize civilian casualties, Mac changed his policy of meeting Gerin intrusions with overwhelming resistance. After a careful study of the Gerin, it was determined that the fleet would set up a major location on the fringes of the Gerin home region. This should result in a major response from the Gerin, possibly a pitched battle. Although this meant Mac would be giving up the advantage of fighting in friendly space, it moved the war a step closer to where Mac wanted to be fighting—on Gerin Prime. It was a major chance, gaining the initiative for the first time, but leaving over a hundred worlds only lightly protected.

The location within the Rift Nebula was chosen because any approaching Gerin fleets would either have to warp in within close proximity of the base or travel at relatively slow rates through the clutter surrounding the area. The warping in would inevitably result in confusion and ragged formations. Approaching slowly would provide extra time to prepare to meet them. Finally, should the battle go badly, the nebula would provide extra cover for the retreating League fleet. There were no planets in the system; this would be a space battle. It would involve the type of combat the Gerin were best at. The result was far from a foregone conclusion.

The battle actually occurred in three phases. Before any fighting began, Mac ordered a number of preparations to be made. The first phase began when, as predicted, a Gerin force of over a hundred ships approached through the nebular cloud. The Gerin were met by a force four times their size and wisely withdrew after a short, intense fighter combat. Mac restrained the pursuit, saving his ships for the larger battle he knew would follow.

The second phase consisted of a hit-and-run raid by the Gerin. Four Gerin carriers warped in almost within the human fleet itself. Each carrier dropped thirty fighters and then tried to warp away again. So great was their surprise that two escaped unscathed. The fighters then dived suicidally at the nearer League ships, firing as they approached and exploding on contact. Well timed and executed, this enemy raid resulted in the loss of over a dozen cruisers and shook everyone's confidence.

Three days later the Gerin fleet appeared in strength. We were later to learn that it included virtually every combat-ready ship left in their empire. They approached cautiously, correctly judging that they were superior in numbers.

Mac made no speech about the importance of victory or the consequences of defeat, as he had in earlier battles. Every ship he commanded was gathered. Defeat would ensure the slaughter of billions of humans and allied aliens. In place of a speech, each combat screen and trivid monitor ran a silent series of images—DuQuesne, New Athens, Lyra, and the other worlds devastated by Gerin attacks. On some ships men roared themselves to a fighting pitch; on others the memories of what they had lost were met with determined silence.

As they emerged into the open space at the center of the nebula the Gerin fleet unfolded into a near-perfect circle one ship deep. The formation was designed to take the greatest advantage of their superior numbers. If the League fleet expanded to meet the approaching wave of ships, they would be spread much less densely and outgunned at every point. If the humans maintained a similar density, their fleet would be flanked on all of its edges.

Mac chose to do neither of the expected things. Instead he ordered the heaviest ships to gather on one flank. Then, to the astonishment of virtually everyone, the admiral ordered a slow retrograde by his entire force. This new formation gave the human ships a distinct advantage in the area where they were concentrated. It also meant that the bulk of the Gerin fleet would be met by a much less thickly deployed line of more lightly armed ships.

Finally, with a single word, Mac halted the retreat. Less than a minute later both sides launched their fighters. Again the combat computers tallied the sides and found the humans badly outnumbered. Still everyone was shocked when before they even met the enemy, Mac ordered the fighters to return and cover the battle line. Harsh words were needed to convince the contingent crewed mostly by New Athenian survivors to obey. Even then several of the highly individualistic D'Tarth and Leassei allies continued on to meet the enemy.

The questioning covert glances on his own bridge told Mac what everyone had to be wondering. Had he lost his nerve? His expression unreadable, Mac waited until the first of the Gerin fighters entered into beam range and then ordered most of thousands of neutron mines he had placed days earlier ignited. For a moment almost too brief to be seen, the space occupied by the Gerin fighters glowed brighter than the stars at the nebula's heart. Hundreds of Gerin fighters, and those of the League allies who had failed to obey his earlier orders, were caught in waves of deadly radiation. Dead tentacles at their helms, most of the Gerin fighters either self-destructed or were blasted easily as they approached the League formation. For the first time in anyone's memory, Mac smiled.

Even after the loss of the bulk of their fighters, the Gerin still outnumbered and outgunned the League ships. The Gerin had been hurt, but not so badly that they could not crush or cripple the fleet facing them. Now the heavies began to come into range. Mac had hurt them, and many expected the admiral to order a general retreat before his forces were trapped in combat. Instead, he actually ordered the reinforced wing forward. Why he did this became apparent as every few seconds yet more mines exploded in front of the weaker flank of the League fleet. Not so many this time, but enough to slow or stop the attacking Gerin. Every few seconds more mines exploded, effectively denying the League's weaker flank. At the same time, the League heavies and fighters threw themselves against the end of the Gerin formation.

Before the aliens could reorganize and swing to reinforce their own threatened flank, it had been scattered and destroyed. Then the still closely packed League ships turned and began to roll up the rest of the Gerin formation. No longer superior in numbers and still unable to attack the weakened forces to their front, the Gerin navy broke apart. Hundreds were destroyed in the pursuit.

Within weeks, League forces had begun landing on the planets within the Gerin empire.

GRENADIER
by Rick Shelley

THE smash-and-run went exactly as planned, rare as that is. Our two cruisers dropped out of FTL space, closer to the world than the book allows, and launched their shuttles before engaging the one Gerin ship in orbit around Grenadier. Two companies of marines landed near the only Gerin complex on the surface, engaged in a short firefight, and made an effort to grab prisoners— an effort that ultimately failed . . . exactly as planned. Our forces suffered relatively light casualties. The marines returned to their shuttles and rendezvoused with the cruisers above, which bugged out as quickly as they had arrived.

Our role was different. We came down hot. It was meant to look as if our shuttle had been damaged and was going to crash—several klicks east of the Gerin base, safe from direct ground observation. With a fight going on upstairs, we hoped that no one on the Gerin ship would notice the deception. The way we slewed to a stop, I thought we were going to pile up for real. But I started shouting out our deployment sequence and we hopped out of the shuttle before it came to a stop. I hurried the men off into the jungle, out of sight and away from the shuttle. Captain Ebersoll was the last man out. We couldn't afford to have a navy jockey tagging along, so the captain had flown the bird in himself. As he ran clear of the shuttle, explosive charges went off. Fire and explosion: the engineers had also rigged smoke pots, and we had been leaving a smoke trail on the way down.

"We got everyone, Sergeant Teel?" the captain asked when he caught up with the rest of us.

"Aye, sir."

"Let's move out before somebody comes looking."

We moved north, scrambling through two klicks of moderately thick jungle in twenty-five minutes, damn good time for soldiers loaded down with double their usual quota of gear. Most of the trees had large hanging fronds. Something about them irritated skin on contact. We finally went to ground in a muddy gully to wait for the raid to end. I posted sentries and warned everyone not to use the radio or active sensors. When everyone was set, I took a long look around our position myself—using all the electronics I carry—to make sure that we weren't sitting in the lap of the enemy. Then I went to sit in the mud with the captain. We listened to the battle talk over the radio net.

It wasn't that long a wait. I switched off my receiver and took off my helmet after the shuttles docked with the cruiser. There would be no farewell message to us.

"That's it, Captain," I whispered. "We're on our own."

He nodded and slipped his helmet visor up out of the way. "Make sure everyone's full power-down," he said in a tired voice that might scare anyone who hadn't been in action with him before. Once we hit the dirt, the captain always sounds like he's ready to collapse from exhaustion.

"Aye, Captain." The first thing I did was check my own controls. Then I went to work on the captain's. He shook his head and chuckled.

"Okay, Ducks," he said, resigned. The start of a mission is sometimes a little tense. You need to be up for it, but not wound too tight. I winked, relieved that we weren't going to start out on the wrong foot. The captain is one of the few men in the regiment I don't mind calling me Ducks. He's earned the right over and over in the years we've served together. I've never been able to shuck the nickname, but most people just use it behind my back. I gave up explaining that my name is spelled T-E-*E*-L, not T-E-*A*-L, before I got out of school. It never helped anyway, and using fists to get my point across got old even before that.

"You check Bravo Squad. I'll take Alpha. We'll finish faster that way," the captain said when I finished checking his switches.

I grinned and nodded. That gave us each eight men to check. The captain and I handpicked the two recon squads. There wasn't a man on the team who hadn't been a combat veteran before the war with the Gerin started. The war changed life for us, though. When news reached our home base on Carthage that the Gerin had slaughtered a million-plus civilians on DuQuesne, Colonel Gregory mustered the entire regiment and made a speech. Afterward, he put the question to a vote and the regiment voted overwhelmingly to enlist en masse under Admiral Mac for the duration. We went from being mercenaries to being part of Mac's forces, but still as a separate regiment. Sure, there was a lot of "loyalty to our kind" and thirst for revenge in the vote, but that wasn't nearly all there was to it. We were *professionals*. War was our business. But it didn't take much for most of us to see that we couldn't do business as usual while the war with the Gerin was going on.

"Sarge, why the hell we totin' all this gear if we can't use it?" Ace Reynolds asked when I checked his switches.

"You'd be out of uniform without it," was my first reaction. I've been a noncom too long. "We'll be using it soon enough," I added. It was all covered in our briefings and drills, but I went ahead and repeated the line. "We don't want the Gerin to know we're here. They'll be monitoring for electronic signatures now, looking to pick up anyone left from the raid." I pitched my voice just loud enough that most of the team would hear. I didn't want to have to repeat myself.

"Maybe we should be looking for stragglers too," Liri said.

"No way!" the captain said. The way Liri spun around,

he hadn't realized that the captain was so close. "Any strays are on their own."

We finished the power check quickly. "Okay, Liri, you've got the point," the captain told him. "You know how to get us to those caves?"

"If we're where we're supposed to be now, I'll get us there," he said.

"We're right on the money," the captain said. "Move out. We want to be inside before dark."

We used most of the afternoon reaching the caves we had chosen from the mapboards on the *Cardigan*. The survey team that first explored Grenadier did a first-rate mapping job. Liri, and Jacobs in Alpha Squad, had been on the survey team. That's always been one of the regiment's sidelines, finding and surveying new worlds. Sometimes that gets even hairier than combat.

The cave entrance was nearly two meters wide, but barely high enough to crawl through without taking off our packs. Liri and I went in first.

"Don't switch on your visor until we're inside," I told him. The limestone and dirt would block any Gerin scanners, even if they were locked right on the cave formation.

"I'm not happy about sticking my head in a hole without knowing what's in there," Liri said.

"You think I am?" I asked.

We slithered in for nearly three meters before the cave opened up enough to let us stand. That first chamber was only about six meters in diameter, but it would do. Two narrow passages led deeper, but exploration could wait. At least the cave didn't seem to be inhabited by anything large enough to contest occupancy with us.

"Stay here," I told Liri. "Rig a baffle behind the entrance. A couple of field blankets. Then you can light a candle." I crawled back out to let the captain know that the place would do. We started the others moving inside. After the captain was sliding in, I grabbed Ace Reynolds and Purl Jacobs and stayed out till the end.

"You two set up in the entrance," I told them. "You've got the first watch. Passive scans only."

The cave wasn't all that homey, but it would do for the time we needed it, once we exterminated the little nippers that infested it. We had electric candles for light and didn't even have to worry too much about keeping quiet. We settled in to wait. This time for three days.

"Let's take a look at the mapboard, Ian," the captain said as soon as I got back inside after posting our sentries. He rarely calls me Ducks when there are others around. He knows I'm sensitive about it.

"Right, Cap. Let me get people looking around first." I grabbed two guys to check each of the passages leading out the back of the room—we couldn't leave them forever, and one would have to be designated latrine before much longer—then I went back to the captain. He was sitting against a wall, mapboard on his knees. I dropped my pack and sat on it, close enough to see what we had to work with.

"The new pictures look good," he said.

A mapboard is a dedicated computer with a flatscreen monitor that folds to make it convenient to carry. You can start with a view of the whole world as it appears from space, clear as looking out a ship's port, showing rotation and everything, then zoom in to the most detailed scale available for that world. The original survey of Grenadier gave us 1.5-meter detail for all landmasses. Coming in this time, the mapboards were netted into the ranging and navigation systems of all the shuttles to give us updates and more detail. I watched while the captain scrolled around the area of the Gerin complex and out to where we were hiding.

"Looks like seventy-five-centimeter resolution for almost the whole area," I said after a few minutes. Only a few small strips still showed the lighter shading of 1.5 meter. "That should make it a little easier for us."

"If anything can," the captain said softly.

I got out my own mapboard and slaved it to his. I was getting a crick in my neck looking over the captain's shoulder. The Gerin had one large concrete building, single-story, right on the water's edge at the back of a tiny cove on the western coast. The cove was fed by a shallow small river and by a couple of even smaller creeks. There was one gun emplacement at the ocean end of the cove and another back by the building, both right down by the high-water marks.

"You'd think they never heard of high ground," I mumbled.

"They must have it staked out somehow," the captain said. "Observation posts, weapons, even if it's just automatic systems."

We had plenty of time to examine the new shots on the mapboard, and we eventually spotted a couple of points on the slopes upstream, automated gun emplacements. And one strip of underbrush along the river and the south side of the cove had been cleared and leveled for use as a landing strip. We'd known about that coming in. The raiding party had been warned against damaging it.

"They can't have much of a force here, Captain," I said after we spent several hours on the mapboards. "Maybe no more than a half-dozen triads on the ground now, after the raid." About as many of them as us.

"Don't get any wild ideas, Ian. We're not here to capture Grenadier all by our lonesome, and don't forget, they've got a ship overhead."

"I know, Cap, but still . . ."

"But nothing. You know what we're here for."

"Aye, sir." I knew *what* we were there for, that is, what we were supposed to *do*, but I sure as hell didn't know *why*. The captain didn't either. Our briefings carefully skirted any mention of motive. I could see that. What we didn't know we couldn't be forced to tell if we were captured. Stripped of all the dotting-of-i's and crossing-of-t's that a full briefing includes, we were to set up observation points and keep out of sight, monitor Gerin activities, learn whatever we could about how they did things, and try to discover what they were doing on Grenadier. Intelligence had several guesses and hoped we'd provide the raw data to remove the question marks. Was Grenadier merely a resort for some Gerin warlord? Was it being set up as an R&R facility? Was some important conference going to take place there? Or was it something else, maybe something so alien that our people couldn't even guess at it?

That was the *what*. The *why* had to be extremely important—at least to the staff-level geniuses who'd dreamed up the operation. To cut loose two cruisers from a fleet that never had enough ships as it was and risk them on a raid that was only cover to drop eighteen of us into the jungle behind the Gerin . . . well, I *hoped* it was for something more important than to settle a bet between a couple of intelligence analysts.

One other topic was carefully avoided during our briefings, the question of when we would be picked up. We were carrying food for six weeks, if we stretched it, but nothing had been said about how close to that limit, or how far beyond it, we might have to go. Another safeguard, I guess, and not for us. If someone was captured and forced to talk, knowing when our pickup was due would give the Gerin a chance to ambush the ships that came in. I don't *think* that Colonel Gregory would send us in without definite plans to retrieve us. A mercenary doesn't waste men like that. I hoped the colonel was still thinking like a merc.

Seventy-two standard hours after we entered the cave, Bravo Squad was back outside ready to march again. Because of Grenadier's shorter day, it was dawn rather than late afternoon.

"See you at pickup, Cap," I said before I crawled out to join the squad.

"Don't be late." He hesitated a moment, then stuck out a hand and we shook. We had served together a lot of years. He had gone from cadet lieutenant to captain while I climbed from corporal to company lead sergeant. The handshake was an admission that this might be the last time we'd be together. I didn't like the feeling it gave me.

"We'll be three hours behind you, Ducks," the captain said. I just nodded. That was safer than talking. The time lag wasn't anything major. Bravo Squad simply had farther to travel to get into position. We had the south side of the cove. The captain was taking Alpha Squad along the north side—where the Gerin building and our cave were. If we had to do any fighting when our ships came back, Alpha would tackle the barracks, or whatever it was, and Bravo would secure the landing strip for our shuttles.

After I crawled out of the cave, I stood up and stretched as far as I could. It felt good to be outside after three days in the cave. My muscles were cramped from being in the damp and unable to move around freely for so long. I started Ace on point and we went upstream for a klick, farther away from the Gerin, before we turned right, south. If we happened to be spotted—not that it was very likely while we were so far off and not moving toward the Gerin post—I didn't want to give away the location of our cave. That wasn't entirely because Alpha squad was still inside. We might need to use the cave again before we got off Grenadier.

By the time we made our second turn, back west toward the ocean, I had decided that I didn't much care for Grenadier, Gerin or no Gerin. All the native animals had too many legs. It looked like bugs were the evolutionary progenitors of everything that moved. Even the birds had six or eight legs. The original survey of Grenadier hadn't gone into much detail about animals. The sightings the team made had been listed, but there was no systematic inventory. And we sure didn't have time now. We couldn't be sure which animals were dangerous and which weren't. That meant that we had to use weapons several times.

"Beamers only," I warned. "And no skying a shot, nothing that shows above the trees." There was still a chance of discovery, but unless the Gerin were still actively searching for people left behind after the raid, they wouldn't be scanning close enough to get the backwash of our helmet electronics or the odd beamer flash. The garrison was too small. But we couldn't risk slugthrowers. Those can echo for kilometers, and there's no mistaking them for something else, not on an undeveloped planet like Grenadier.

Liri was on point when we reached the river that led down to the cove. The river made me nervous, even though we were fifteen kilometers from the Gerin post. Water was one place where the Gerin had us hands, or tentacles, down. Amphibs. They were as much at home in water as on land, more so, according to some reports.

"It's not deep," Liri said. I nodded. This far above the cove, the mapboard didn't show anything deeper than a meter. It wasn't much deeper than that at the mouth.

"There's nothing close bigger'n a mackerel," Ace said after he dropped a monitor in the stream.

Still, we crossed in two elements. I wanted some of us on dry ground all the time. Liri took his fire team across first. I followed with Ace and the other team. We got across and moved on.

Hiking wet is miserable, but the next hour gave us time to dry out as much as we were likely to. We were almost on Grenadier's equator. The day was hot and humid. We did a lot of sweating.

"Must be a law against fighting a war where it's comfortable," Ace whispered when we took five beyond the next low ridgeline, after making our turn west. Ace's mouth ran too much at the wrong times. That was why he was still a corporal instead of a platoon sergeant, though he was as qualified as any man in the regiment otherwise. He liked to brag about it when he was drinking. "I wise off enough to keep 'em from promoting me, but not enough so's they got to bust. I like it where I am just fine." When I mentioned that to the captain, he laughed and said he had a mind to promote Ace just to prove him wrong.

Liri tapped me on the shoulder and pointed to the pocket where I keep my mapboard. I pulled it out. Liri unfolded it and zoomed the controls down in a hurry, putting our position at one edge of the board and the Gerin base at the other. He drew his finger along the screen, tracing a route toward where we wanted to go. Then he raised his hand, flipping the palm to make it a question. I nodded. Liri didn't talk when he didn't have to on an operation. He was already on the list for platoon sergeant, next opening in the company. With a big war on, that probably wouldn't be long.

Hiis took the point after our second break, a couple of hours later. We had a low ridge between us and the river.

We were getting close to the cove. Not long after we started up with Hiis in front, he stopped and brought his fist up quickly. The rest of us froze in place, weapons at the ready, senses cranked up as we looked for telltales on our helmet visors. There was no sign of Gerin or anything else, but I waited for Hiis to work his way back to me. He pointed at the ground five meters past where he had stopped. I needed a minute to see what he had spotted—something like a small pipe sticking up about four centimeters. I looked around to make sure that everyone was paying attention, then brought a hand up to the side of my head, thumb over my ear, little finger over my eye, so they would know why we had stopped. I used hand signs to get everyone to look around to make sure that we hadn't walked into the middle of a full spotter array.

I didn't know how sensitive Gerin equipment was. *Our* perimeter monitors can pick up the vibration of a single footstep ten meters off, and the cameras transmit visible and infrared pictures.

Hiis tapped me on the shoulder, then put his hand to the sides of his eyes like blinders and looked down toward the creek. Then he put his hand over his ears, angled the same way, and mouthed, *Directional pickup.* I nodded even though it didn't make much sense.

When nobody found any other spotters, I pointed Hiis off at an angle, above the spotter he found. That took us off the animal track we had been following, but slow progress through the bush was better than announcing ourselves to the Gerin. Once we were far enough above the spotter to be safe, I passed the word to be extra careful looking for more of the little buggers. Even if Gerin didn't use the same kind of array we would, I couldn't believe that there would be only one.

"They're only interested in things moving down low, by the creek," Liri whispered when we were a little farther off. "We'da had spotters aimed along the trail, where *people* would be." I hesitated. One thing that gets drummed into you early is to always expect the enemy to do the smartest thing in any situation, to be at least as savvy as you.

"They don't have any idea that there might be *people* here," I whispered. Liri nodded. That was what we had been hoping all along, that they wouldn't even suspect that we were peeking over their shoulders—or whatever they have. I didn't bother to voice the questions that remained. Why have sensors out at all then? Was it just routine? Or was it that the Gerin didn't understand us any better than we understood them?

We moved more slowly after our brush with the spotter, looking for more. But we didn't see any and no Gerin came rushing out to intercept us. Maybe there only *was* the one, crazy as that seemed.

An hour after noon, local time, we planted the first of our spotters on the ridge overlooking the cove and the Gerin installation and moved on to plant two more. Since we planned to stick around to monitor them, we used remote-control binoculars with attached microphones. Even less shows above ground than with the Gerin spotter. Two fiber-optic stalks with one-millimeter lenses and directional mikes are left just barely above ground. The rest of the apparatus is buried except for the knob of the transmitting antenna, and *that* is scarcely as big as one of the lenses. Then the observers can move back to safer ground, anywhere within line of sight of the transmitter—up to about five-hundred meters. The transmitters are very low-power to minimize the chance of detection. Our three snoops looked down at the cove, the landing strip, and the barracks. We spaced them three-hundred meters apart along the ridge, then moved into positions on the opposite slope, above the next creek.

After putting normal perimeter bugs behind us and in each direction along our valley, we split up into two fire teams and dug in about fifty meters apart. Each team's trench was covered with field blankets to shield us from IR detection. Then—again—we settled in to wait. We made our trenches as comfortable as we could. We had no idea how long they would be home.

The active spotters on the ridge would run constantly, feeding everything they saw and heard into a computer pack for later analysis. We also monitored the feed to keep track of what the Gerin were doing. By slaving a spotter to our helmet electronics, we could scan as easily as holding a pair of binoculars to our eyes—left, right, up, down. The thin fiber-optic stalks were a lot less likely to be spotted than a head poking up in the same place.

Night came before I was ready for it. We had our essential work done, but I wasn't acclimated to Grenadier's shorter days yet. In the cave, we hadn't worried about the local cycle. I didn't sleep much at all, and I was awake to stay well before dawn. That's rare for me. A soldier has to be able to sleep whenever and wherever possible. But not that night. I'd doze for a few minutes, then wake, take a look at what our spotters were seeing—nothing, mostly—and take forever to doze off again. I guess we all had trouble sleeping. Although we rotated sentry duty in each fire team, there was usually more than one person awake. I finally gave up and lifted a corner of the field blanket to stare at the sky, hoping to cool off a little. The insulated blankets keep us from showing up on IR scanners, but the insulation also makes them hotter than blazes to hide under in tropical heat.

The brief flash I saw in the west *might* have been a meteor. Then a second flash, almost overlapping the first. Okay, maybe *two* meteors, close together and coming from the same swarm. It was possible, but somehow I doubted it. I used my helmet radio to whisper the others awake, then checked our spotters to make sure that nothing was going on at the landing strip or over by the Gerin barracks.

"You think that's our pickup?" Liri asked skeptically.

"Can't be," I replied. We both whispered even though there didn't seem to be any Gerin stirring. It didn't make sense to pick us up so soon, not after everything that had been staged to put us into position. "It could be just about anything," I added, still linked to the spotters. I switched from one remote to the next.

Lights went on around the landing strip, diffuse panels that glowed more than shine. "Gerin traffic coming in," I whispered. Three shuttles landed, one right behind the other, as close as if they were on a combat run. Five

Gerin triads hurried out of each shuttle as soon as it braked to a stop near the end of the landing strip.

It was my first real look at Gerin, though I knew what to expect from the stills and videos. Still . . . *I know why they call them slime* was my first reaction. Just a look at them sent a strange feeling galloping up and down my back. They came out of the shuttles armed and alert, as if they were expecting a fight, or hoping for one. Only one triad went into the building—one warrior and his two slaves or apprentices, whatever they are. At the door, the warrior stopped and looked back toward the end of the landing strip. The other triads were already setting up temporary shelters near the inland end of the cove, on the north side of the stream not far from the end of the landing strip.

The shuttles took off again as first light hit the water. Thirty minutes later, three more shuttles landed—it was too soon for the first group to have made a round trip. Another fifteen triads disembarked and moved supplies off with them before they made camp with the others.

We're going to earn our pay this time, I thought. I wondered how big a mess we were in, how many Gerin were going to come down and park in our laps. Before the shuttles started bringing in these reinforcements, it looked like we might have a slight numerical advantage, parity at worst. Now we had to be on the short end of at least six-to-one odds.

"Would you think I was out of my mind if I offered a guess that at least one more Gerin ship has come to Grenadier?" I whispered.

"I wonder what Admiral Mac had in mind when he sent us in," Liri said. "Did he know something was going to happen or was it just a lucky guess?"

"I'll ask him the next time we have tea," I said, and that ended that conversation.

The arrival of so many extra Gerin put me more on edge than I had been before. And when they started sending out patrols, I felt very naked and vulnerable—and I didn't like it. Two more shuttles came in and disgorged their complements of Gerin that morning. We were getting deeper and deeper. All of a sudden there were more than ten times as many Gerin around as when we landed.

As long as it was light out, we couldn't do anything but sit still and age. But when night fell and the Gerin brought in their last patrols, I had to do something, even if it was futile and dangerous.

"Let's move back a little," I said when night was firmly in place. It was a nervous detail, filling in the holes we had been using, making that ground look undisturbed, and digging new trenches. We worked silently but fast, worried that the Gerin might decide to send out a patrol our way. I sent Ace and his team back to dig their new home first while the rest of us covered them from our original position. Then Ace's team returned the favor while we retreated the forty meters we could afford without losing touch with our three spotters. Forty meters wasn't much, but it made me feel a little better. I went to sit with Ace's crew for a while then.

"You think they know we're here?" Ace asked when I dropped into the trench next to him.

"No, but they're bound to stumble over us sooner or later," I said.

I didn't think it would take nearly as long as it did.

Three local days. We sweated under our field blankets through the hours of daylight and were very careful about trips out after dark, even though the Gerin didn't patrol at night. We got used to three or four Gerin patrols along our valley every day—usually one triad moving along the creek. We made like dead whenever that happened, just one man on the corner watching with a fiber-optic system in case the Gerin got too close. Maybe they weren't real patrols the way we would have mounted them. It might have simply been a Gerin warrior out for a stroll with his two flunkies along from habit.

By the third day, there were over two hundred Gerin on the planet. Every day more triads came down, and none seemed to be leaving. We were ready to crawl out of our skins, even when no slimers were in sight. And when the patrols came around, it taxed our discipline just to stay quiet, even though there was nothing else we dared to do.

Most of the patrols came along the valley, but late on the third day after reinforcements started to land, one patrol came directly over the ridge. It was just a little before sunset, later than any of the other patrols had been out. I swallowed hard as these three Gerin moved past one of our spotters on the ridge and started down the slope, not directly toward me, but close enough that I worried that they might spot the fiber-optic stalks I was watching them through.

They'll turn at the creek and follow it, one way or the other, I told myself. The Gerin always seemed to follow the water when they could. This time I was wrong. The warrior waded upstream for a few steps, but then he came out on the near side, and his stooges followed.

"Turn, dammit," I whispered. But they didn't. They were heading straight for the trench where Liri and his fire team were hiding.

I didn't have much time to consider alternatives. Sure, our orders were to keep out of sight, not let the Gerin know we're around, but one way or another, we were about to get found. There wasn't even time for doubt. I was going to get up and start shooting. That gave us a slight chance. If the Gerin just tripped over Liri's position, we'd likely lose four men straight off and the Gerin warrior would get on his radio link the instant he spotted humans. Then we'd have all the slimers down on us in minutes.

Unless I could pop the Gerin warrior off with one shot. But he was in battle armor. I wasn't sure that even a direct hit would kill him fast enough, not from behind. I had to make him turn around without tipping him off so I'd have a chance of putting a beam through his throat or into his face below the helmet.

It takes longer to tell than it did to do.

I said one soft word on the radio. "Ready." Then I stood up fast, like an idiot from some third-rate adventure, popping the field blanket aside while I brought my beamer to bear on the Gerin warrior.

I quacked once, very loudly.

People have taken ducks to a lot of the worlds with them. But Gerin would have no reason to recognize the call or associate it with humans. The warrior and his stooges turned toward me, toward the sound. I got off the critical shot that took out the warrior. Before the others could return fire, Liri and his men were up behind them, and the whole skirmish was over in less than twenty seconds.

"No signal," Ace said at my shoulder. "They never had a chance, Ducks."

"Knock that crap off," I said. "We're still in deep."

"What now, Sarge?" Liri asked when we got over to the dead Gerin.

"If we move back any farther, we risk losing contact with our spotters," I said, and we couldn't move the spotters either. I looked down at the bodies. Four more steps and the slimers would have been in the trench with Liri.

"Why not make it look like these two fried their boss?" Ace asked, poking a body with his boot. "These burn marks don't carry signatures."

"Will Gerin believe that?" Hiis asked.

I shrugged. We had no way to know. But I also couldn't come up with any alternative that sounded more plausible.

"We'll still have to move them," I said.

"I knew it had to be you, Sarge, even without the radio," Liri said, loosening up a bit. "No one else would have quacked like that."

"Well, just forget about that," I said, sharper than I intended. "I had to do something." *Am I gonna have to live with that from now on?* I asked myself. Talk about above and beyond the call.

"We'll dump them in the creek. These things belong in the water." I pointed. "Downstream of our last spotter." We could get them about six hundred meters from the nearest trench. That was the best we could do. But there was no posse screaming over the rise yet, so maybe we could get away with our deception a little longer. If nobody saw us moving the bodies or returning to our holes, we could sit around some more and hope that our people came back for us in plenty of force before the Gerin went ape.

I didn't sleep a wink that night. I hardly closed my eyes long enough to blink. *Somebody* had to miss the dead Gerin. But no one came for the bodies until morning, just after first light. Three triads came together, over the ridge, in skirmish formation. We sweated out the operation, not moving a hair while the Gerin homed in on the bodies. Then the Gerin stood around their dead comrades for several minutes, talking. One or another of the warriors—it was easy to identify the head slimer of each triad—scanned the valley constantly. When one looked back to the bodies, another took up the scan. Cautious, well-trained soldiers. Or maybe it's instinct with them. Who knows?

I tried to figure odds. We *might* be able to take out all nine of these Gerin as long as we held the edge of surprise, but not fast enough to keep them from blowing the whistle on us. And we wouldn't be able to evade all the Gerin on Grenadier very long once they knew we were around.

After a time—maybe no more than fifteen minutes—the three warriors started back toward the cove. Their stooges picked up the bodies and followed, and they really had to hump to keep up. We kept watch, directly until the Gerin crossed the rise between us and the cove, then with the remotes. The bodies were hauled to one of the shuttles that were on the ground. One triad got in with the bodies. The rest headed for the permanent building on the shore. Before they got there, the shuttle was in the air.

And I started breathing again.

"We may not have bought much time," Hiis said when he saw me relax. "If they do good autopsies, they may figure out that something's wrong."

All I could do was shrug. "So what choice did we have? All we can do is stay alert and hope our people get back before our position here gets, uh, untenable." That's a word right out of the manuals. Every grunt knows exactly what it means before he gets out of boot camp.

Bend over, stick your head between your legs, and kiss your ass goodbye.

The shuttle carrying the bodies hardly had time to clear the atmosphere before three more Gerin shuttles landed. From the way the troops on the ground snapped to, it wasn't hard to guess that there had to be at least one big shot among the new arrivals. One Gerin from the second craft got a lot of attention from everyone else. Then those shuttles were taxied off the landing strip in a hurry and three more shuttles landed. And even the big shot from the first group snapped to when this latest batch unloaded.

"Are we here to spy on their general staff or something?" Liri asked.

"Your guess is as good as mine." I didn't take my eyes off the scene the remotes were shooting me. "But if intelligence knew this was coming, our fleet should have been tracking their ships." And if so, our ships should be dropping out of FTL space right about then—with any luck at all—ready to take on the Gerin and pick us up. I hoped.

Why is there never a bookie around to take my action when I guess right?

The only indication I saw of the battle in space over Grenadier was one massive explosion—so bright that it was like a second sun in the sky for more than a minute. Two of our dreadnoughts and six cruisers surprised four Gerin ships and destroyed three of them, losing only one cruiser in return. But I didn't hear about all that until later. I was too busy on the ground.

We heard a series of sonic booms as shuttles punched into the atmosphere attack-hot, and then I had the captain's voice on my radio. "That's our ride home, Ian. Get up to the ridge and give them some cover. We'll be on the other side, so keep your fire down." He had to be getting orders from someone upstairs.

"On our way, Cap." I got up out of the foxhole, tossing the field blanket aside as I clicked back to the squad frequently to get everyone moving. We jogged toward our positions on the ridge, ranged between two of our spotters. My knees were so stiff from all the squatting and sitting that I must have waddled the first few steps, but the stiffness worked itself out in a hurry. We were finally going to move into real action. There's no place for cranky joints when that happens.

Alpha Squad got in the first shots, but we weren't far behind. It was—you should pardon the expression—a duck shoot. We flopped into steady prone firing positions and opened up with everything we were packing—beamers, slugthrowers, rockets, and grenades. After all the days of tension and cramped muscles, we were all a little trigger-happy, high on adrenaline.

Gerin can be surprised, even if they recover quickly. After the sonic booms, they were looking to the air for attack. Before they had time to get crews to the big guns, though, Alpha Squad hit them from the ground. As the Gerin responded to that, we showed up in back of them and surprised them again. The few seconds they needed to shift their thinking each time provided all the advantage we needed. We lowered the odds in a hurry, and the Gerin had almost no room to maneuver once our shuttles started coming in.

The mayhem wasn't all one-way, though.

Ace got a few centimeters too high while he fired a rocket into the concrete building across the cove. The rocket went in the door, but Ace was dropped before it blew. Smoke and flame belched out of the building, though it didn't collapse. We used the rest of our rockets on the Gerin shuttles on the ground.

Hiis fell when three Gerin triads got their act together and charged up the slope at us. All nine of those Gerin went down in payment. It wasn't enough. It never is.

But then, Gerin never know when enough is enough. They don't surrender, no matter what. We knew that already. When the captain clicked back to me and said, "We'd like prisoners if possible," all I could do was laugh. "I know," the captain said, "but they want us to try anyway." I rogered and passed the word to my people. A couple of them laughed too.

The Gerin never tried to flank us, never managed to use the numerical advantage they started with. They didn't have much chance at all for initiative. They fought from cover when they could, but a lot of them finally got around to standing up and charging. It wasn't enough to keep dropping them. They kept coming, even when they had to crawl, and no matter how badly they were hurt, they kept shooting, providing covering fire for their comrades even as they bled to death.

Finally, our piece of the action came down to one last Gerin triad.

"Hold your fire," I told my men as the Gerin warrior walked out into the open below us, his two shadows right with him. The warrior shouted something while several of his limbs churned. A challenge, I think. I've heard that's something Gerin will do. He wanted us to come out and fight like Gerin.

"What's that all about?" Cord Witters asked over the squad frequency.

"I think he just gave us the finger, Gerin-style," I replied.

I raised my head just a little to shout, "Throw down your weapons and surrender!" That brought a few chuckles over the radio. I shook my head, then lifted a hand to show the Gerin the finger, human-style.

"Aim to disable, not to kill," I said. I took the first shot. All three Gerin went down fast enough, but none of them gave up. They kept shooting as long as they could hold their weapons.

"Don't those bastards ever pass out?" someone asked on the radio.

"They're losing buckets of blood," Liri said next to me.

The stooges finally stopped moving, dead or so close that it didn't matter. But the warrior kept dragging himself up the slope toward us. His gun was gone. He was clutching a knife now.

"Let's reel him in," I said, getting to my feet. Maybe we could get a prisoner after all. I kept my gun trained on the Gerin, in case he was hiding another gun or a grenade or something, waiting for one last chance to take out some humans. But all he had was the knife. And when he saw the crowd of us approaching, he used the blade.

On himself.

Two hours later, we were back on the *Cardigan*, standing in the showers hosing a week of Grenadier's grime off while the ship accelerated away from the planet. Eighteen of us landed. Fifteen made it back off, and only two of them had wounds requiring serious treatment. Colonel Gregory was aboard to welcome us back personally. He shook hands with everybody and clapped us on our shoulders. The cooks laid out a banquet to make up for our days on concentrated field rations. A couple of bottles of hootch appeared in the squad bays that night.

Three weeks later, we were eleven light-years away, dropping out of FTL space for a rendezvous with a little rest and recreation dirtside. Before we shuttled down from *Cardigan*, though, Colonel Gregory gathered us in the mess hall to read a "well done" message from Admiral Mac.

I suppose the text is around somewhere if anyone has any real interest. There was nothing in it about *why* we were dropped on Grenadier. Nobody has ever bothered to tell us that. But Mac carried on in the usual way about how our bravery and professionalism might shorten the war by years and save millions of human lives—that kind of snake oil.

My face turned red while the colonel read the message. It's not that I'm easily embarrassed by compliments, but all that crud about professionalism reminded me of an unfortunate incident that happened on Grenadier, after the last of the Gerin went down to stay.

I was leading Bravo Squad toward the landing strip to meet Alpha Squad and some of the reinforcements. The captain was leading his people across the river. Reunion time. The captain had a tired grin on his face. I was feeling pretty good myself. The fight was over and we were both still alive—despite that "this might be the last time" handshake in the cave. I guess I forgot that the captain and I weren't alone, that there were a lot of other guys around with nothing to keep them busy. For a minute, it was just the captain and me, together after a fight again, the way we had been so often over the last fifteen years. I waddled a few steps and quacked loudly every time I moved a foot . . . until everybody started laughing.

God, I'll never live that down.

The League of Man

When Mac convinced the League of Free Planets to join his crusade, pride and legalities prevented the League from placing itself under another government. With a burst of insight, the problem was solved when Mac simply ordered those worlds and ships under his command to apply for membership in the League. Mac, of course, was appointed admiral of the now reinforced League fleet.

As time passed, the League of Worlds gradually merged into the League of Man. If the Gerin had been a less determined opponent, the intensity of xenophobia developed might have been less. Certainly the total destruction of all life on three worlds and over thirty million civilians on virtually every League world inspired the League's early policies. There can be no question that repressed guilt over the fate dealt to the Gerin inspired many of the League's late excesses. Nor can the Mac's own fanatic hatred of the Gerin be underrated. Certainly as its first chairman, Chu Lee MacDonald was obsessed with ensuring no other race could repeat the havoc wrought by the Gerin.

REUNION

by Diane Duane

IT was the good time for him, the quiet time: the time when no one shot at him anymore, the time he had dreamed of for so very long. Lel Askhenazy had survived the war. Sometimes he found that miraculous.

In retrospect it seemed to have gone on forever, some ways. His first battle had been with the Castleman's fleet, when they hit DuQuesne. That was the time he had almost died. Beginner's luck, everyone had said: explosive decompression in the weapons room of the *Bantry Bay*, his body picked up and slammed against a stanchion—the only thing between him and the howling, snow-swirled tornado of freezing air bursting out of the hull. The one man in a pressure suit, the one man who had managed to hang on, who had grabbed him and managed to drag him into the airlock when the air was all gone, and seal it, and save them both: that was Revi Abhrahindar, who hated his guts. He was dead now, his ship dragged out of warp by a Gerin cruiser and fried, somewhere in the Battle of Ten Moons.

In fact, most of the people he knew were dead. Lel sat back in the command seat, thinking that this line of recall was morbid; but a man had to grieve sometimes, didn't he? He thought of the people on board *Crimea* when he had been transferred there, all the medical staff and the crew. He had been barely more than a skin-bag of shattered bones, which they had carefully, patiently pieced back together like an old familiar puzzle. McLuhan, the crazed neurology specialist, who took such cheerful pleasure in running unnecessary tests on the response of Lel's healing nerves; Irisai and Vuuonen, the nurses, completely "ignoring" him while they changed one after another of his numerous dressings, and discussed his probable social life in improbable detail; Spencer, the captain-surgeon, as comfortable with a laser as with a scalpel: all gone now, blown up when the Gerin went after the support craft responding to the bombing of Klaremont, and *Crimea* fought rearguard so that some could get away.

And all the crews of *Maestricht* and *Prinz Willems Land*, which Lel had served on after he was stitched back together: also gone during Ten Moons, every mother's son and daughter of them. Cruiser crews tended to get to know one another too well, so few of them in so much ship—there was a tendency to band together against the size of the thing, the way party guests in a large ballroom will clump in a corner, as if there were no more room for them at all. Lel remembered Katya, from *Maestricht*, and the way she used to laugh at him of nights, and push him down on the bed. Gone, she and her blond hair both.

And *Azusa*, that had been his first command, and the one Lel loved best: gone too, a month after he had left her, with all hands, at the Battle of Olympus. Mad Rostropov, his exec, and big hairy dark Leif, Leif the Turk, as everyone called him, for some reason—Lel never found out why. And Mary Turner, the weapons officer, with her little sly smile, and Murik Janislav, and Ceyrat, and Bergues, and Illhauesern—all gone. Ghosts.

But a few, somehow, had survived. He was going to see one of them. There was some consolation in that. *We survivors*, he thought: and then let out a breath of laughter at his own pretentiousness. There was no great honor in still being alive. Some skill, a lot of luck—that was all.

"Lorne," he said over his shoulder to his exec, "how close are we?"

"Another half hour of warp, sir," Victoria said in her soft little voice. "We can accelerate a bit, if you like."

"No, we're fine."

She nodded and turned her attention back to her navigation board. Lel looked at her, wishing she would say a little something else. *Like what, though?* he thought. *Only a month with this group, and they're a little skittish yet. Give them time to sort you out.* And no question, they must find the tall, hunched, black-eyed, grim-faced figure somewhat difficult to deal with. Even the surgery of the day had not been able to do much about some of his scars: and as for his face . . . "I'll have you know" he remembered Spencer saying, annoyed, "that I took six hours carving you that face out of our last piece of osteo, which could as well have gone for that compound fracture of Wallis's. Not to mention the time I took installing it. And it wasn't *my* fault that the stuff had been in storage past its sell-by date. You don't like the workmanship, fine. Come on in my office and we'll take it off. Shouldn't take a minute." And Spencer had run his hand over his bald spot, the way he always did when trying to keep from punching someone.

Lel sighed at the memory. It vanished like a ghost.

But it's not just me that these people are reacting to. They're going to have to have time to sort out not being shot at.

That was the strangest part of it all, really. After what seemed a lifetime—after *Crimea* and *Maestricht* and *Prinz Willems Land* and *Azusa,* and then *Boston II* and *Raden Mas* and *Irizar*—then had come the fall of Gerin Prime, and suddenly there was no more war. Crews used to living holding their breaths suddenly had to learn how to let those breaths go, and draw new ones. It was difficult at first, as the fleets were reshuffled, as Mac bent his great talents to a new task: bringing order out of the chaos the Gerin had left.

For chaos there was. The League of Man found itself an enemy without an enemy left for its allies to fight: and such a vacuum was dangerous. The allies were dangerous, too. Alien creatures—

They fought alongside us, Lel thought. *But it doesn't change the fact: there's no telling with aliens. Their mindset isn't ours . . . and allies today might be enemies tomorrow. Worse enemies than the Gerin . . . for they know our secrets, now. . . .*

Lel got up out of his seat and paced around the cruiser's cramped little bridge, trying to work one of the numerous kinks out of his back. *Boyne* was a good ship, but she always seemed smaller than the other ones he had commanded. Though that was ridiculous. She was *Stockholm*-class, as they all had been.

Is it just that we're not fighting?

He sighed. Certainly going out as a part of a formation, to bomb another tactical group, or attack a planet, was more straightforward work than what was ahead of them now. Mac was as nervous about the alien allies as the commanding admirals of the other human worlds were. They must be made . . . secure. Usually this meant visiting their homeworlds and seeing how the ''people'' there viewed the rule of the League of Man. If they welcomed it, or accepted it, well and good. Hostages were received and guarantees taken, and a tax was levied to support the armed forces of the League and protect the worlds associated with it from any further trouble. However, if the planet proved hostile in attitude, or lukewarm, stronger measures had been prescribed. They came in measured levels, according to response. They ended with the destruction of the planet. Fortunately, that had been needed only once or twice.

Lel had the whole careful set of instructions on tape, on data solid, and in a big looseleaf book in his cabin. It made poor bedside reading, he had found, and he had left it strictly alone after his first couple of dips into it. Depressing stuff. But policy was policy: without secure boundaries, and neighbors it could be sure of, the League of Man would have no certainty of peace in the future. And that was what the worlds were crying out for: peace. There would be no future for them without a quiet time to grow and heal.

Lel, at least, had a slightly more pleasant mission than some of late. He had done some wangling for it, had sent repeated polite communiqués through every channel he dared: and finally someone in Mac's office—he hardly dared think it was Mac himself—had probably said, ''Oh, give him what he wants, and get him off our cases.''

And so the orders had come through for Lel to go to en'Harha, and take the mandate of the League of Men to the D'Tarth.

He had almost felt like hugging himself at the time.

He almost felt like hugging himself right now. For Irrhun was there, and she was expecting him. Irrhun was one of the ones who past belief, past expectation, was still alive. It was odd—how the mere fact that she had made it, as he had, made him feel somehow more alive himself. They would sit down and talk over old times, they would—

He walked over to his hot seat again and sat down, trying to maintain some measure of control. There was no controlling the smile, however crooked it drew the lines of his face. That was one of the things Irrhun had never seemed to care about. The smile grew to a grin, thinking about it.

"Fifteen minutes, sir," Victoria said.

Lel nodded, savoring the way he felt. It was an odd feeling, a sensation of homecoming, though there was no real cause for that. It was three years since he had set foot on Luyken, his last home, and he wasn't even sure whether the Gerin had hit it again after the first strike, which had killed his parents and sent him into the military. All that seemed very far away now: only the old hatred of the Gerin was at all immediate. And even that no longer had a proper home, with the Gerin fleets hunted to extinction, and Gerin Prime bombed into the stone age . . . since plague and famine were doing for the few remaining millions what the bombs had not.

Lel sighed and let the thought go. For a little while he watched his bridge crew go about their business, quiet and efficient.

How will she look? he thought. The last time he had seen her was at her decoration, with numerous other officers, after the Battle of the Red Giant. There was rather less to her uniform than to his: considering that she spent her days wearing a fur coat, it seemed only fair. D'Tarth officers wore a sort of harness, suitable for their insignia and equipment, and with pockets and holsters for their voders and sidearms. Irrhun had been resplendent that day, every fitting shining, the leather gleaming softly— where she had come by saddle soap, Lel had no idea. And when she rose up on her haunches to accept the White Cross, with both clusters, Irrhun had snarled right in the face of the admiral making the presentation. He

hadn't flinched, to his credit: but Lel still doubted
whether the man knew that Irrhun had been joking with
him. One only snarled at one's friends, or one's potential
food.

Lel chuckled softly to himself, and all over the bridge,
heads turned. He glanced over at Victoria: she looked
hurriedly away, and said, "Three minutes, sir."

"Very good," Lel said, and breathed out softly, looking out the port at the stars swirling by, slowing gently
toward the drop-out point.

D'Tarth was a large planet, by most standards: the kind
of place where one could look out toward a horizon and
find it unusually high up the sky. There was less sea than
usual, and more land: the oceans were small and land-
locked. Rivers were plentiful, and there were mighty
mountain chains: the ice caps were large, and there was
a greenish tinge to the atmosphere, something to do with
higher-than-usual percentages of nitrogen and argon. By
the standards of human worlds, there were very few cities, and most of its people were scattered far and wide
over the planet. Not to say that they were backward, by
any means. Their communications network was among
the best in all the worlds: by use of personal comm equipment and public comm establishments, you could be in
touch with anyone on the planet in a matter of seconds,
whether he was in a town dcn or thousands of miles from
anyone else, out in the open country.

Lel had *Boyne* land in the place prepared for it in the
planet's eastern-hemisphere spaceport. The number of
landing cradles and repair facilities suggested that the
D'Tarth fleet must have been quite something before the
war: they did not differentiate between military and civil
spacefaring, and both kinds of ships shared the field. But
only one dock in ten had a ship in it: even allowing for
those out trading, Lel had to shake his head at the punishment their fleets had taken.

The delegation came out from the nearby official buildings, a cluster of bright glassy bubbles, to meet the shore
party. Lel stood with Victoria and Asbury, his tall lean
scowling weapons officer, and watched the five D'Tarth

come, loping along the scorched, stained surfacing in
that long easy gait that he had become used to with Irrhun. She had always made it look more graceful, though,
a sort of cheeky, leisurely dance along the ground. The
only time that grace had deserted her had been in free
fall: she would twist and swear and spit as she tried to
orient herself. Most D'Tarth had less trouble with it: Irrhun's inner ear had simply refused to make the adjust-
ment. But when the power to life support and grav went
out in *Anderal* that time, and the whole ship was plunged
into a dark that drove humans screaming mad of disori-
entation and fear, *she* had kept her head, fought her way
down through the corridors to the backup control room,
and brought everything back online again. Lel remembered the hot, feral gleam of her eyes when the lights and
gravity came back on . . . and how she had been most
loathsomely sick immediately afterward.

Most of the approaching D'Tarth had a similar look on
their faces, though it seemed to Lel that they were trying
to control it. Lorne and Asbury showed no sign of seeing
anything unusual about their expressions . . . well, they
had had less practice than Lel had. In all but one case,
the D'Tarth's great lips were wrinkled up and back, as
if they smelled something bad; their whiskers bristled,
and the stiff bright ruffs of fur around their faces seemed
ruffled too far forward. The fifth D'Tarth, white-muzzled,
his plush gray-striped coat scarred with old burns, had a
face as impassive as a carved lion's on a monument.

They paused a few feet away, rose up on their haunches
in courtesy, and greeted the shore party politely enough,
giving their names: Commander Lahhim, Port Admiral
Eher, Commodore Juhhir, Captains Khirrith and Rhai.
Lel greeted them as gravely, introduced himself and his
people, and walked with them back toward the port
buildings, watching the discomfort evident in the way
they moved, and wondering why Irrhun was not with
them. Surely she knew he was coming: word had been
sent days ago.

The meetings took the rest of that morning and most
of the afternoon. Lel sat down cross-legged at the low
round table in the meeting room, looking over to where

the huge feline forms lay at what looked like their ease, and patiently spelled out the terms of the League of Man as regarded the D'Tarth. There were many disgruntled glances, but no overt gestures, and no words of disagreement. Port Admiral Eher, who seemed the most senior of the group—and seniority counted for a great deal among the D'Tarth—accepted, on behalf of the planetary government, the dictates regarding how many human forces were to be garrisoned on and around the planet, at the D'Tarth's expense; accepted the tax, which Lel privately found close to extortionate; and almost graciously offered to arrange for the hostages himself. Lel accepted all this, and found himself wondering why he wished they would make more trouble for him. He searched the old port admiral's great green eyes, as they talked, for some kind of hint; but there was no expression in them that he was able to read, and shortly Lel began to feel like a child trying to stare down one of his elders.

Finally they finished: the last of the documents of co-operation—*submission, actually*—signed and saved to data solids and to the curious liquid-gallium memory storage that the D'Tarth used for data. The less senior of the D'Tarth officers made their goodbyes, all politely, and loped out of the big bleak office where they had done their work. Only the port admiral hesitated, and Lel seized the moment.

"Sir," he said, "I was hoping I might see one of your people here today, before we have to leave."

The port admiral blinked at him, a sleepy-cat look: but there was nothing sleepy about the eyes, not oblique now, but alert. "One of my staff, *rrhn*-Askhenazh'?"

"No. I mean, not now, but formerly. Senior Commander Irrhun."

"Ah." It was a sound that seemed as if a growl might have followed it, but was being restrained. "My apologies, *rrhn*. She was detained. She left a commcode for you, and coordinates."

Why did he wait till now to mention it? Lel thought. *Well, never mind—business before pleasure, after all.* "Thank you, sir," he said.

The port admiral recited a series of figures and standard characters, then said. "The coordinates are at some distance. We would be delighted to loan you a lowflier if it will expedite your visit."

—*if it'll get you out of here quicker,* Lel heard under the rumble of words. He nodded. "Port Admiral," he said, "I thank you very much."

Lel dismissed his crew to the ship and followed the port admiral a thousand meters or so across the field to a little fenced area, where several trim little hoppers stood. All their control couches were made for D'Tarth, naturally, so that a pilot would work on his belly rather than sitting up, but Irrhun had taught him the way of it a long time ago, and flying cat-style was no problem for Lel. He walked around the craft with the port admiral, accepted the starter solid from him, thanked him, got into the craft and sealed it up, and began his preflight checks.

Several minutes later, as he eased up into the air, he saw the old D'Tarth standing there gazing up after him, the big age-whitened muzzle still wearing no expression he could read.

Hatred? Lel thought. *Who could blame them, after we treat them this way?*

But the thought smelled of treason. Lel put it uncomfortably aside, and turned his attention to the flight.

The coordinates were indeed a good distance away: Lel considered himself lucky that he hadn't tried to take public transport. At least four hundred klicks he had to travel, not mentioning the detours to avoid various D'Tarth air traffic control facilities; it was surprising how much air traffic there was, considering how few real cities there were. Tiny ports were scattered all over the place, and little craft came and went everywhere, stopping as frequently as the trams of old.

But Lel's flight took him away from the small ports at last, out over the country. For a while it looked the way Luyken had out in its countryside, little fields parceled apart by hedgerows: a long, lovely patchwork of greens and golds and the occasional pewter shine of water, with high golden-tinged clouds piled up in a turquoise sky, and the high horizon leaning against that sky with the dim jagged outline of far away. Then the fields gave out and the country became sparser, dryer: pale golden grasslands, overlying gently rolling hills. *Her country house?* Lel wondered. *Or is she staying on a hunting preserve?* For the D'Tarth made a point of staying in touch with their roots as solitary-hunting carnivores, even though their food usually came from distribution facilities instead of being caught bloodily on the veldt.

But finally he found the coordinates, and there was no country house there, no game preserve—nothing but a little dirt road leading to an ordinary-looking complex of buildings, of the bubblelike architecture favored by the D'Tarth. Several of the bubbles were clustered together around a central pool, which looked from the air as if it wanted cleaning: it seemed murky.

Lel circled once, found nothing that looked like a landing pad per se, and finally settled for putting the hopper down nearby, in a patch of long dry grass. He cracked the canopy and climbed out to stand and look around him in mild bemusement. *What's Irrhun doing out here in the middle of nowhere?* But it was a nice nowhere, he had to admit: a clean wind blowing cool, rustling softly to itself in the grass: wide views, peace. *You could get to like a place like this. . . .*

Lel walked over to the buildings, and found that he had to walk right around before finding a door. *Odd.* But the door was open, and dilated for him: and inside, she was waiting.

She was not a whisker different from when he had seen her last. Irrhun was tall even for a D'Tarth when she stood up, and strikingly marked—the particular pattern of the striping of her red-gold coat, she had told him once, meant that she was descended from one of the old D'Tarthi king-houses. Had a council of world government not long since supplanted the kingly house in her little part of the world, she would have been counted a princess of the blood, one whose fur it was death to ruffle. Time had ruffled that fur a bit, during her service with the forces; there were cut places and burn marks on her hide here and there, where the fur had refused to grow back, even with regeneration technology what it was. The warm green eyes were the same too, and the way she grinned at him. The gesture was not one that belonged to her people: she had learned it from the humans she served with, and made "smiles" at them when the situation was appropriate—though sometimes those smiles curdled the blood of those not prepared for them.

"Hlel," she said: the old dear mispronunciation. He went to her and hugged her, because he knew she wouldn't mind: and she hugged back—the D'Tarthi did have *that* gesture—and kept her claws in.

Then he let go of her, and said, "Irrhun, you weren't at the port—was there a problem?"

"No problem, Hlel," she said. "Just work." Her tone was cheerful enough. "Come and we'll go where we can talk."

She led him from the large bare circular anteroom where they had met into the next bubble over. It was a garden bubble, from the looks of it, with tall green and blue plants towering up against the clear roof, and spicy-sweet smells in the air. Lel looked around and said, "The government has you running a nursery?"

She looked at him oddly for a moment, then said, "Not quite. I'm head of a research program."

"Into what?"

She made another human-style smile for him. "Alien relations," she said. "I'll show you shortly. . . . Tell me, Hlel, how have you been?"

"Not too many complaints." He shook his head. "It's just that . . . there seem to be a lot fewer people to complain to than there used to be."

She twitched her tail in a gesture of agreement. "The War has taken its toll," she said. "Of all of us. . . . Did you reach agreement with the people you came to see this morning?"

"Agreement," he said, and frowned a little. "A little too much of that."

She glanced at him in amusement. "What were you expecting?" she said softly, as they passed out of the greenhouse bubble into another one, this one blocked off into office space, with screens and consoles, and perhaps ten D'Tarth working here and there. "You have us rather outgunned, Hlel."

"Oh, come on, Irrhun. We would never—"

"—do what you did to Arkheit, and Downlow? Indeed I hope not." But her eyes looked unconvinced, and Lel felt a little shudder run down his back. It was always the eyes, with a D'Tarth; their eyes would tell you what was going on, if anything could.

"Seriously, Irrhun." He reached down to touch her back as she loped along beside him, so that she stopped and looked up at him. "We've fought together. Nothing would make me—"

"Nothing?" It was soft enough to be a purr. "Not even Mac's direct order? Suppose he told you to glaze our world over: would you do it?"

Lel frowned. "He'd never do such a thing—you're our allies. And even if he did—there would have to be a reason—"

She would not look away from his eyes, and it suddenly occurred to Lel that she was reading him more accurately, perhaps, than he had ever managed to read her. The old fear raised its head. *Aliens, you can't trust them—*

"Irrhun," he said finally, "if that order ever was given, I would pray I wasn't the one who had to implement it."

"And if you were?" Her voice was casual. Her eyes were not.

He looked back at her, suddenly finding that he was sweating. "I would have to think about it," he said finally, very softly, as if he were afraid someone might hear.

Her tail swung from side to side in slow agreement, or approval. "Yes," she said. "That's what I thought you'd say. Come on, Hlel. I have something I want you to see."

They crossed out of the office bubble. Lel was aware of movement at his back, then realized it was every D'Tarth in the office, suddenly released from stillness, all of them having been perfectly motionless for the little while he was having that exchange with Irrhun.

What is going on here—?

The next bubble had an airlock to it. Irrhun palmed it

open, waved Lel through, then let the door shut before palming the next one.

They walked through the doorway. Lel looked around him and saw what appeared to be row after row of plastine tanks; over at one side of the bubble was a shut-in office space. The other side of the bubble gave onto the pool he had seen from outside. There was some sort of channel cut in from that pool, along the ground outside, and through the wall of the bubble, to a pool inside this room.

"My research facility," Irrhun said, and made another human smile at him.

They walked among the tanks, and Lel glanced down into one of them. There was nothing much to be seen: the water was murky. A little aquatic greenery poked up out of it, or waved gently under the surface.

"It was an odd job at first," Irrhun said. "They wouldn't tell me what it was. You know how the military can be? Governments are worse. They simply insisted that I was the best-qualified returning officer for this job." She laughed after the manner of her people, a soft *chuff!* in the throat. Lel looked down into another tank as they passed it.

"I can't tell what it is either," Lel said. "Looks like you're raising fish here."

"The whole matter came as something of a surprise to our government," Irrhun said as they strolled. Her tail was twitching gently. "There was just suddenly a visitor to our system one day: a little ship that didn't have any of the usual ID, nothing but shields of an unusual type. We didn't even know it had come into the system until it had already crashed, not too far from here."

"Another alien species?" Lel said, more interested than surprised.

"It was surprisingly advanced in design over anything we had seen before," Irrhun said, as they walked past another rank of tanks, larger ones. "But there was nothing in it but tanks like these. Many of them were ruptured. Most were intact, though, with the instructions."

Lel looked in the next tank they passed. The water in this one was clearer, except for something down in the bottom of it, a grimy-looking, jellylike mass. "We set up a facility as much like we found in the ship as we could," Irrhun said, peering into that tank as well, "and waited to see what happened."

They walked on. "So what happened?" he said. "Are you getting results?"

"I would say so," Irrhun said. She paused by a third row of tanks, looked in. Lel looked over her shoulder.

In the end of the tank were tiny tentacled shapes, not more than an inch long, many less than the size of his thumbnail. They wriggled and jetted gently about in the water, having barely enough color to make them visible in it. They swam in threes.

They were baby Gerin.

Lel stopped stock still, and stared.

"Our people are terrible in war," he heard Irrhun's voice saying. "Isn't that so? We were one of your best allies because of that. Solitary hunters the One made us, and so we remained. There were no fighter pilots like us, and even you humans had to admit it sometimes. But there's another side to that haunch, Hlel. Hunters we are, but we are also fosterers. We care for our young like no one else—"

"Your young!" he whispered.

"We also," Irrhun said, "adopt."

There was a long silence.

"You're trying to tell me," Lel said, "that the Gerin sent some of their eggs here—"

"*All* of their eggs," Irrhun said. "Their last chance. Hlel, do you know how long it's been since a Gerin actually reproduced in the sea? Their technology allowed them to switch over to creche-based reproduction long ago. So many more of their children survived that way. Where are their creches now, Hlel? Your people bombed Gerin Prime until barely anything that generated energy stood: the creches and their fail-safe power stations were the first to go. Billions died in the war and the fall of the planet. Of the few million still living, how many of those are going to manage to rear children, if there are any left at all? How many are even going to find a way to spawn?"

Lel's eyes were narrowing. "Seems better that way,"

he said, "considering what they did to *our* children when they had the chance."

Irrhun sat down opposite him, looking at him cool-eyed for the moment. "You're the victors," she said. "No question of that, on Gerin Prime or anywhere else. You have won your war. You've been making it plain enough to your allies, as well. No harm in that, I suppose. But you have no right to destroy an entire species."

"When it does what they did—" He stared down into the tank with loathing, as the little almost-transparent shapes jostled and glided and bumped into each other.

"No right," Irrhun said. "This ship came to us with a message begging us to take care of their children, who now had no parents. What would you have us do?"

Lel drew his sidearm.

Irrhun got up and rose up on her haunches, and stood in front of him, her eyes glittering. *Did D'Tarth cry?* Lel found himself wondering: rather absurdly—it would be wiser to ask whether he thought he could do anything about this place, when a creature with three-inch canines and inch-long talons was reared up in front of him like black-and-gold death.

"Hlel," she said. "Listen to me. Put aside your shock for the moment. I brought you here willingly because I knew you would come looking for me, and might otherwise discover the truth on your own. I wanted to be truthful with you from the start, and have a chance to talk to you, my old friend. We desperately need an advocate with the League."

Lel began to laugh at the absolute madness of it. "An *advocate?*"

"Listen to me! Our government put me here because I had more experience with aliens than almost anyone else. Meaning you humans," she added softly. "And because they knew I knew you, and they knew you were coming here. We need someone to help us save these children's lives. If you hadn't found out, sooner or later someone else would have. And at any rate, soon they'll be too large to conceal any more . . . nor *should* they be concealed. They deserve the right to be free, to grow up under sky, in clear water, to learn to be other than their parents were—''

"They deserve nothing," Lel said, "except maybe to be dead. Didn't the children on Luyken, and half a hundred other worlds, deserve to live and grow up, instead of being bombed out of existence, or—'' He was in such shock that his mind was refusing to catalog the atrocities for the moment. "They need to be dead," he said.

Her green eyes held his. "The killing must stop somewhere," she said. "If you do not stop it now, all your people, it will hang around your necks for all the rest of your lives, and make them something that should never have been lived.''

"If these, these things grow up," Lel shouted, gesturing with the gun at one of the tanks, "they'll do exactly what their parents did. And why shouldn't they? They'll grow up in freedom, right?—that's what you want for them?—and in freedom they'll find out what we did to their parents. Wouldn't *you* be angry? They'll find a way to come at the humans again—revenge was always their style. It's a species trait. And then we'll have to kill them all over again—but more of *our* people will die in the process.'' He flicked the safety off the sidearm, activated it, listened to the soft, building hum. "Better to get it over with now.''

Something weighing about thirty pounds hit his hand and sent the gun spinning. Lel cried out and clutched the hand, not sure it wasn't broken. Irrhun settled back to her haunches and folded her paws neatly again. "Hlel,'' she said, gentle-voiced, "remember the Rift battle? You owe me a life. And again, at the Red Giant? If not for my flying, and my squad's, *you* would be among those people who are missing, and to whom nothing matters anymore. Not all the Gerin you kill will bring your dead back: not all the humans they killed would have brought back their dead, whom they loved as you loved yours. I fought the war, yes: they were a danger, and that danger is over now. These six million eggs and embryos are no danger to anyone or anything except your own fears. I ask you, by the life you owe me, twice over, maybe three times if we count that last fighter that almost took your cruiser out: help me save them, Hlel. Do this for my people, if nothing else. The One requires it of us. If we turned away the helpless, we would not be D'Tarth any more. And nothing is worse than that: not even death."

He stood there, wringing the hurt hand, looking into those green eyes.

Ghosts whispered to him. *Bantry Bay,* they said. *Crimea. Luyken.*

"They are no more a warrior race than humans are," Irrhun said, reaching one pad of one paw down into the water. A largish baby Gerin, perhaps three inches long, slipped up to the paw and butted the pad of it gently, stroking it with its tentacles. "It's early for the programming to begin, but we do know that the 'threesome' paradigm is easily broken; we'll teach them to be social solitaries, like us. We know that best. They'll learn the truth—and learn to deal with it, as we have." She raised ironic eyes to him. "After all, we have been your good allies and staunch friends—and still have acquiesced to such treatment as you, in all your superior force, have seen fit to mete out to us. All for the sake of peace, of course." She made a human smile at him, but there was more than the usual face-wrinkling about it.

He shook his head. "I couldn't understand why you didn't fight it harder—"

She blinked at him, a deceptively lazy look. "We're solitary hunters, as I said. We don't care much about the internal politics of running a pack. We'll buy our peace, if we have to, and go about our business." And she glanced down at the tank. "Life . . ."

Death, the ghosts whispered.

But here was Irrhun, always his friend, always truthful, who had indeed saved his life—more than just three times, too. "You think they can be trained to be . . . useful?"

She looked at him sharply. "Are *you* useful? Do you prefer other sentient beings to think of you that way? They'll be alive. If they're lucky, they'll find purpose. If they're luckier still, they'll find joy. More than that, none of us can say."

The ghosts were whispering loud. Lel shook his head,

then very gingerly reached down into the tank, slipped one finger into the water.

One of the baby Gerin slipped up to it, hesitated, touched it with gently probing tentacles, then slowly wrapped them around his finger and squeezed: just a little squeeze.

His newborn cousin Marl's little fist had felt the same way.

On Luyken . . . said the ghosts.

"What do you need from me?" he said finally.

Irrhun's eyes held his, then glanced away. "Find a way to tell them what we're doing," she said, "a way that won't endanger your own status . . . but will also let us keep doing it. Find some way to make the League of Man understand that these babies are no threat to them. This is our best chance for peace with this species: to bring up its children as our own, and tell them the truth, and then perhaps let them go home, someday, to tell the truth to those living there. . . . "

As if it would matter, the ghosts said. *The Gerin left on the planet would call them traitors, and kill them.*

The same way the League would call the D'Tarth traitors—and kill them—no matter who brought them this news. Mac himself couldn't pull it off—

With an effort, he put the ghosts aside.

"Let me think of what to do," he said. "But your secret is safe with me."

Irrhun touched her paws to her forehead in the great thanks, which he had never seen a D'Tarth use on a human before. He didn't know what to do in return but hug her.

Then, "I have to get back to my ship," he said. "They'll be wondering what happened to me."

"Peace," she wished him, and would have seen him out the way he had come: but he shook her off, and went alone.

It seemed a long flight back to the spaceport, and he wasted no time getting into the ship and getting her out into orbit. Victoria and the others wondered a little at his manner, but said nothing, being used to his occasional black mood.

He sat in the command chair for a long while, looking out the port. Finally, Victoria said to him, "Shall we break orbit?"

"Not just yet," he said. "One last thing to take care of. A discretionary punitive."

The crew looked at one another, and shrugged. It was within a mission commander's discretion, on a mission of *this* sort, to make an "example" of some feature of a planet, if he felt it needed a weapons demonstration. He gave Asbury the coordinates. "Pulse lasers," he said. "About a bevawatt's output should do it."

"Aye, aye," Asbury said, and executed the command.

"That should do it," Lel said. "Take us out."

They broke orbit. Lel stayed where he was for a long time, listening to the engines, listening to the quiet conversation of his crew at work, hearing none of them. He heard only ghosts: one more in particular.

It had to be done, he thought desperately. *Better me, who loved her, than someone else. And it would have been someone else, sooner or later. No way to stop it. Let the war be over, over at last. They're better dead.*

But that ghost would not answer him. The only one that would . . .

. . . felt like a baby's fist.